Tragedy in the Dark

An Inspector Reynolds of Scotland Yard Mystery

By Elaine Hamilton

Originally published in 1935

Tragedy in the Dark

© 2015 Resurrected Press
www.ResurrectedPress.com

Published by Resurrected Press

This classic book was handcrafted by Resurrected Press. Resurrected Press is dedicated to bringing high quality classic books back to the readers who enjoy them. These are not scanned versions of the originals, but, rather, quality checked and edited books meant to be enjoyed!

Please visit ResurrectedPress.com to view our entire catalogue!

For updates on future releases, LIKE us on Facebook:
http://www.Facebook.com/ResurrectedPress

ISBN 13: 978-1-943403-00-4

Printed in the United States of America

Resurrected Press Books in A. E. Fielding's *The Chief Inspector Pointer Mystery* Series

Death of John Tait
Murder at the Nook
Mystery at the Rectory
Scarecrow
The Case of the Two Pearl Necklaces
The Charteris Mystery
The Eames-Erskine Case
The Footsteps that Stopped
The Clifford Affair
The Cluny Problem
The Craig Poisoning Mystery
The Net Around Joan Ingilby
The Tall House Mystery
The Wedding-Chest Mystery
The Westwood Mystery
Tragedy at Beechcroft

RESURRECTED PRESS CLASSIC MYSTERY CATALOGUE

Journeys into Mystery
Travel and Mystery in a More Elegant Time

The Edwardian Detectives
Literary Sleuths of the Edwardian Era

Gems of Mystery
Lost Jewels from a More Elegant Age

Anne Austin
One Drop of Blood
The Black Pigeon
Murder at Bridge
Murder Backstairs

E. C. Bentley
Trent's Last Case: The Woman in Black

Ernest Bramah
Max Carrados Resurrected:
The Detective Stories of Max Carrados

Agatha Christie
The Secret Adversary
The Mysterious Affair at Styles

Octavus Roy Cohen
Midnight

Freeman Wills Croft
The Ponson Case
The Pit Prop Syndicate

J. S. Fletcher
The Herapath Property
The Rayner-Slade Amalgamation
The Chestermarke Instinct
The Paradise Mystery
Dead Men's Money
The Middle of Things
Ravensdene Court
Scarhaven Keep
The Orange-Yellow Diamond
The Middle Temple Murder
The Tallyrand Maxim
The Borough Treasurer
In the Mayor's Parlour
The Saftey Pin

R. Austin Freeman
The Mystery of 31 New Inn from the Dr. Thorndyke Series
John Thorndyke's Cases from the Dr. Thorndyke Series
The Red Thumb Mark from The Dr. Thorndyke Series
The Eye of Osiris from The Dr. Thorndyke Series
A Silent Witness from the Dr. John Thorndyke Series
The Cat's Eye from the Dr. John Thorndyke Series
Helen Vardon's Confession: A Dr. John Thorndyke Story
As a Thief in the Night: A Dr. John Thorndyke Story
Mr. Pottermack's Oversight: A Dr. John Thorndyke Story
Dr. Thorndyke Intervenes: A Dr. John Thorndyke Story
The Singing Bone: The Adventures of Dr. Thorndyke
The Stoneware Monkey: A Dr. John Thorndyke Story
The Great Portrait Mystery, and Other Stories: A Collection of Dr. John Thorndyke and Other Stories
The Penrose Mystery: A Dr. John Thorndyke Story

The Uttermost Farthing: A Savant's Vendetta

Arthur Griffiths
The Passenger From Calais
The Rome Express

Fergus Hume
The Mystery of a Hansom Cab
The Green Mummy
The Silent House
The Secret Passage

Edgar Jepson
The Loudwater Mystery

A. E. W. Mason
At the Villa Rose

A. A. Milne
The Red House Mystery

Baroness Emma Orczy
The Old Man in the Corner

Edgar Allan Poe
The Detective Stories of Edgar Allan Poe

Arthur J. Rees
The Hampstead Mystery
The Shrieking Pit
The Hand In The Dark
The Moon Rock
The Mystery of the Downs

Mary Roberts Rinehart
Sight Unseen and The Confession

Dorothy L. Sayers

Whose Body?

Sir William Magnay
The Hunt Ball Mystery

Mabel and Paul Thorne
The Sheridan Road Mystery

Louis Tracy
The Strange Case of Mortimer Fenley
The Albert Gate Mystery
The Bartlett Mystery
The Postmaster's Daughter
The House of Peril
The Sandling Case: What Would You Have Done?

Charles Edmonds Walk
The Paternoster Ruby

John R. Watson
The Mystery of the Downs
The Hampstead Mystery

Edgar Wallace
The Daffodil Mystery
The Crimson Circle

Carolyn Wells
Vicky Van
The Man Who Fell Through the Earth
In the Onyx Lobby
Raspberry Jam
The Clue
The Room with the Tassels
The Vanishing of Betty Varian
The Mystery Girl
The White Alley
The Curved Blades

FOREWORD

Tragedy in the Dark is the seventh installment in the mystery series involving Scotland Yard's Inspector Reynolds. Written by Elaine Hamilton, the nine books in the series were published during the 1930's, that period of time often referred to as The Golden Age of British Mysteries. Other than her authorship of the series, there is little biographical information about Hamilton available.

Unlike the flamboyant amateur detectives that had been so popular during the previous decade, Inspector Reynolds is, at least on the surface, a professional policeman of the style of mystery that has been dubbed "Hum-drum" for their reliance on methodical investigative methods rather than intuition or inspiration. This style became popular in the 1930's in the works of writers such as Freeman Wills Crofts, A. E. Fielding, and Ngaio Marsh. Reynolds, far from being an eccentric character of quirks and moods as many of his predecessors were, is a thoroughly amiable chap, happily married, and not at all adverse to a good honest dinner when the opportunity presents itself. He is well respected by his colleagues and thought of fondly by those who work for him.

A central feature of all of the Reynolds mysteries is the presence of young women of good breeding and education who, due to circumstances, finds themselves caught up against their will in some criminal enterprise. The novels deal as much with how these young women manage, with Reynolds' help, to extricate themselves from this trap—and find romance in the process. The series was clearly aimed at a target audience who could identify with these heroines. As the series progressed, elements of melodrama were added and the books take on more of the aspect of a thriller. In many ways, they resemble Agatha Christie's *The Man in the Brown Suit*.

The crime in *Tragedy in the Dark* involves the murder of a man in a crowded London cinema, who is stabbed while watching the film without attracting the notice of any of the other patrons. To Inspector Reynolds' surprise, the victim is a man who had visited Scotland Yard earlier in the day claiming to have received a threatening letter. The clues in the case are limited, consisting mostly of the observation of a sharp-eyed concessionaire that she had seen a young woman enter with one man and leave with another

Tragedy in the Dark is one of the best mysteries in the Inspector Reynolds series, entertaining and fast paced while toning down the less believable melodramatic elements that mar some of them. In that way, it resembles the first book in the series, *The Westminster Mystery*, more than some of the later installments.

The works of Elaine Hamilton are hard to find these days, particularly the second through fifth books which are particularly rare, yet they are well worth seeking out. It is, therefore, with some pleasure that Resurrected Press offers this new edition of *Tragedy in the Dark*.

About the Cover

The cover of this book contains a re-worked portion of the original dust jacket for the first edition of the book, published in 1935.

About the Author

Not much is known about Elaine Hamilton other than she wrote a series of mysteries in the 1930's featuring Inspector Reynolds of Scotland Yard. *The Westminster Mystery* published in 1930 was the first of these. Other titles in the series include *Murder in the Fog* (1931), *The Green Death* (1932), *The Chelsea Mystery* (1932), *The Silent Bell* (1933), *Peril at Midnight* (1934), *Tragedy in the Dark* (1935), *The Casino Mystery* (1936) and *Murder Before Tuesday* (1937).

Greg Fowlkes
Editor-In-Chief
Resurrected Press
www.ResurrectedPress.

TABLE OF CONTENTS

I. SHADOWED 1

II. A BIRTHDAY PARTY 9

III. MURDER 17

IV. A HARRIS TWEED COAT 23

V. PIKE ANDREWS' PARE 31

VI. IN ROOM 134 30

VII. THE BRASS DISC 45

VIII. INTRODUCING BOB DEANE 53

IX. BEFORE THE MURDER 61

X. A RAT ON THE RUN 69

XI. DAPHNE MAKES A SEARCH 77

XII. IN THE CINEMA 87

XIII. A TERRIBLE AWAKENING 97

XIV: DEANE ON THE CARPET 105

XV. MICHAEL LEARNS THE NEWS 111

XVI. VISITORS FOR REYNOLDS 119

XVII. A FIND AT WATERLOO, ... 129

XVIII. MRS. REYNOLDS ON THE TRAIL 135

XIX. THE LONELY MONUMENT 141

XX. MICHAEL FINDS DAPHNE 149

XXI. AN UNCLE FROM SCOTLAND 157

XXII. ALLEN'S STORY 165

XXIII. MICHAEL'S PATIENT 171

XXIV. IN ALLEN'S FLAT 179

XXV. PRIMROSE 185

XXVI. NEWS FROM AUSTRALIA 191

XXVII. A JEALOUS WOMAN 197

XXVIII. PAT 205

XXIX. A BUNDLE OF MISCHIEF 215

XXX, PRIMROSE SPILLS THE BEANS...223

XXXI, SLUG TAYLOR'S DISCOVERY...229

XXXII, THE THEATRE DRESSING-ROOM... 237

XXXIII, THE MISSING BRACELET 249

XXXIV, THE NET DRAWN TIGHTER..259

XXXV, THE HOUSE ON THE MARSHES 269

XXXVI, AT BAY 275

I. SHADOWED

Tuesday, November 20th.

INSPECTOR REYNOLDS laid down his pen and frowned as the door of his office at the Yard opened. "What is it, Jenkins?" he asked with a touch of irritation. "You know I have an urgent report to do before noon."

Detective Sergeant Jenkins looked worried. He regarded the Inspector's wish as his law, but this morning circumstances seemed to warrant the interruption. At least, he hoped so.

"A man wants to see you on a matter of life and death, sir."

The Inspector smiled.

"They all say that. Who is he?"

"He won't give his name, address or business to any one but you. He's well-dressed, apparently well educated, about thirty-eight years of age, and might be considered good-looking if he weren't so white and jumpy. The constable on duty says the man has waited more than an hour although he was told that you would not him unless he filled in the form."

"Show him up, Jenkins. You might get on with the routine part of this report while I find out what is scaring the mysterious gentleman."

There was no doubt that his visitor was badly frightened, Reynolds decided, as he noticed the trembling hands and nervous gestures of the man whom Jenkins presently ushered in.

"Are you Inspector Reynolds?" the caller demanded in a low shaky voice.

"I am. Take a seat and tell me your name." Reynolds' tone was curt.

The man sat down, and took an envelope from his pocket.

"Look at that," he urged. "it came by the first post this morning."

Reynolds drew a card from the envelope. On it in block letters was printed:—

TO-NIGHT

Underneath was the day's date. November 20th.

"And what is going to happen to-night?" he asked his visitor.

The man gave a mirthless laugh.

"Murder, Inspector."

"Do you expect to be the victim?"

"I certainly do or I should not have come to Scotland Yard this morning."

Reynolds' grey eyes, with their quiet abstracted gaze, gave no hint that he was studying his caller closely.

"Have you had any previous intimation of this nature?" he inquired.

The man nodded.

"Four or five, Inspector. They contain definite threats. I disregarded the first two. Then, becoming uneasy, I tried to do some amateur detective work myself without success. I've got too many enemies, you see."

"I can't see," Reynolds said crisply, "unless you tell me who you are and why you have so many dangerous enemies."

The man slid a finger round inside his collar and glanced towards the corner of the room where Detective Sergeant Jenkins sat writing.

"Couldn't I speak to you alone, Inspector?"

"No. That is my assistant, who works with me on every case I take up," Reynolds informed him "Get on with your story. What is your name?"

"Gill. Jabez Gill. I'm a money lender," the man hesitated, "among other things. My office is in my flat at

20 Wingford Mansions, Bayswater Road. Not far from the Marble Arch."

"I know Wingford Mansions, Mr. Gill. What are the 'other things' you do besides money lending?" Reynolds inquired bluntly.

"I'd rather not go into that"

"You'd better do so and fully, if you want my help. Money lending alone, if the business is properly conducted, is not an adequate reason for receiving threats of murder."

"My business, or the lack of it, led to side-lines. Bits of private inquiry work with," Jabez Gill paused, "perhaps unorthodox results," he finished.

"In plain English, blackmail," Reynolds supplemented.

"I don't like that word, Inspector."

"Perhaps not. But people have been paying money to you?"

"Yes," the man admitted. "That's why I was afraid to come here this morning."

"Have you any suspicion as to which of your victims has the greater reason for designs on your life?"

Gill flinched at the cold contempt in the C.I.D. official's words.

"It might be any one out of a dozen," he muttered. The Inspector raised his eyebrows.

"So bad as that? Well, Mr. Gill, you must give me details concerning your clients."

Jabez Gill wiped his moist hands.

"I'm afraid I can't," he said. "Even with a threat of murder hanging over me, I'm not willingly going to put myself within the reach of the law again."

"Again!" Reynolds caught at the word.

"I started as a youngster in a stockbroker's office, got mixed up in a betting crowd and embezzled some money," Gill explained. "I did eighteen months in the second division, came out of prison at the end of the War and have had to scrounge for a living as best I could ever

since. It was pretty hard going until I got into a moneylender's office and later took over his business."

"H'm. Presumably the 'going' is considerably easier
now with the addition of the less savoury sidelines,"
commented the Inspector. "The rental of flats at Wingford
Mansions is high. As you decline to lay your cards on the
table, Mr. Gill, I don't see why you came to see me," he
added in a casual manner.

Scribbling a few words on a slip of paper, he turned to
his assistant. "Get that seen to at once, Jenkins, will
you?"

Jenkins took the message and went out.

"Follow this man," he read.

Gill leaned over the desk when he was alone with the
Inspector.

"Can't you protect me in some way," he begged
desperately, "without knowing everything? If I tell you, I
risk a term of imprisonment."

"And if you don't," Reynolds replied, "you risk your
life. Make up your mind, Mr. Gill. You can't play pitch
and toss with the laws of England."

"Even if I am what you call a blackmailer," Gill
brought out the word with difficulty, "surely I am entitled
to have my life protected."

"Certainly you are. How do you suggest that it could
be done?" There was disarming innocence in the
Inspector's question.

"If I could have a couple of C.I.D. men to look after me
until to-morrow I should be safe, shouldn't I?"

"Do you propose to clear out to-morrow?" asked
Reynolds pointedly.

The man reddened at Reynolds' unexpected thrust.
What a fool he had been to come here. To-morrow his
passport would be ready and he could be out of the
country. To-day he must spend in the danger zone of his
flat, burning his damning documents and packing. With a
couple of detectives watching the flat, he would have been
safe.

And now, this Inspector, with the vague-looking grey eyes, had touched on his secret. The best thing would be to get out of Scotland Yard quickly and take a chance. The threat said "To-night." It was only a little after noon now. Three hours he would allow himself at the flat. When that business was finished he'd go to a cinema and spend the night at a hotel.

Puffing himself together he rose and forced a smile to his lips.

"I'm sorry to have taken up your time, Inspector. Maybe it was only a silly threat. Sleeplessness has played the dickens with my nerves lately. A couple of good nights' rest and I'll be laughing—"

"Good day, Mr. Gill," the Inspector cut in.

Jabez Gill drew a sigh of relief when he was outside the grim walls of Scotland Yard again. In fancy he had felt the firm fingers of the law gripping his shoulder while he was in Inspector Reynolds' office.

At the moment the threat he had received that morning seemed a shade more remote than the risk of being arrested on a charge of blackmail through coming here. Terror had forced him to flee from one danger to another. All he had to do now was to destroy the incriminating papers in his flat and hide himself in London until the morning. Then, once he had his passport, he could cross the Channel to safety.

Meanwhile it was most unlikely that anyone had followed him to the Yard, but it was as well to be sure.

He stood on the pavement and looked up and down Whitehall, scanning the passers-by. Not one of them seemed to show the slightest interest in him.

And then he noticed the man in the fawn mackintosh on the other side of the road. The man's head was bent over a newspaper and Gill could not see his face.

Fighting back an uneasy feeling, he walked briskly up towards the Strand and entered a tobacconist's shop near the corner. Through the window he saw the same individual saunter slowly by—on this side of the street now.

Gill paid for his purchase and chatted with the assistant for a few minutes. Panic shouldn't make a fool of him a second time to-day. The man was probably aimlessly wandering around. He'd be out of sight by this time Gill walked boldly from the shop.

But the man was reading his newspaper, a few yards away.

Jabez Gill's heart missed a beat. Jumping into a passing taxi he ordered the driver to go quickly to Oxford Circus. The intervening traffic blocked his view when he looked through the back window of the vehicle.

He paid off the driver. Close behind was the man in the fawn mackintosh paying his taxi fare.

There was no doubt now. Gill knew he was being followed. Probably the sender of the anonymous missive did not intend to lose sight of his victim even if he would not strike until to-night.

For a moment Gill had the daring idea to go up to a constable and state that this man had designs on his life. He rejected the thought, remembering his difficult interview at Scotland Yard.

The owner of the fawn mackintosh could not attack him in a crowded street and might be eluded by the exercise of strategy. A big restaurant at the corner seemed a likely place for the maneuver, with its second exit opening into a side street.

Gill strolled into the vestibule, fully aware that his shadow was almost on his heels.

Inside the lift he caught a glimpse of the man's face. It reminded him vaguely of one of his "clients," called Vickers, who had shot himself a few weeks ago. Perhaps, he thought in dismay, this was a relative of Vickers bent on revenge. Vickers had been very profitable!

By a few deft movements Gill continued to keep close to the gates. The lift porter was closing them when a woman tried to enter.

"Full up, madam," she was told.

"Let her take my place," Gill said quietly to the porter. "I'll walk up."

In a second the change was effected, the lift shot up with its burden, including the shadow, and Gill walked out of the restaurant, free.

Arriving at his flat, he worked with frenzied haste. The task of getting rid of his papers and packing took longer than he had anticipated. It was nearly half-past six when he carried his bags down stairs and called a taxi. He was giving the driver the address of a hotel near Victoria when he saw the man in the fawn mackintosh again.

Things began to look serious, Gill reflected during the journey. Still, the man couldn't do him any harm in public.

Gill booked a room at the hotel. Driving to the West End he had dinner at a grill-room and went to a large cinema near by, where a popular film was being shown.

There was no sign of his follower, and Gill's hopes rose.

"Any seats?" he asked the commissionaire.

"Not yet, sir. There'll be plenty presently. Take your place in the queue outside, please."

It was about twenty minutes before the line of people began to move towards the entrance hall. Gill was near the ticket office when he stepped out of the queue and looked along the line. About ten people divided him from the man in the fawn mackintosh. Gloomily he resumed his place.

And then, just as he was buying a ticket, his luck changed.

"That's all for now," said the commissionaire, and held up the queue.

Gill passed into the darkened hall and sank into a seat thankfully. There were over two thousand people in the building and at least until the lights went up the man in the fawn mackintosh couldn't possibly find him.

Inspector Reynolds lifted the receiver as his telephone bell jangled that evening.

"Hello, Jenkins. You've had a long day, I'm afraid. Any luck?" he inquired.

"Nothing's happened to Gill up to now, sir, and I don't see anybody hanging about," the detective replied. "He gave me the slip in a restaurant lift at one o'clock, but I guessed he'd go to his flat afterwards. At six-thirty he drove to a hotel in Victoria where he's dumped his luggage. I've got the number of his room. Now he's in the Royal Imperial Cinema. Shall I go back to his hotel and wait there?"

"No. I'll put another man on. You go and get some food. Good night."

II. A BIRTHDAY PARTY

Tuesday, November 20th.

A FILM had been running for ten minutes when Mrs. Weston and family, by dint of slightly unfair methods in the queue, entered the Royal Imperial Cinema.

Followed by her husband and children, she marched proudly down the carpeted aisle, looking for seats. It was her birthday, and she had celebrated it in style by taking three-and-sixpenny tickets, plus a couple of glasses of port before starting.

"There's five seats in that row, Ma," her young son pointed out.

"They ain't together," objected Mrs. Weston. "It's a pity to be separated. Perhaps them folks in between would shift up," she suggested in clarion tones to four people in the middle of the row.

Three of them showed no signs of having heard the remark. The fourth, a gentleman, remarked coldly that he preferred to stay where he was.

"Never mind, Ma. We can join up later," Mr. Weston said in an embarrassed whisper.

"Righto," agreed his wife. "Arthur, you and Lily push past those people and take those two empty seats. Me and Dad and Marjory'll sit here at the end. Maybe some folks'll remember they've got homes soon and give other people a chance," she added darkly.

"Gimme some of the sweets, else Marj will eat 'em all," her son demanded, pausing in the "push past" authorised by his mother.

"Move along. You're standing on my feet," said the gentleman who had declined to change his seat.

"Here y'are, Arthur." Mrs. Weston thrust a paper bag into her son's hand. "Divide 'em up fair like a good boy between you and Lily, mind."

"Hush."

"Sit down in front," came from indignant voices behind.

"Hush yourself," retorted Mrs. Weston generally. "I paid for my seat same as you."

"Then sit in it and be quiet," requested the gentleman who had refused to change his place.

Mrs. Weston sank down heavily next to him with "Marj" and her husband on the left between her and the side aisle. Before settling in her place to enjoy the film she leaned forward to find out if Arthur and Lily further along the row had obtained their three-and-sixpenny rights. Her eyes were becoming accustomed to the darkness and she was reassured to see that her offspring were engrossed in the picture. She cast a resentful glance over the quartette who had broken up her party.

One of the four was a woman, and Mrs. Weston idly wondered which of the men she belonged to. Probably not the obstinate toff who was her own neighbour. Mrs. Weston felt particularly bitter towards him, for he was staring dully ahead with his eyes below the level of the screen obviously uninterested in the picture.

She determined to make herself as unpleasant as possible. Pulling off her fur, she flicked it across his face and stuck her elbow sharply against his arm. His only response was to draw himself slightly further apart.

Baulked for the moment, Mrs. Weston sucked a peppermint audibly. The double port she had imbibed and the heated atmosphere were making her drowsy. She loosened her coat with a yawn and felt something drop from her lap. Her handbag and fur were there, so it must be her gloves. Bending down, she fumbled about the floor.

"What's the matter now?" demanded her neighbour testily, after she had knocked his leg twice.

"I've dropped my gloves," she explained. "They must be under your feet."

"Then they must stay there. You can get them when the show's over."

"I s'pose you call yourself a perfect gent," exclaimed the woman.

"I've not called myself anything," the man retorted, "but I can describe you as a perfect nuisance with entire truth. You've not been quiet a moment since you came in."

Mrs. Weston muttered something under her breath and subsided. Presently she drifted off into a pleasant doze. The doze had developed to sound sleep with a remarkable dream when she was roused by someone stumbling clumsily past her.

"What's up? Is it over?" she demanded of her daughter, only half awake.

"No, Ma. You've been asleep. It's only some people going out."

"Well, I hope they haven't kicked my gloves away and lost 'em. Is this still the same film?"

"Yes, Ma. It's lovely. That girl who was only the typist has gone on the stage and is a star. Ma, can't I go on the stage? I love dancing."

"No, you can't," her mother snapped shortly. "Honest service is going to be your stage, my girl. Dad, directly this picture's over, strike a match and see if you can find my gloves."

"Pity you hadn't kept 'em on," growled back her husband. "It'd have saved a lot of fuss for everybody. Hold the bag of sweets, Marj, while I look for the dratted things. Now then, Ma, where d'you think they are?"

"They was on the floor between me and this gent on my right. He hadn't the manners to pick 'em up for me."

Mrs. Weston peeped slyly at her neighbour as she spoke, in the hope that he would show annoyance at her remark, but his head had tilted forward, in the attitude of slumber. Between him and Arthur and Lily there were now three empty seats, evidently vacated by the people who had awakened Mrs. Weston as they walked out.

"I say, Dad," she remarked to her husband, "if the sleeping beauty on my right would shift up, Arthur and Lily could come next to me."

"Oh, do stop fidgeting, Em. They're all right where they are," Mr. Weston replied. "You can't disturb folks just to let you and your kids sit in a row." He pulled out a box of matches and knelt down. "I'll find your gloves and then perhaps you'll give me a bit of peace. Keep your legs out of the way."

Mrs. Weston tucked her feet under her seat and awaited results. The match flickered out as her husband extended his search past her and felt carefully round the feet of the sleeping man.

Suddenly his wife heard an exclamation and Mr. Weston crawled back to his seat. She saw him strike another match and extinguish it quickly.

"Did you find 'em?" she demanded.

"Shut up, Em, for Gawd's sake, and don't speak or move till I tell you," came from her husband in an agonised whisper. "Something terrible's happened."

In the darkness she could hear him breathing hard. Was he going to have a stroke like his father had, she thought fearfully. Perhaps stooping down after an unusually heavy tea had sent the blood to his head Awed to stillness, she wondered if he'd go off sudden and leave her alone with three children to bring up.

She cast a frightened look at her husband. What she saw did nothing to console her. He was straining forward, his face gleaming white, staring with wild eyes at the figure of the man on her right.

With a dreadful caution, Mrs. Weston turned her head slowly and tried to see the cause of her husband's alarm. The overcoat collar of the man next to her was turned up and his head bowed as if he were sleeping naturally, but one glance told her the truth. She had seen death before and was not afraid of it. Neither was her husband who had fought in the War. It must be something worse than that to have terrified him, she reflected. Besides, he had been kneeling on the floor when she heard him make that exclamation.

Her eyes travelled down from the man's still countenance. His overcoat was open and just over his heart she caught the glint of steel. Imagination filled in the blanks.

Holding her hand to her trembling mouth she suppressed the first instinctive desire to scream. There was danger, grave danger, here for her husband. People in the row behind could state that he had been kneeling beside the man who was now dead.

Dead? He must have been murdered. Suspicion might fall upon her man the moment the crime was discovered. She must act at once and save him somehow. As he seemed too scared to think of anything, she must do the best she could. The seats immediately behind them were vacant now. Maybe they could all get out without being noticed. . .

"Listen, Marj," she said softly to the child next to her, "I feel bad and we must get home at once. Slip along to Arthur and Lily and tell them to leave by the other gangway. Dad and me will meet you at the back. Don't bother me with questions, there's a good girl"

Her urgent tone impressed Marjory.

"All right, Ma. I'll make them come with me," she promised.

Her mother lifted her bodily over the dead man and thrust her forward with a murmured injunction to hurry.

"Come on, Dad, let's clear out of this stuffy place," she said, making an effort to speak naturally. "I feel quite faint."

Mr. Weston nodded and followed her up the, aisle in a dazed fashion. The three children were waiting for them at the back of the hall. They gazed curiously at "Ma," who was rarely ill and had chosen such an unfortunate moment for her indisposition. They trailed after their parents obediently.

Mr. Weston thrust violently at a door. It was one of the emergency exits, ordinarily used after the final performance each night.

An attendant hurried forward.

"You can't go out that way," he informed the party sternly. "The exit—"

Mr. Weston lost his head.

"I must, I must," he cried. "Let me out, quick."

"Be quiet, Dad," his wife said in a warning tone as the attendant caught her husband's arm.

"What's all this noise about?" The question came from an individual in evening dress who had been standing near.

"This man wants me to open the emergency exit, sir," the attendant explained. "He's in a hurry to go out."

"My husband feels faint, sir," put' in Mrs. Weston.

"Why, it's you who feels bad, Ma!" piped her little daughter indignantly.

Mrs. Weston shook the child's shoulder.

"Hold your noise, Marj," she ordered.

The manager instructed the attendant to let the party out by another door. He was moving away indifferently when a shaft of light from the screen illuminated Mr. Weston's light check suit.

The manager's eyes met those of the attendant in a significant glance. Together they conducted Mr. and Mrs. Weston and the children into the brilliantly lighted foyer.

"You youngsters stay here for a minute," the manager said, and turned to Weston.

"Had an accident?" he inquired mildly.

Weston moistened his dry lips.

"No, sir. The heat inside made me and my missus feel a bit queer. That's all."

"How do you account for that?" The manager Pointed to the man's light trousers and coat cuffs, which, bore large crimson stains, obviously still wet.

Weston's eyes darted from his besmeared garments to the relentless eyes of the manager and then to his wife.

"Don't you say a word, Em," he cried, and made a leap for the street.

Instantly the commissionaire caught him and grasped him firmly.

"Hold on to him while I telephone for the police," ordered the manager. "There's something about all this that needs an explanation."

III. MURDER

Tuesday, November 20th.

THE commissionaire led Weston to the manager's office. Telling the frightened children to sit quietly in the vestibule, Mrs. Weston followed.

The manager was already telephoning when she entered the office.

"There must be a silly mistake, sir," she began in the desperate hope of getting her man released before the police arrived or the murder was discovered. "You see, he's been doing up our parlour and I expect he got himself plastered with red paint without us noticing it."

"You'll only make it worse, Em, by telling lies," her husband said wearily. "The manager knows this ain't paint. But all the same, I haven't done anything wrong."

"Then why such haste to leave the cinema?" inquired the manager bluntly. "And why, did you try to bolt when I saw your clothes?"

"I was scared," Weston admitted. "I don't know how my clothes got stained. It's enough to scare any innocent man. I don't believe you've got any right to keep me here," he ended boldly.

The manager wasn't oversure on that point either, but he did not intend to admit it.

"Well, innocent or guilty, you can explain to the police how those marks came to be on your suit and why you acted in such a suspicious manner," was his answer. He glanced at his watch and spoke to the commissionaire. "News reel just about to start, I suppose?"

"Yes, sir. A good crowd is coming in. Cheaper seats are full but there are plenty of three-and-sixpennies. They thinned out during the last picture."

The manager frowned as an idea occurred to him.

"What seats were you in?" he asked the woman.

"Three-and-sixpenny," Mrs. Weston answered with pride. "All the lot of us, 'cause 'twas my birthday. Good money wasted. We weren't in there an hour when—" she broke off in dismay, wishing she had not said so much.

"When you all decided to hurry out!" finished the manager. "Where were you sitting?"

"On the, right hand side," Mrs. Weston lied, catching a warning look from her husband.

At that moment the door was burst open by an anxious-faced attendant who hurried in and said something in an undertone to the manager. From the vicinity of the hall screams could be heard, screams that came from a human being and not from the news reel.

The screams grew louder. Evidently the owner of the voice had rushed out into the vestibule. At the door of the manager's office a police sergeant and constable suddenly appeared.

"Thank Heaven you've come!" the manager said with relief.

"What's the trouble?" asked the sergeant. "Who sent for us.?"

"I did. My name's Milner. I'm the manager. A man has been found dead in the stalls, I hear, officer. I don't know whether it's a case of suicide or murder."

"It can't be suicide," put in the cinema attendant who had entered so hastily a few moments before.

"Why not?" demanded the sergeant.

"Because he has a knife thrust right into his body. I've not touched him." The attendant shuddered. "We're keeping that section of the theatre clear."

"I'll go and have a look," said the sergeant. "Detain these people," he added to his colleague, glancing significantly at Weston's clothes "I shall be back presently."

In a few moments he returned.

"Well?" inquired the manager anxiously.

"I've left a constable in charge there, and your men are putting screens around until the doctor comes," the sergeant told him "Now then," he went on, turning to the attendant, "who discovered the body?"

"Two people who tried to pass into that row of seats which was nearly empty. There was more light in the hall then."

"Has this man anything to do with it?" the sergeant indicated Weston.

"He was acting suspiciously and—" the manager began.

"Leaving in a hurry isn't acting suspicious," Weston interrupted defensively. "My name's James Weston and I've lived in Pimlico for more than ten years."

"His clothes were in that state," the manager continued, "so I asked him to wait and telephoned for you. I didn't know about this horrible business then."

The sergeant wheeled round as a little girl came in timidly.

"Whose is this child?"

"She's mine, sir." Mrs. Weston put arm round her daughter's shoulder. "Marj, dear, Ma told you to stay out there with Arthur and Lil. You shouldn't have come in. These gentlemen want to talk to me and Dad."

"Somebody was screaming, Ma, and we got frightened." The child whimpered. "Let me stay with you."

"I found this near the feet of the dead man," the attendant said, giving the officer a brown crumpled object.

The sergeant unrolled a pair of gloves, stained with crimson in places..

"Why, Ma, that's your gloves!" exclaimed the child. "My! Fancy having two policemen in to find them!" she added in awed accents.

"They're not mine," Mrs. Weston declared firmly.

"Yes, they are, Ma. Look, that's the button I broke in half," the child pointed to it in triumph. "They're not half messed up, though."

"I'll ring up the police station," the sergeant informed Mr. Milner, "and get the doctor and ambulance men along."

"The hall shall be kept as dark as possible until they come," promised the manager. "We'll prevent a crowd from gathering round."

The sergeant put through his telephone call. As he replaced the receiver he glanced at a tall, grey-eyed man who had just entered the office.

"I'm Inspector Reynolds of Scotland Yard," the newcomer remarked "I had a man under observation in this cinema to-night and looked in for that reason. Anything wrong, sergeant?

"Murder!" said the sergeant grimly, and crisply outlined all that he knew.

"While you're wasting time keeping my husband here, the murderer is getting miles away," Mrs. Weston ejaculated bitterly. "Jim wouldn't harm a fly. Besides, the man must have been dead when we went into the cinema. Come to think of it, I noticed the man who sat next to me was hunched up all funny and never moved all the time we was there."

Her invention was promptly quenched by the sharp voice of her little girl.

"Why, Ma, you forget. That was the man who wouldn't move when you asked him to. He said he liked it where he was. You must have thought he was asleep when you lifted me over him and told me to get Arthur and Lily out by the other gangway quick."

"Hold your tongue, Marj," exclaimed her distracted mother. "You don't know what you're talking about."

"On the contrary, Mrs. Weston, I think your child is not far wrong," the sergeant remarked.

Tactful attendants had calmed a few excited people in the vestibule, and cleared them away by announcing that someone had been taken ill, when Inspector Reynolds, accompanied by a doctor and the sergeant, crossed the foyer.

The entire back of the left block of seats was concealed from the public and empty of occupants. Empty, save for one still figure in the fifth row down.

By the aid of an electric torch Inspector Reynolds and the doctor threaded their way along the vacant stalls until they reached the victim.

In silence the C.I.D. man waited while the doctor made his examination. It was a silence punctuated incongruously by the humorous talkie in progress and occasional outbursts of laughter from the vast audience who were unaware of the tragedy in their midst.

The medical man closed his bag.

"Nothing that I can do, Inspector. He's been dead about an hour; perhaps less. Death must have been instantaneous. Stabbed through the heart."

"A pretty strong blow," commented Reynolds.

He extracted the weapon and showed it to the medical man.

"I've never seen a stiletto like this before," commented the doctor.

"Nor a handle like this either," Reynolds said, regarding the shaft which was of steel, square-sided and notched deeply at intervals. "It reminds me of—well, that can wait. Here's the Yard photographer. We'll let him get on with his job. I want the ambulance man to take the body out before the audience leave. We'll go back to the office and talk to the man they're holding."

"The manager seems pretty certain that fellow in the office committed the crime," the sergeant remarked.

Reynolds' eyes had a quizzical expression.

"I don't think it's going to be as simple as that," he replied. "One minute, doctor. Raise his head a bit, will you? I want to see what type he was."

Hitherto the light of the torch had been concentrated on the body of the man, and his head, sunk deeply in the upturned collar of his overcoat, had been in shadow.

The Inspector gazed closely at the face of the victim. It was the man who had called at Scotland Yard that morning! The sender of the anonymous message had fulfilled his threat.

"About forty years of age, well-dressed, might be something in the City," suggested the doctor.

"Very likely," Reynolds agreed vaguely. At the moment he was not giving away the information that he knew the dead man. "What have you found in his pockets?" he asked.

"Plenty of money but nothing that supplies any clue to his identity." The sergeant's tone was despondent. "No cards or letters. That may delay things a bit, Inspector."

Reynolds I nodded.

"It may," he admitted with inward satisfaction. He would get a few hours' start before the Press opened up details concerning the crime. "Let's see what this chap Weston and his family can tell us."

In the vestibule the medical man wished them goodnight. Reynolds went into the manager's office with the sergeant.

IV. A HARRIS TWEED COAT

Tuesday, November 20th.

"YOU were frightened when you saw blood on the floor while searching for your wife's gloves with a lighted match," summed up the Inspector as Weston finished his story.

"That's right, sir," the man acquiesced. "Then my missus saw something had upset me and said we'd go."

The manager frowned. In his opinion the C.I.D. official was inclined to think too lightly of Weston's share in the crime.

"I still maintain that Weston and his wife acted in a most suspicious manner, Inspector," he observed.

"How would you like to get hung on circumstantial evidence when you was innocent?" Weston exploded. "I tried to do a bunk because I was scared."

"We are all apt to act unwisely on the spur of the moment," was the Inspector's calming remark. He pivoted the subject to another angle. "Try to tell me all you can, Weston, about the people who went out from your row of seats, *before* you looked for the gloves."

Weston bit his lip.

"I'm sorry, sir. I didn't notice them. You know how it is in a cinema when a film is on and folks push past you. One was a woman, I fancy, but I don't even know how many people went out."

"Three, Dad," piped the shrill voice of his little girl.

The Inspector turned to the child with a smile.

"That's splendid, Marjory. Did you notice if they were men, women or children?" he asked in kindly tones.

"There were no children," she assured him. "First there was a man and a young lady. And about a minute later another man. He stumbled against the gentleman who was sitting next to mother."

"I wonder how you came to notice that he stumbled." Reynolds suppressed his eagerness. This child was giving valuable information, but he must proceed with caution or she might venture beyond the bounds of accuracy.

"The first two blocked the picture from me so I looked to see how many more wanted to go out," the child explained. "I saw there was another man standing up. He tripped over the gentleman's feet; sort of fell on his chest. Then he went out too."

"Was he with the first man and woman, do you think, Marjory?" Reynolds inquired.

"I dunno, sir. I didn't want to miss the picture. It was lovely and exciting."

"Did you notice anything about these people, Mrs. Weston?"

"No, sir. It was very hot in there and I was sound asleep," the woman confessed. "But Marj is right about the last being a man and stumbling. It was that that woke me up. He knocked against me too. I was too sleepy to see what he was like, and it was pitch dark just then. I remember calling him a clumsy hound and that's all. Perhaps the attendants could describe him," she added.

Reynolds shot an interrogative glance at the manager.

"I should think it is most improbable," Mr. Milner replied. "People are coming and going all the time and there was a biggish crowd, entering the vestibule."

"Pity you didn't make a fuss earlier and stop the right man," Mrs. Weston cut in with bitterness.

The manager ignored the comment. He considered that he had done his bit by holding the Westons, and now this easy-going Inspector was apparently going to let them slip off scot-free. He decided to wash his hands of the affair, and picked up some letters on his desk with an air of bored disapproval.

"One moment, Mr. Milner!" Reynolds said sharply. "I need your attention." Turning to the Westons, he inquired, "I want each of you to tell me as near as you can what was happening on the screen when these people went out."

Weston rubbed his forehead and looked sheepish.

"Well, sir, to tell the truth, my mind was mainly on Tottenham Hotspurs. I send in football coupons weekly, for a prize," he explained. "I was sort of looking at the picture without taking it in, thinking over different teams' chances."

"And I was dead asleep, sir," added his wife ruefully.

"I know," came Marjory's voice in triumph. "The uncle was just accusing his nephew of stealing the money from the safe when the first two people passed in front of me."

"You're getting this, I hope, Mr. Milner," the Inspector said in a curt undertone.

"I hear it, of course," the manager retorted sullenly, "though I can't understand what it has to do with me."

"It will check up the time of the murder." Reynolds' tone was cold with annoyance. "You can surely ascertain how long the film took to reach that point, can't you?"

The manager sat up alertly. At last he saw what the Inspector was driving at.

"Almost to a minute, Inspector," he agreed, rising. "Shall I ask the film operator?"

"Yes, please, when we've heard the child's reply to my next question. Tell me more about the film, Marjory," Reynolds asked the little girl. Was the nephew angry with his uncle?"

The child puckered her brow.

"Yes, they had a real row, and I think the young man knocked his uncle down."

"Didn't you see him do it?" inquired Reynolds.

"No, sir. I was looking sideways at the man who stumbled and then he blocked up my view when he scrambled past me. When I could see the picture again the uncle was lying on the floor and his nephew had gone."

"Got that, Mr. Milner?" Reynolds demanded swiftly.

The manager nodded and rose.

"That ought to fix it exactly. I'll let you know what our operator says," he promised.

Marjory Weston, on being further questioned, was sure that the man who went out was tall and big. "Like that man," she added, pointing to the commissionaire. Also that he wore a cap, and a rough overcoat because it touched her hand and felt like a blanket.

"It had a funny smell," she finished.

The Inspector felt anxious. So far he was convinced that the child's story was accurate. Was she now, he feared, beginning, to draw upon her imagination? It was most unlikely that a man who intended to commit a cold-blooded murder would be so stupid as to use perfume beforehand.

"What kind of scent was it?" he asked dubiously.

"It wasn't like a scent. A funny smell," the child persisted. "Like Mrs. Milligan's room, Ma," she said, turning to her mother.

"She's an Irish neighbour of ours, sir," Mrs. Weston explained, "and has a peat fire sometimes."

Reynolds glanced at the door, behind which the manager's overcoat was hung.

"Shut your eyes, Marjory," he said, "and we'll have a guessing game. I'll give you a box of chocolates if you can find that funny smell again. Sniff this." Beneath her nostrils he held his own cloth overcoat. "Is that it?"

"No, sir," she replied instantly, obediently keeping her eyelids closed.

He tested her with various things and received negative answers. At last he tried her with the manager's overcoat.

"That's it, sir," she cried. "That's the funny smell I mean."

Very little to go upon, Reynolds reflected, but at least he had proved that the probable murderer had worn a Harris tweed overcoat.

Mrs. Weston's eyes suddenly gleamed.

"Does that mean the manager committed the murder, sir?" she breathed.

The commissionaire snorted indignantly.

"That overcoat's been there hanging up ever since Mr. Milner came in at seven o'clock," he stated "He's dressed in evening clothes and was standing at the back of the stalls when all this bother began. If an alibi's needed for him, there's plenty of the attendants could prove—"

"We don't need an alibi for Mr. Milner," Reynolds interrupted "Mr. Weston, you and your family are at liberty to go home." He put a coin into the man's hand. "Buy Marjory some chocolates. You will probably be called to attend the inquest to give evidence, but there is nothing alarming about that. Good-night."

A few moments later the manager returned from his quest.

"The particular episode the child mentioned was shown on the screen at about twelve minutes past nine," he reported. "If that's all the clue you have to help, I don't envy you your job, Inspector."

Reynolds himself didn't feel over-cheerful.

"I'm going to question every member of your staff was in the vestibule at that time, Mr. Milner." The manager grinned.

"If they were obeying my instructions, they were attending to people who were coming in and not those who were going out. However, go to it, Inspector. I wish you luck."

Reynolds felt he had need of it as he went from one to the other of the vestibule staff. He picked up an unexpected trail at last from the girl at the sweet stall.

"A pretty girl came out of the left exit with a gent at ten past nine," she declared. "He wanted to buy her some chocolates. I said I'd just shut my stall for the night but he could get some from the automatic machine if that would do. He hadn't any small silver. Just then another chap came out of the cinema by the same exit, and the first man—the one with the girl—" she broke off awkwardly.

"Call the first man A and the second man B," Reynolds suggested.

"That'll be easier. Well, A left the girl and asked B if he had change for half a crown. B snapped out, 'No, I haven't,' and hurried out."

"What happened then?" Reynolds inquired.

"A seemed disappointed. The pretty girl with him said it didn't matter and anyhow, she asked, why should he bother about her? I think they'd only made friends in the cinema," the girl added confidentially. "They went out together and I saw her get on a 'bus. He stood on the cinema steps for a minute and then walked away. I expect he thought, 'there goes another busted romance.'"

"Would you recognise either of them again?"

"Well, the man, A, I mean, was just ordinary and he didn't cut much ice with me. But the girl was lovely; a sort of Constance Bennett type. I'd know her anywhere and her clothes too."

"Did any other people come out by that door into the vestibule soon afterwards?"

"Nobody until that family who kicked up a shindy and were kept in the manager's office," the girl replied positively. "I was watching for my friend who is an attendant at that side of the house. A woman came out screaming blue murder shortly after and we had a rare job getting her quiet."

It seemed pretty evident that this girl had described the three people who had left the row of seats where the murdered man was discovered.

"Will you write down a description of A and the pretty fair-haired girl?" Reynolds requested. Walking across to the manager meanwhile he asked if the girl in charge of the sweet stall was to be depended upon, as her information, if inaccurate, might be seriously misleading.

"Miss Oliver is as sharp as a needle, Inspector. She has been here over four years and I've found her most reliable," Mr. Milner replied. "Her memory for faces is excellent. At times she is a bit pert with clients who try to be 'fresh' with her, but that's all."

Reynolds felt distinctly encouraged by the manager's assurance. His spirits reached an even higher level when he read Miss Oliver's clear notes on the man A and his pretty companion a few minutes later. Even of A, who, she had said, was "ordinary," she had given a tolerable description, while that of the pretty girl was a cameo of detail.

"Thank you, Miss. Oliver," he said, placing the paper in his pocket. "You've been of great assistance. Of course you cannot tell me what the second man, B, was like?"

"Can't I?" she demanded with a touch of the pertness ascribed to her by her employer. "I've still got the use of my tongue."

Reynolds reflected that so long as she talked to some purpose she could be as pert as she liked.

"See if it works as well as your pen has, will you?" he bantered. "Would you know B again?"

"Would I know my own brother-in-law?" she retorted.

"Your brother-in-law!" Reynolds repeated incredulously. "Surely B wasn't—"

The girl flicked her fingers in a gesture copied from the screen.

"You go too fast, mister. The gent we're calling B wasn't my 'in-law' but he's the very spit of the bloke my poor sap of a sister married last week. She's down at Margate on her honeymoon with him now, Heaven help her. She'll need it too. Took all her savings he did to furnish their home! However, he hasn't been wished on to your family so you don't have to worry about him. D'you want him described too?"

The Inspector certainly did and said so.

Miss Oliver pulled on her coat and hat.

"I can't remember now because I'm hungry," she remarked pointedly. "But maybe I could after sausage and mashed and a cup of coffee. That is if your pocket money'll run to that."

"I think it might," Reynolds gravely agreed. "There's a restaurant across the street."

"I'm most annoyed that Miss Oliver has been so impertinent," the manager remarked in a vexed undertone to Reynolds. "I've never heard her speak in such a fashion before. Shall I give her a hint that you're an *Inspector*?"

Reynolds' eyes flashed with amusement

"Not on any account; Mr. Milner. I'll get more out of her if she is natural. The girl is a jewel. Sausage and mashed is a small price to pay for what she can tell me."

V. PIKE ANDREWS' PARE

Tuesday, November 20th

INSPECTOR REYNOLDS kept his promise nobly and made no attempt to question his guest while she was dealing with the sausage and mashed. She thrust away her empty plate and gave him a speculative glance.

"I've mopped that up," she announced. "Go ahead. What d'you want to know?"

"What about some trifle?" he invited.

"It wasn't in the bargain."

"We'll throw that in for information already received," Reynolds told her, and gave an order to the waitress.

Miss Oliver opened her handbag and after a search pushed some snapshots across the table.

"You can look at those while I'm eating. I forgot I had them with me."

Reynolds studied a photograph of a bridal pair with eager interest.

"This is your sister and her husband, I suppose. You say that he closely resembles the man who came out of the cinema to-night?"

"You've caught the idea, mister. Mum says I've got the brains, and my sister's got the looks in our bunch. Beauty and the beast, I call her and her husband. He knows it too. There's no love lost between us."

"How tall is he?" Reynolds inquired, anxious to turn the domestic recital to a subject nearer his heart. "About the same height as the man you saw to-night?"

Miss Oliver accepted the lead.

"Yep. Call it five feet ten, and broad shouldered. He wore a lightish brown overcoat made of rough tweed and had on a darker cap. Black hair and eyes, biggish nose and a heavy jaw. A sort of prize fighter's jib, if you get me."

"I get you," Reynolds replied, mentally noting that the description indeed tallied closely with the face of Miss Oliver's brother-in-law. "You were very quick to observe all this in the minute or two when the man came out of the cinema."

"No, I wasn't," she rapped back bluntly. "I noticed him before the show, about eight o'clock. He was in the queue in the vestibule. I pointed him out to the commissionaire, and said, 'That chap's exactly like my sister's husband.' He'll remember if you ask him."

"Your word is good enough for me, Miss Oliver. Did the man you observed do anything unusual in any way before he took his ticket?"

The girl puckered her brows thoughtfully.

"Not exactly unusual; or if he did, I didn't see it. But I remember one thing that maybe was queer. The queue was getting near the box office and he was behind a well-dressed man in a dark blue overcoat and grey felt hat."

The murdered man had a dark blue overcoat and grey felt hat, Reynolds reflected.

"The well-dressed gent stepped out of the queue and walked to the door as if he were watching for somebody. Instead of taking his place, I saw the bloke you're after deliberately hold back until the gent returned."

"You're sure of this?" inquired the Inspector.

"Positive," the girl affirmed. "Because I said to myself, 'Well, if you're like my blasted—beg your pardon, mister—brother-in-law in looks, you ain't in ways.' He'd have snatched the gent's place, I'll bet."

"Can you spare me one of these snapshots?"

"You can have the blooming lot if they're any use to you. I don't want 'em." The girl's eyes lighted with malicious glee as an idea occurred to her. "Why not print copies of that photograph and send 'em to the Press? I'd love to see that mug's face under a 'Wanted for murder' headline."

The Inspector's mouth twitched.

"Your brother-in-law might not share your joy, I'm afraid, Miss Oliver."

"He hasn't got a moustache and this chap had," she objected. "You stick one on this snap, mister. A short Ronald Colman sort of affair it was."

"I'll remember. Thank you for your help, Miss Oliver. I'm sorry to have kept you so long."

She rose and fastened her coat.

"So long as I've earned my supper, it's all right by me," she remarked nonchalantly. "Anyhow, I've told you the truth. And in case you think I'm a Nosey Parker, you try standing at a sweet stall hour after hour with very little to do but watch folks going in to enjoy themselves. You'd begin to notice a thing or two like me unless you were soft, and," she added kindly, "I don't suppose you'd be a sergeant at Scotland Yard if you were. G'night."

The Inspector chuckled to himself as he walked back to the cinema. He had learnt a lot from the bright little cockney girl's fearless tongue and her final remark would help to keep him humble.

The commissionaire met him with the news that the body of the dead man had just been taken away in an ambulance.

"All nice and quiet by the side door, sir," he added. "Mr. Milner won't allow anyone to touch that section of the stalls until you give permission."

"Good." Reynolds drew the man on to the pavement. "Do you see anybody in the street now who might have been here an hour ago and noticed people leaving the cinema? Newsboys, taxi-touts, for instance.?

The commissionaire looked up and down.

"There's usually an Evening Record boy outside about that time. He's gone now though." He paused a minute. "There's a cunning old rascal who hangs round most evenings. I wonder if he saw anything. He was here to-night, because he fetched a taxi for the woman who rushed out screaming. Probably he's in the pub round the corner. The Black Dog. You can't mistake him, sir. Everybody calls him 'Fish and Chips' and you can smell him at half a mile."

The barmaid behind the counter at the Black Dog favoured Reynolds with a coy look as he entered. She knew good clothes when she saw them, and decided that their occupant was worthy of her most ingratiating manner. Her smile changed to a bleak expression upon hearing his request.

"Yes, I know old 'Fish and Chips,'" she replied icily "He's over there in the corner. If you want anything, you'd better order it now. It's nearly closing time, and the police are pretty hot round this way."

Carrying a pint of ale, Reynolds walked over to the spot the barmaid had indicated. There sat an ill-kept old man, his garments apparently held together by string. He shot a crafty glance at Reynolds who set the glass of ale before him.

"You can do with a drink, I fancy," the Inspector remarked casually.

"Thank'ee, sir," the old man replied. "And what can I do for you?"

"You fetched a cab for an hysterical woman at the Royal Imperial Cinema to-night."

"Fish and Chips" took a long drink before he nodded.

"Did you notice any of the people who went out of the cinema immediately before that?" Reynolds pursued.

"There wasn't many to notice."

Reynolds fancied he detected a touch of evasion in the man's answer.

"Try to remember," be urged. "It might be worth your while."

"Fish and Chips" peered under his rheumy eyelids at the Inspector.

"You one of them 'flatties'?" he inquired in mild accents.

Reynolds skirted the question by asking why.

"Oh, nothin'," replied "Fish and Chips" wearily, "only I hate 'em. Got a pinch o' baccy, sir?"

A cigarette was the nearest thing Reynolds could manage. It helped to bridge the awkward subject of detectives. By a little subterfuge of feigned interest in the girl who had left the cinema with the man he had called A, he was able to glide on to the subject of his quarry in the Harris coat.

"Yes, I saw 'im come out in a 'urry. I offered to get a cab," the old man stated. "He was one of them mean ones: jes' pushed me away and got one 'imself."

"You didn't hear the, address he gave?"

"Fish and Chips" shook his head.

"No, I wasn't near enough," he said. "Pike Andrews may remember. He drove the gent. Pike's on the rank by the side of the cinema most evenings. Much obliged, sir, I'm sure. No offence at what I said about 'flatties,' I hope."

"None whatever," 'Reynolds assured him.

Pike Andrews was not on the rank, he discovered a few minutes later, but a fellow taximan was able to give his address.

Reynolds tried to decide between two courses of action open to him. Should he wait here for Andrews?

Or should he go to the murdered man's hotel?

Obviously it was most important that he should see Pike Andrews at once and ascertain where he had driven the man in the Harris tweed coat. On the other hand, Andrews might not return to the rank to-night.

"If Andrews comes back, ask him to ring me up at this number," he said to the taxi-driver's colleague. "What time does he usually finish for the night and go home?"

"It's his own cab and he won't be late to-night, sir," the taximan answered. "Pike told me his missus was very bad with 'flu and he was going to knock off early for once. He may be home now."

"In that case, drive me there," Reynolds requested. "I'll chance it."

Near the block of flats in Praed Street, where Pike
Andrews lived, the taxi-driver stopped.

"That's him, sir," he said, pointing to a man walking
on the footpath. "Hi, Pike, this genel'man wants to speak
to you."

"You picked up a fare outside the Royal Imperial
Cinema about a quarter past nine to-night," Reynolds
said.

"What of it?" Pike's tone was belligerent. "That's what
I drive a taxi for, isn't it?"

"Of course. I want to know where you drove that
particular fare."

"Aw, do you?" This time Pike was definitely
aggressive. "Well, you can *want*. He paid what was on the
clock and a bit over, and where he went's no business of
yours or mine. I've seen you private 'tees before to-day.
Dirty unsporting lot. Trailing round trying to trap some
poor devil of a man or woman and bring a divorce case
against 'em. You don't get no evidence from me, and
that's flat."

Reynolds appeared unmoved by the outburst.

"I am an Inspector from Scotland Yard, Andrews. The
information I want from you is not for divorce but," he
paused impressively, "murder."

Pike Andrews was startled.

"Murder! Lumme, d'you mean to say the chap I picked
up outside the cinema did the job?"

"I don't mean to say anything," Reynolds replied. "I
want his address, and I may need you to identify him
later on. Where did you drop him?"

"I think I'd know him again, sir. Tall, biggish chap he
was, with a heavy sort of face."

Reynolds produced one of the snapshots that Miss
Oliver had given him.

"Is he like anyone amongst that group?" he inquired,
holding his magnifying glass over the photograph to aid
the taxi-driver.

Almost at once Pike's finger indicated the man who had recently claimed Miss Oliver's sister for a bride.

"If that ain't him, it's his twin brother," he declared. "Only I fancy my fare had a moustache. Murder, eh?"

"Where did you drive him, Andrews?" Reynolds' voice had a hint of impatience. "Hurry up, man. Time is important."

"You'll have a job to trace him at the address I took him to, guv'ner."

"Why?" Reynolds demanded.

"Waterloo Station's a big place," Pike retorted with a sardonic grin.

VI. IN ROOM 134

Tuesday, November 20th.

OUTSIDE the hotel in Victoria where Jabez Gill had booked a room earlier that evening, Reynolds found his assistant, Detective-Sergeant Jenkins, waiting.

The Inspector pursed his lips in mock severity.

"I put Detective Yelland on to this job," he observed, "and told you to get some food."

"Yes, sir," Jenkins replied with a placating smile. "After supper I came along here and relieved Yelland. Thought I'd like to see our bird Gill roll home from the movies. It must be over by this time. He may be back at any minute."

"The cinema is doubtless over, but Gill will never come back," Reynolds told him. "He was murdered. Stabbed whilst a film was in progress."

Jenkins listened intently while the Inspector related the history of the last hour or so.

"The murder was probably committed at twelve minutes past nine by a powerfully built man in the thirties, wearing a Harris tweed coat. He left at nine fifteen and drove to Waterloo Station. And that," Reynolds summed up, "is virtually all I've discovered up to now. Not much to work upon, eh?"

Jenkins tried to take a more optimistic view.

"The photograph Miss Oliver gave you must be a pretty good likeness of the man you want if the taxi driver recognized his fare from it. It ought to come in useful, sir. Couldn't the Press print copies of it; requesting information from anyone who had seen the man?"

The Inspector's lips curled to a grim line.

"There is one snag that cuts out your idea. Miss Oliver's brother-in-law might quite reasonably object to such unpleasant publicity. I have his name and address and there's no cause to suspect that he is anything worse than the unfortunate double of the man in the Harris tweed coat."

"Also," Jenkins put in, "the man we want has a moustache."

"He *had* one, my lad, false or real. By this time he is probably clean-shaven. In which case he will resemble even more closely the man in this snapshot!" The Inspector passed it to Jenkins, "Have a good look at it. Did you by any chance spot him in the cinema queue tonight?"

Jenkins stared hard at the picture for a minute or two.

"No, sir, I'm sorry, to say I didn't. It's hard that a C.I.D. man should be beaten by a sweet-stall girl and a taxi-driver. Even old 'Fish and Chips' did better."

"You were keeping your eyes on Gill," his chief said consolingly. "Miss Oliver might not have noticed this man at all but for the resemblance to her sister's husband. Anything suspicious happened here since you came?" he added, glancing at the hotel before they were standing.

Nothing. Yelland stationed himself in the lounge where he could watch the board where the keys are hung. Jabez Gill's room number is—was 134. Yelland said no one took his key from the hook."

Reynolds nodded.

"Good. We'll do that now. Come along. With luck we'll find something interesting in Gill's luggage."

The two C.I.D. officials entered the hotel and Reynolds asked to speak to the manager.

"Mr. Fleming is probably engaged," the haughty blonde at the reception desk announced pertly. "What is your business?"

Reynolds drew out his pocket-book.

"My business is urgent and private. Send in this it once, please," he requested.

The blonde cast a casual glance at the name and, flushing under her rouge, ordered a page to take the card to the manager.

"Of course, Inspector, if I had known—" she in apologetic tones.

Reynolds was indifferent to her pertness or apology.

A trace of anxiety was on the manager's suave face when he appeared. The presence of Scotland Yard officials was no asset to the welfare hotel.

"I hope nothing is wrong!" he murmured.

Reynolds explained what had happened.

"I should like to see the dead man's room, Mr. Fleming," he added.

The manager conducted the Inspector and Jenkins' to the lift.

On the second floor he led his visitors along a corridor and, stopping at the door numbered 134, opened it. Two large suitcases were stacked against a wall and a dressing-case rested on the luggage stand. An unopened parcel stood on the dressing-table.

Reynolds tried the locks of each of the bags, and cast a significant glance at his colleague.

"The gentleman, Mr. Jabez Gill, who booked a room soon after half past six this evening, did not come up here at all," the Inspector observed. "He engaged it at the office, left his luggage and went away at once."

"That is quite a usual proceeding if a guest is in a hurry," replied the manager. "I was naturally not aware of it in this case. I presume you were watching this Mr. Gill."

"My assistant, Detective Jenkins, was doing so. Who has been in this room since six-thirty or had access to the key?" Reynolds inquired.

"No one except the chambermaid who has her pass," the manager assured him. "She comes in between seven and eight o'clock to lower the blinds and turn down the beds. She will be on duty until midnight if you would like to speak to her."

"I should." Reynolds rang the bell and, walking over to a communicating door, studied it. "Where does this lead?" he asked.

"Into the next bedroom. There is another on the other side of the room but it is blocked by the wardrobe."

"Then we needn't concern ourselves with that one," Reynolds replied.

The remark was cryptical to the manager.

"Nor the other," he observed a little stiffly. "There are bolts on both sides of all communicating doors in the hotel."

"I've noted the bolt on this side, Mr. Fleming. Ah, here's the chambermaid." Reynolds turned to a middle-aged woman in cap and apron who tapped at the open door. "Come in. Did you see anyone enter this room before or after you turned down the bed?" he asked in kindly, tones that bore no resemblance to his usual crisp manner.

"No one could do so without obtaining the key from the clerk," interrupted the manager. "The chambermaid has nothing to do with the ordinary keys."

Reynolds ignored the comment.

"Please answer my question," he said again to the maid.

"Are you the gentleman who has booked this room, sir?" she inquired respectfully.

"How did you know it was I and not a lady who intended to occupy it?" Reynolds parried with a smile. "The luggage is not unpacked and has no name on it."

"I shouldn't have known, sir, but for the young lady. I mean your sister who has the next room."

Reynolds shot a warning glance for silence at the manager who had made a faint exclamation.

"Tell me what happened," he urged the maid gently.

"The young lady from 135 came out into the corridor about seven o'clock just as I had finished this room and was closing the door. She said, 'I want to leave this parcel for my brother. He needs it and I may be asleep when he comes back."' The maid pointed to the dressing-table. "There it is, sir, just where she put it. She said you'd be sure to see it there."

"Where were you when she came in with the parcel?"

"Picking up the things from her handbag, sir. She dropped it by the door. She wasn't in the room for more than a few seconds."

"Not then," Reynolds reflected to himself. Aloud he remarked, "And then she retired to her room and you went along the corridor."

"Yes, sir," the maid agreed. "I hope there was nothing wrong in letting her go in with the parcel. I was going to take it in when she let her bag fall."

"You merely acted as she wished," Reynolds told her. He tore the paper and string from the package and opened the box inside. It was empty.

"My, of all the tricks!" exclaimed the maid.

"Well, we've looked inside the parcel," Reynolds observed. "We'll now look inside the room next door."

VII. THE BRASS DISC

Tuesday, November 20th.

LEAVING Detective-Sergeant Jenkins in Gill's bedroom, the inspector and Mr. Fleming followed the maid into the corridor.

Outside the door of 135 she hesitated.

"Shall I knock, sir? The young lady said she was going to bed and didn't want to be disturbed as she had a bad headache."

Reynolds' eyes met those of the manager with an amused expression.

"If the young lady went to bed at seven, she will have had a nice rest by now," he said to the maid gravely. "Knock, please. I think it won't do any harm."

The maid tapped, waited a few seconds and tapped more loudly.

"The lady's coming, sir. Oh!" she exclaimed as the door was opened and the tall form of Detective Jenkins stood before them. Why, however did you get in here? Where's the young lady, sir?"

"I don't know where she is," Jenkins replied, "but I came through the communicating door which was not bolted on either side."

The hotel manager rubbed his chin uneasily.

"Was that door fastened properly this morning?" he demanded of the maid.

"I'm sure it was, sir. The housekeeper is always very particular about that when she inspects the rooms daily"

"You stooped down to pick up the things from the young lady's handbag, didn't you?" Reynolds inquired.

"Yes, sir, Some of the things had rolled into the corridor."

"So she would have had the opportunity to draw back the bolt at that side of the door after she had placed the parcel on the table?" pursued Reynolds.

"I expect so, but she only seemed to walk straight in and back without stopping." The maid bit her lip. "I'm very sorry, sir," she added, turning to the manager.

"Can you remember if any letters dropped out of the handbag?" Reynolds asked her.

The maid shook her head. "Only a few coins and trinkets, sir. Lip salve, a pencil and vanity case. The young lady was very pretty and spoke so nicely. I'm sure she can't have meant any harm."

The manager frowned.

"Did she give you a tip?" he demanded sharply.

"She gave me a shilling, sir," the maid replied. "At least I expect she thought it was. I thanked her and slipped it in my pocket and when I took it out later I found it was this." She drew out a coin and handed it to Reynolds. "I meant to give it back to her in the morning."

It was a token of some kind and not a coin of the realm, Reynolds saw.

"I'll take charge of it. You may go now," he said to the maid.

He and the manager went into room 135 which the girl had booked. The bed was untouched. On the luggage stand was an attaché case. It was unlocked and contained nothing but old magazines, evidently thrust in to give the impression of a packed case.

"I'll go down to the desk and ask for particulars of the girl who took this room, Inspector," the manager offered.

"You needn't, Mr. Fleming. My assistant is already doing that. He'll be back in a minute. We'll go into Mr. Gill's room again."

They passed through the communicating door and Reynolds opened the dead man's dressing-case.

"Forgive my ignorance," the manager said with a puzzled air, "but how did you guess that someone had been in this room?"

"All his bags were unlocked, Mr. Fleming. The dead man had far too many secrets to conceal to leave his things like that. Also the communicating door was unbolted."

The manager sighed.

"It's pretty obvious, even to me, Inspector, how the girl acted. She only had to go into her own room from the corridor, slip back her bolt on the door into 134 and get to work on these bags." He examined the locks. "Standard pattern cases. Easy enough to unfasten. What did she steal?"

"She may not have stolen anything," Reynolds stated. "I shall have to take this luggage with me and go through it carefully. As Mr. Gill never entered this room I have no further use for it."

"Thank you. Publicity of an unpleasant nature can work havoc with the reputation of a hotel. I'll tell a porter to put these bags in a taxi for you."

"Also the attaché case in 135, please. I'll send along a Yard photographer in case we can get any finger-prints from the girl's room."

While the luggage was being taken down Reynolds obtained from the maid a description of the pretty occupant of 135. It tallied in every particular with the girl whom Miss Oliver had seen. Jenkins joined him a moment later.

"A Miss L. Thorpe signed the register and booked this room immediately after Mr. Gill took his to-night," he told the Inspector. "Her name is written beneath his."

"Somebody besides you must have been watching outside his flat this evening and have followed him here," the Inspector said reflectively.

"I expect Gill noticed my fawn mackintosh," Jenkins admitted ruefully. "I was so afraid of losing him that I hung on closer than was wise. I'm certain he spotted me in the queue outside the cinema and probably thought that *I* was his enemy."

"And was unaware of the real source of danger! I wonder if Gill saw the man in the Harris coat," Reynolds ruminated. "You remember he spoke this morning of a client or victim of his by the name of Vickers who killed himself a few weeks ago. We'd better trace up that case of suicide. Perhaps one of Vickers' friends has avenged him."

A porter approached the Inspector and stated that the luggage from rooms 134 and 135 was in a taxi. Reynolds thanked him and, wishing the hotel manager good night, he and Jenkins went downstairs and drove to the Yard.

They were searching one of Gill's cases when the telephone bell sounded.

"A Miss Oliver has rung up and wants to speak to you, sir," the constable on duty said.

"Put her through at once," Reynolds ordered.

Presently a girl's voice demanded over the wire:

"Are you the gent who asked me all those fool questions at the cinema and stood me a posh supper to-night?"

"I believe I answer to that description, Miss Oliver."

"Well, you'd better be sure who you are or I shan't shoot the works," was her retort.

"My name is Inspector Reynolds. Shoot."

"That's the stuff, mister. I don't know whether it matters two shakes of a dog's tail, but I've remembered something. I'm sure that that ugly chap like my brother-in-law was talking to the pretty girl *before* he went into the cinema. She was standing beside him in the queue."

"A pretty girl, or the one who came out later with another man?"

"*The* pretty girl who I said was a bit like Constance Bennett," came in positive tones from Miss Oliver.

"Then she went in with one man and came out with another," Reynolds commented

"I didn't say so," the girl flashed back "I saw her speak to the big chap in the tweed coat, but didn't notice if they went in together. But she came out of the cinema with the shorter man and went off with him."

"Did she appear to recognize the taller man when her companion asked him for change?"

"Nope," Miss Oliver said decidedly. "P'raps she'd had a bust-up with him and given him the bird. I'll know her again even if she changes her snappy little bat. That's the news bulletin, mister. Now I'm switching off to bye-byes."

Reynolds replaced the receiver, and repeated the conversation to his colleague.

"The girl in room 135 was in all probability the same girl Miss Oliver saw at the cinema to-night," he added. "She was searching Gill's luggage in his hotel bedroom presumably while her accomplice in the Harris coat was trailing Gill before they all arrived at the cinema."

"The telephone clerk at the hotel says he put a call through to room 135 about twenty minutes to eight, and a lady's voice answered. A man who didn't give his name rang her up."

Reynolds pursed his lips thoughtfully.

"We can guess the nature of that call. It must have been to tell her where to join him. In the cinema they must have agreed to leave separately and pretend not to know each other. Possibly she deliberately picked up a chance acquaintance to come out with. We know that they parted outside the cinema and she took a 'bus."

"While the man in the Harris coat took a taxi to Waterloo, and of course vanished."

"Exactly. There are times, Jenkins, when I wish I were a bloodhound instead of a detective. This is one of 'em. All we have to help us towards solving to-night's affair is the weapon the murderer used, the time he used it and the place he jumped off; plus a good working description of his looks, build and overcoat. I'd scrap most of that for some clue to his identity." Reynolds sighed and bent over the dead man's suitcase again. "We may have got some light on the subject here, though I doubt it. If

Gill left any letters or papers locked up, the girl probably took them."

The task begun in faint hope ended in despair. Stacked on the floor were suits of clothes, shoes and underwear, evidently packed in a great hurry.

"Not even an envelope!" groaned Jenkins. "My hat, Gill had some trousseau, hadn't he? This little lot must have cost him a tidy pile."

"His was a nasty but lucrative profession. Pass me over that ghastly purple thing "

Jenkins handed a silk dressing-gown to his chief. Reynolds eyed the garment with distaste as he searched the two side pockets.

"Here's a letter! " he exclaimed.

The two men looked eagerly at the envelope which bore a London postmark and a date six days old. It was addressed to Jabez Gill at 20, Wingford Mansions, Bayswater Road, London, W.2. Inside was a card on which was written in block letters:

IN A FEW DAYS YOU WILL BE KILLED.
THIS IS NO IDLE THREAT."

"A bit like a Lyceum melodrama, isn't it, sir?" Jenkins commented. "A man who meant to commit murder must be crazy to threaten his victim first."

"Maybe all murderers have a kink. I wonder why this one sent a preliminary notice of his intentions to Gill."

"It's written in the same style as the card he received this morning."

"Quite so," Reynolds agreed. "They may both be warnings and not threats. We must not disregard that possibility. Somebody, suspecting that murder would be committed, might have sent these to Gill to put him on his guard." He studied the envelope under a magnifying glass. "Compare the W of Wingford Mansions with the one giving the district. They are totally different. The latter is an ordinary block capital; the former is almost in the style of script. The writer was careless or perhaps she was in a hurry."

"*She*!" echoed Jenkins.

"It's barely more than a guess on my part, but I fancy that a woman's hand formed that letter W. It has a feminine touch. Also we know that a girl was mixed up in to-night's tragedy. Possibly she wanted to prevent the crime for the murderer's sake."

Jenkins pondered the point.

"You may be right, sir," he admitted. "Was there much in the clothes Gill was wearing, to-night?"

"His body," Reynolds replied tersely, "also a considerable amount of money, handkerchief, gloves, penknife and the keys of his flat. Nothing else. We'll go to Wingford Mansions now. I have his keys. It's after midnight but I daren't wait until morning or some charwoman may destroy useful traces."

The flat which Gill had occupied bore signs of his hasty departure. Torn newspaper and discarded clothing littered the floor, and the grate was full of burnt paper.

"Absolutely nothing but ashes!" Jenkins muttered. "Gill took no chances with his letters if he did with his life! There's not a scrap of anything in this place to tell us who the pretty girl was, or the man in the Harris coat."

"No, but if we are patient, there may be," Reynolds said. He smiled as he saw his assistant's blank face and added, "His correspondence will come along as usual to-morrow; possibly his clients also. You or I must be here to receive both."

"The murderer won't write or call," was the objection raised by Jenkins.

"I know that, but some letter or caller may give me some idea as to who Gill's clients were. It's a forlorn hope, I know, my lad. Don't quench it. It's about all I *have* got. Lock up. I've finished here. We'll dig out the caretaker on our way down."

A surly man answered their summons.

"I scarcely knew Mr. Gill by sight," he said in answer to the Inspector's inquiries. "He got his own breakfast and went out for his other meals. My wife kept his rooms clean."

"Please call her," Reynolds requested.

The woman blinked sleepily when she arrived. "I never saw any of Mr. Gill's visitors," she declared. "Nobody but him was ever there when I was in his rooms. A horrid bully he was, and I'm glad he's gone away. It's a furnished flat, let by the month. He paid up to-day and never give me a tip or a thank you."

"And that," Reynolds remarked as he and Jenkins stood waiting for the 'bus, "looks remarkably like a dead end, unless you can make anything out of this." He dropped a small object into his colleague's hand.

Under the light of the street lamp Jenkins examined it. It was a small brass disc, a little larger than a shilling, with a hole pierced in it. One side of it was blank; the other bore an engraved inscription.

"Please take me home."

Above the request a name had obviously been filed out: a faint "TR" was visible only.

Jenkins returned the disc to the Inspector.

"That helps a lot, sir, doesn't it? Who the dickens is 'me' and where is it to be taken?" he inquired.

"I'd give a whole lot to know," Reynolds observed with feeling. "It might be a cat or dog and this disc might have fallen from its collar. The girl might or might not have owned the animal. If it had a pedigree, it might be registered at the Kennel or Cat Club or whatever the thing is called. Ifs and Mights don't get us anywhere, this 'bus will. Hop on."

VIII. INTRODUCING BOB DEANE

Wednesday, November 21st.

"COME, come, Inspector, this won't do. You're late again this morning. I shall have to put you back on point duty."

Reynolds closed his office door on the morning after the murder and faced the young man who had greeted him with this facetious comment.

"Good morning, Deane. There are five sound chairs in this room. You might get off my desk and try sitting on one of them if you must inflict yourself upon me. By the way, why are you here?"

"Just a friendly visit," Deane suggested, taking out a packet of cigarettes. "Got a light?"

The Inspector tossed across a box of matches.

"Well, you can consider you've paid your call and get out. I've no time to waste on prying little reporters who are too lazy or stupid to fill their columns without the Yard's help."

Deane whistled.

"You've said a nasty mouthful, sweetheart. Not getting jealous, are you?" he inquired anxiously. "I'm the crime expert on the *Evening Record,* I'd have you know, Mr. Reynolds."

The Inspector raised two fingers in salutation.

"Pleased to meet you, Mr. Deane. At least I may be— one day. Meanwhile I can bear up if you push off."

Deane transferred his body to a chair and placed his feet on the desk.

"We poor journalists are sadly misunderstood," he mused plaintively. "Night and day in all weathers we slave to present our vast public with hot news—facts with which they should be made acquainted, at once."

"When you have facts, you distort them, and when you haven't any, you make 'em up," was the Inspector's terse observation.

"You misjudge me, officer. Promotion has hardened your finer feelings. Now when you were a fat-faced bobby keeping a football crowd in order, you were a lovable soul and I'd have given you half my orange any day. As it—"

"As it is," cut in Reynolds with a chuckle, "your jibes leave me unmoved. I know what you're here for, and you won't get it."

"Night and day in all weathers," chanted Deane solemnly, "I slave to obtain items of news, while jumped-up Inspectors dash off in high-powered cars and gloat over juicy murders in cinemas."

"Where and at what were you 'slaving' at nine-thirty last night?" Reynolds inquired. "Playing snooker at the club, I bet."

Deane looked pained.

"Just marking time. Pushing a cue mechanically while my ears were strained for the whisper of your S.O.S. over the wire, begging me to come and help you solve some mystery. Who's the murdered bloke, Inspector?" he demanded in a crisp tone.

"Certain facts will be given to the Press in due course, Deane."

"I want to be ahead of the band. Be a sport. Open your heart and tell your little pal all about it."

Reynolds studied the eager face of the young journalist. Bob Deane was not only a brilliant craftsman but his ingenuity had been useful in the past. Also, he could give Scotland Yard the precise amount of publicity they wished for on this case. On the other hand, Deane could prove a confounded nuisance by snooping round and rushing into print with details that hindered the Yard officials in their task of tracking a criminal.

"If I let you in on this case," the Inspector said slowly, "will you promise not to play any tricks as you've done before?"

"It's a bargain," Deane promised. "Open up the throttle and if I can help you, I will."

He listened eagerly while Reynolds told him of Jabez Gill's call at the Yard yesterday morning with the threatening message, and of Jenkins' surveillance that ended at the entrance to the cinema. Briefly he related the unwitting part the Westons had played in the tragedy and the other information he had obtained from various sources, suppressing the description of the fair-haired girl.

"Phew! " Deane whistled. "You've a nice tangle to sort out. I'd like to have a talk with the girl in charge of the sweet stall at the cinema. What's she called?"

"Her name is Oliver. All right. See her, but stick to the truth in your writing, mind. Here, I'll keep those snapshots, thank you," the Inspector rapped out as Deane's fingers closed lovingly over the photographs which Miss. Oliver had given him. "They're not for Press reproduction."

Reluctantly Deane handed them back.

"Very well, Great heart," he agreed, taking out a notebook "I'll jot down a description of the man in the Harris tweed coat and let it go at that." He brightened suddenly. "I say, what about the golden-haired wench who must have been his accomplice?"

"What about her?" Reynolds echoed.

"A photograph of her might help."

"It would if I had one. I hear she was wearing a black coat and jaunty little black hat—one of those flat berets. And that's all I know."

Deane patted his chest proudly.

"Ah ha, my bonny boy. That's where you're lucky in having me for a friend. I'll get Miss Oliver to give me a clear description of 'Harris tweed's' lady friend. That will give me something meaty to work up. Keep your shirt on," he added as the Inspector raised a swift objection. "I'm not going to do anything your delicate soul could jib at. Our artist shall make a few imaginary sketches based on details I'll drag out of this girl Oliver. Whichever one she selects we'll use."

"After you have shown it to me," Reynolds enjoined.

"Oh, sure," came Deane's glib reply. He thrust his hat on the back of his head. "I'll go and get something out of that sweet stall lass now. What's her type, Inspector? I'm a 'wow' with all ladybirds. You see I classify 'em and suit my style of approach accordingly. Charm, personality, tact, bluff: I can turn 'em on at will."

"You may not find yourself so successful as you think. Miss Oliver is no fool."

A moment after Deane had gone, Detective-Sergeant Jenkins came in.

"Has that conceited pup been worrying you for news, sir?" he inquired.

"He came here for details of last night's crime." Reynolds bit his lip. "Deane is clever and ingenious. He has been and could be of service to us, but I don't trust his discretion."

"Neither do I," Jenkins said with conviction. "Deane would put his grandmother into jail if he could get good copy out of it."

"Have you traced the report of Vickers' suicide?"

"Yes, sir. He worked as cashier in a big firm, and was found shot on Clapham Common. The firm's money was short by over three hundred pounds. He'd done a lot of betting and had been to a moneylender named Gill."

"We know the rest of that story." Reynolds ran his eyes over the newspaper cutting. "H'm. Identified by a fellow clerk and his landlady. No known relatives. It looks as if we can wipe out any idea of Vickers' relatives or friends having avenged his death. I'm going to see Miss Oliver before Deane can get at her."

Half an hour later the Inspector rang the bell at a small house in Camden Town and, stating his errand to the buxom woman who opened the door, was invited inside.

"I'm her mother," she explained "Rita told us you'd been questioning her, sir, about that dreadful affair. She's a truthful lass but she's rare handy with her tongue, so I hope you'll excuse it."

"The main thing is that she's truthful," Reynolds observed "Will you please tell her I should like to see her, Mrs. Oliver?

Presently the girl came into the room.

"Cheerio," she remarked. "Thought up a bit more catechism during the night?"

"Yes," Reynolds admitted. "Tell me if any of these resemble the girl you saw last night," he said, producing a carefully chosen selection of photographs from the Rogues' Gallery.

Rita Oliver scanned the pictured faces carefully. There were several at which she paused. Finally she pounced on two:

"They *might* be the girl," she declared. "Only you can't see her colouring or tell her height by these head and shoulder affairs."

"I can give you those details," Reynolds replied, and read aloud the description that he had concealed.

"Golden hair, large grey-blue eyes, small features, cleft in chin, short upper lip, even teeth, slim figure, height five feet three inches."

"Fits like a glove with the girl I spotted last night," Miss Oliver exclaimed.

Reynolds tucked the collection into his pocket.

"I should be glad if you tell no one about our interview. No one," he repeated firmly as he heard the front door bell ring and a familiar voice ask for Miss Oliver. "Good morning, Mr. Deane," he remarked pleasantly a moment later, on passing the journalist in the hall. "Miss Oliver is in there. Don't dazzle her too much with your charm and personality, will you?"

"You bet I will," avowed Deane with heat. "Tried to get in ahead, of me, did you? You wait!"

"Sorry, I can't. Although I fancy you won't be long," was Reynolds' parting shot.

Hat well back on his head, Deane strode into the sitting-room.

"Hello, kid," he began blithely. "Uncle's come to have a nice little talk with you."

"I've all the relatives I want and one that I don't," retorted the object of his visit. "You're not one of them, I'm glad to say."

Deane changed his tactics

"Do you know that with a bit of boosting from me you can be famous?" be demanded. "Your picture in the newspapers. 'Observant cinema attendant tracks down murderer,' etc. No more sweet-stall work for you after that."

Miss Oliver's chubby face had an uncompromising look upon it.

"What makes you think I want to lose my job?"

"You wouldn't need it," Deane asserted. "After that publicity you could easily get a star part on the movies as a clever girl detective."

"So easy as that!" she jibed. "Well, bright boy, you've said your piece and you can go, hat and all," she added with a pointed glance at his head.

Deane flung his hat on a chair with a muttered apology. Things weren't going quite so smoothly as he had anticipated.

"Miss Oliver, you're a smart girl and I'd like to put things on a business footing. I'm Bob Deane from the *Evening Record,* and my paper will be willing to pay for first-hand information. All I want is a full account of what you witnessed at the Royal Imperial Cinema last evening."

"Well, if your paper likes to hand out money for that, here goes." Miss Oliver raised her eyes to the ceiling. "I saw a large crowd of people buy tickets at the box office. My stall is close to it, you see."

"I know that," Deane said impatiently. "Go on with the rest of the story. You told the detective last night that you noticed a man who resembled your brother-in-law and a girl who was a bit like a well-known film star."

Miss Oliver raised her eyebrows.

"Did I? My mind is a blank this morning. Anyhow, if he told you, I needn't repeat it, need I?"

"No," snapped Deane. "But you can give me some fresh details. Who was the actress this girl resembled?"

"Marie Dressler," the girl replied, "or was it Marie Lloyd? I forget."

The journalist picked up his hat. Reynolds had beaten him. This girl didn't mean to talk.

Suddenly his eyes fell on four or five picture postcards ranged side by side on a table as if someone had been comparing them. They were all studies of the same actress. With a quick movement he strode nearer.

The girl, interpreting his action, swiftly covered the photographs with a newspaper.

"Beat it," she ordered. "And don't come here snooping again."

"I shan't need to, thank you," Deane answered.

He had recognized the film actress a second before Miss Oliver concealed the postcards.

At four o'clock that afternoon Reynolds walked into his office at the Yard. Jenkins looked up expectantly. "Any news, sir?"

The Inspector slumped into his chair.

"None," he replied gloomily. "How can one hope to find traces of a man in a Harris tweed coat who was at Waterloo station last night? He and the girl who searched Gill's room have vanished."

"You've given details to the newspapers and asked for information from the 'public," put in Jenkins. "That might help. I'd like to know what that girl did after the murder."

"What I want to know," said Reynolds, "is what *happened before the murder*."

IX. BEFORE THE MURDER

Wednesday, November 7th.

IT was exactly a fortnight before Jabez Gill met his doom in the Royal Imperial Cinema when Daphne Ingram climbed the stairs to his flat.

Before ringing the bell she waited to regain her poise. Her anger was at boiling point, anger roused by the letter she had received that morning, and fanned to flame during her hurried journey here.

Her piquant, charming face, capped by waves of pale gold hair, gave no hint of the tumult surging in her heart. Only her eyes, grey-blue and fringed with long smoky lashes, bore evidence of the storm within. Their dilated pupils betokened strong emotions rage, fear, impotence.

Yet Daphne's fear had not robbed her of courage. That quality she had always possessed to the verge of impulsive recklessness. She had read and re-read the letter and then, without consideration of what she would say to Gill or gain by the interview, she had come to his flat.

Now, with her finger on the bell, she tried to evolve a plan of action. Appeals to his better nature he would of course laugh at. The small sum of money she could offer would not satisfy him. Threats of exposure to the police, on her side, would bring about a similar threat on his. Jabez Gill knew his ugly business well and selected his victims with care. Daphne had something to hide and he knew it.

Hesitation already was creeping over her in chill shivers. In a resolve to stem panic and fright, she pressed the bell firmly. It echoed behind the closed door but her summons was unanswered. Again and again she rang, rattling at last the flap of the letter box in the forlorn

hope that Gill would appear. To find that she had braced
her nerves for nothing was an anti-climax.

She jumped nervously as she heard a voice behind her
Swinging round, she confronted a tall, broad-shouldered
man

"Sorry I frightened you," he said gruffly.

"I didn't know anyone was near," she explained.

"You must have been very absorbed in thought not to
hear my heavy feet, and very anxious to see Gill by the
way you rang and knocked "

"Yes, I am—I mean, I must," she floundered.

"I'm afraid you're going to be disappointed. It looks as
if he's out—or away."

"Away!" Daphne's face expressed blank dismay. "Do
you know him?"

The man nodded slowly.

"Oh, yes, I know Jabez Gill."

"If he's a friend of yours, perhaps you can tell me
where he is and when he'll be back."

The man noticed the anxiety in her breathless tone.

"I don't know where he is or when he'll return. He's no
friend of mine and," he added in warning accents, "he
ought not to be a friend of yours."

"Friend!" Daphne gave a mirthless laugh. "Call him
my worst enemy!" she added incautiously.

"As you and I seem to share the same sentiments,"
observed the man, "why not come and share lunch? If I
can do anything to help you, I will. Not for philanthropy,
but to spite Gill. My name's Allen, and you needn't
imagine I shall try to pry into any secrets you wish to
keep. By the time the meal is over you'll feel less
agitated, Mr. Gill may be back on his perch, and you and
he can have your talk. What about it?"

For a moment the girl hesitated.

"Thank you, I'll be glad to come. I'm hungry," she
said. "My temper was too bad for me to eat any
breakfast."

"Temper's a queer thing," remarked the man as they walked along to the restaurant. "Yours apparently is hot and hasty. Mine is slow and nasty. I never forget and can't forgive."

The man's semi-confidential remarks lured Daphne to a similar mood. Fright and worry made her clutch at this fellow-sufferer who was also apparently being penalised by Jabez Gill.

During luncheon he talked frankly, and asked her no questions.

"I've knocked about the world all my life," he told her. "Had a ranch in Western Australia, sold it for a decent bit, and came back to England."

"Are you going to settle here, Mr. Allen?"

"I'll settle *up* here," he replied, with curious emphasis. "After that I'm not sure. I'm a rolling stone. Listen, my girl, I don't want you to tell me your business, and you needn't give me even your name unless you wish, but if you are in an awkward spot with Gill and haven't got a brother or some man behind you, I'll stand by. A girl can't tackle that blackguard alone."

Daphne's lips quivered.

"I've no one behind me, Mr. Allen, and I'm more than grateful to you. But why should you take on fresh troubles when you yourself probably are in difficulties with Mr. Gill?"

The man gave a hard laugh.

"My score with Gill can wait until yours is cleared up." He glanced at her keenly. "Of course, if he's blackmailing you, the easiest thing is for you to call in the police."

"No, no, I can't possibly do that. It's out of the question." Her refusal was almost piteous "And much as I want your help, I can't explain why—"

"Why he has a hold on you," finished Allen. "All right. I understand. Don't give me any details. I'll make a rough guess. Gill knows some secret you wish to keep private."

"Yes."

"He's demanding money or threatening exposure to the police."

"Yes. He has had several sums. Now he wants more. A lot more. The amount can't possibly be found."

"Does he hold any papers? I mean signed documents or letters?"

"No documents, but several letters that would be incrim—damaging if he made use of them."

The man's eyes had a far-away, speculative look in them.

"Would it matter to you if those letters were found by anyone else?" he asked quietly. "The police, for instance, if Gill were arrested on any charge."

A startled gasp broke from the girl's lips.

"The consequences would be terrible if anyone saw those letters," she said in alarm. Suddenly she half-rose from the table as a dreadful thought occurred to her. "Are you connected with the police?"

He laid a calming hand on her arm.

"I most certainly am not," he assured her. "Sit down and have a cigarette. Get this clear. So far as I'm concerned you can walk straight out now and forget you've ever seen me. I don't know who you are or where you live. On the other hand, you can trust me and still keep your counsel about your affair with Gill."

Daphne gazed at the man, trying to read any ulterior motive in his offer. Could it be sheer good nature on his part, or, as he said, the angry desire to thwart Gill whom he also had reason to hate?

In any case, she meditated, Allen could do her no harm if she did not reveal the facts, and she had no intentions of doing so. Exactly how he could be of service she had no idea, but it was some comfort to have a strong figure in the background.

Allen was certainly strong, both in physique and character, she was sure. Whether the character was good or bad she could not determine. His rather heavy features with the wide jaw and cheekbones might have indicated mere muscular power and possibly stupidity, but, for the eyes. They were curiously expressive eyes, with a suggestion of restraint or tragedy behind them.

Psychologically she felt she had no clue to this man's real nature, and in her driven, desperate condition her mental vision was too clouded for judgment

She decided to take a leap in the dark. Perhaps fate had mercifully allowed him to cross her path.

A whimsical smile curved her lips.

"My name is Ingram, Daphne Ingram," she said. "I have a bed-sitting room in Maida Vale. My parents are dead, and as I spent most of my life in school in France and later studying music in Italy. I've no friends in this country."

She was glad that the man did not snatch at the chance to say she had a friend in him.

"Quite recently I came to London because of this affair with Gill," she went on "As I've had several fairly good professional engagements abroad I am not financially on the rocks, unless—"

"Unless Gill swamps your resources," put in Allen. "I'll see that he doesn't. You needn't go into any more particulars. In plain words, what will give you freedom from him?"

"A packet of letters. The first is a signed confession."

"You're sure he's got them, and not bluffing?"

"Sure," she replied steadily. "They were written to him; at first to stave him off, later enclosed with sums of money."

"Nothing but this packet of letters, Miss Ingram?"

"Nothing. Yes, there is something else—the cause of it all—but I'm practically certain that Gill hasn't got it. He couldn't have."

"Let it go at that." The man's manner was coldly businesslike. "Gill probably keeps all such documents as yours in his safe."

"I suppose so."

"Well, I've seen that safe. It's foolproof, I should say, even for an expert safe-cracker, and I'm not even an amateur."

"Then it's hopeless to try to help me, isn't it?" she faltered.

"I might promise to buy the letters for you at Gill's price if I were a mad philanthropist. I'm not, and I'd die rather than give him a penny."

"Of course I wouldn't let you," she interposed stiffly. The man made an impatient movement of his hand.

"Leave pride out of it. If we're going to get anywhere you'll have to pocket a good many nice feelings. Now then, when you can't go down a hole after a rat, what do you do?"

Daphne looked bewildered.

"I don't know. Smoke it out, perhaps."

"Exactly. Gill has to be smoked out metaphorically. Then when he runs, he'll take the precious contents of his safe with him to a place where you'll have more opportunity to get at them."

The man nodded.

"Yes. If I undertake to drive him out, you must do your part. It won't be a pretty, ladylike job. You can back out now if you like."

"I'll do my share, Mr. Allen," she said with spirit.

"Good. It will take all your wits, but I think it can be worked. Of course, Gill might destroy his papers before he leaves the flat and bolts. Probably he'd make for the continent."

Daphne stared at him aghast.

"Would he go to Paris?" she whispered.

"Paris is a good hiding-place. Also it's an excellent jumping-off ground to any other country." The man watched her for a minute. "I understand. Your secret has its roots in Paris. You think that if Gill takes refuge there he will retain your letters, and either conduct negotiations on the spot or probe still deeper into what you want to conceal. Is that it, Miss Ingram?" he rapped.

"Yes. He would not burn the letters, I am sure he means to go there. Oh, please help me to get them. I'll do anything—anything."

Allen's mouth set to a hard line.

"You'll probably have to," he informed her. "It's no use being squeamish at the last minute, mind, or I shall regret delaying my business with Gill to get you out of a hole."

"I won't be squeamish," she promised. "Can't you manage to do yours at the same time?"

"No, I can't," he barked shortly. "And don't try the 'one-good-turn-deserves-another' stunt on me. I don't want anybody's help or interference. All you've got to do is to obey my orders."

Daphne swallowed her resentment at his tone. What manner of man was he, she wondered? She studied his cold, mask-like face and, queer, tragic eyes. There was no trace of any emotion there, save implacable purpose. Had he always been so entirely void of human feeling, or had some impish trick of fate changed the man's whole nature and carved his countenance with those bitter lines?

"When you've finished staring at me, I should like your address in Maida Vale," he said with a frown.

"Thirty-two, Barton Place. It's near Sutherland Avenue, the Edgware Road end."

"Do you know anybody in the house? The landlady, for instance; are you friendly with her?"

"I don't know a soul there. The house is run by an elderly man and one old servant. I only see him once a week when I pay my rent."

"Where's your room?"

"On the ground floor, at the back."

"Who opens the door to you?"

"To me? No one. I have a latch-key," she explained. "I have no callers. It's a very impersonal kind of place."

"Good. Give me your key now. Tell your landlord that you've mislaid it and make him give you another."

"I needn't," Daphne replied "There are several latch-keys in the drawer of the hall table. I can easily take one. But," she added uneasily, "couldn't you write? I may be out when you call."

The mask-like face twisted to a faint smile.

"I never write letters to women I don't know, Miss Ingram. Or even to women I do, for that matter."

He drew a packet of envelopes from his coat pocket and pushed them across to the girl.

"Make yourself useful and address four or five of those to Gill," he ordered. "Print the letters in block capitals if you're afraid."

For a moment Daphne's courage wavered. Then, with a shrug, she did as Allen requested. After all, whatever he put inside the envelopes didn't affect her. No one could trace printed characters.

"There you are," she said, passing the packet back to him.

He placed them in his pocket and rose.

"Now, don't try to see Gill or write to him. Be in your room at half-past nine every night until you see me again. And," the smile changed to a sneer, "in case you're nervous, I'll put your mind at rest. You and your sex don't interest me in the least." He called the waitress. "Two bills, please," he requested.

Pushing one across to Daphne, he walked out of the restaurant.

X. A RAT ON THE RUN

Monday, November 19th.

IN the long days of waiting that followed that strange interview, Daphne was keyed up with the suspense of inaction. From daybreak she was haunted with the fear of Gill's threat; and from nightfall, with the fear that Allen would come and claim her to perform some impossible task.

Each evening she waited up until midnight, shivering over the gas-fire, starting up in alarm every time the front door was opened. When at last she went to bed, dreams in which she played torturing parts racked her nerves. Dreams that caused her to wake imagining she heard a creaking board, or her door handle being softly turned.

Yet not once did she doubt that Allen would keep his word. That much his hard strength had impressed upon her. It was no idle promise made in order to establish easy contact with a pretty girl. He would have been here long ago if that had been the reason.

Her varied experience on the Continent had taught her much about the ways of men. Without appraising her charms unduly, she was quite aware of her beauty and knew how to protect herself from unwanted attention. Had anyone suggested to her a year ago that she should confide her latch-key to a complete stranger, she would have been indignant.

Desperate circumstances change one's point of view, she reflected. In her present humiliating position she had not the power to dictate to the man she had met outside Gill's flat.

Did this delay mean that he had failed to smoke the rat out of his hole? To her, the plan had appeared to be fantastic. Why should Allen imagine he could frighten Jabez Gill from his stronghold?

The arrival of another blackmailing letter made her certain that Allen had not been able to fulfil his intention. Then Allen's words came back to her with a shock. Gill would almost certainly go to Paris; in which case, he could still continue to demand money from her.

At half-past ten that night she was sitting beside her comfortless gas-fire when she heard a faint click. Someone was turning her door handle softly.

In a second she pulled back the bolt and stood aside as Allen brushed past her and entered. His tall, heavy form seemed to fill her small abode.

Taking off his hat, he scanned the room and its furnishings.

"So this is where you live," he remarked. "Not very home-like, is it?"

"No. Still, it contains all I need just now. One has to put up with many things in life."

"A rotten philosophy. If that's your creed, no wonder you got into Gill's clutches."

She smiled bleakly.

"It seems to have been yours also, Mr. Allen, since you, too. are in the same boat."

"I didn't say so," he snapped harshly. "Once, perhaps I was. Not now, though. Indeed, he's in—" the man broke off and glanced from her narrow divan couch to the window. "Your bed's in a draught if you sleep with the window open."

"It is and I do," she snapped back. "What of it?"

"I'll move it. You won't be any use to me if you catch a cold."

He put his arms round the divan and lifted it to a more sheltered position as easily as though it were a light valise.

"Thank you," she said. "That's better. You must be extraordinarily strong. A box-spring mattress is very heavy."

He seemed pleased at the compliment.

"My muscles have had good opportunities for development, Miss Ingram; particularly my arms. However, I didn't come here to boast of being a modern Samson." He frowned suddenly. "You look washed out. Had any more letters from Gill?"

"I had a communication this morning that worried me," she admitted.

"Well, you'll have no more. I suppose you thought this long delay meant that I'd gone cold on the job."

She shook her head.

"No. I knew you would try, but I feared you might fail."

"I might fail yet, but I don't think so. We shall know before this time to-morrow. Are you still willing to take your share of the risk?" he demanded.

"Yes. What am I to do?"

"That depends on what Gill is going to do," he told her, taking out a cigarette-case. "Do you smoke in this room?"

"I've done little else for days," she replied. "So no one's suspicions will be roused if we smoke now. Tell me your plans."

"I've hired a small private car and placed it in an empty lock-up garage. It's almost facing the main door of the block of flats where Gill lives. There's a convenient iron grill in the garage door so that I can sit in the car and watch his exits nicely. Wherever he goes to-morrow, we shall be on his heels."

"Suppose he walks," Daphne suggested.

An ugly leer twisted the man's mouth.

"He won't walk much to-morrow. If he does, I shall go on foot after him. It might be handy, if you could take a turn at the wheel. Can you drive at all?"

"I used to drive my own small car all over Paris."

"If you can do that, you can drive anywhere. But don't get into a smash to-morrow."

"I'll try not to. By the way, I've no English driving licence."

"That doesn't matter. You'll be breaking more laws than that before the day's over, my girl." He drew a large bunch of keys from his pocket. "Bring these with you. I've bought one of every conceivable variety to fit suitcases."

Daphne's heart sank as she put the keys in her handbag. Would Allen expect her to burgle Jabez Gill's room?

"I'll try not to fail," she murmured

"You'd better not," he retorted grimly. "I shan't be there to back you up, mind. Meet me at the garage at ten o'clock to-morrow morning. You can't miss it."

"I'll be there. Shall I bring some sandwiches? We may have a long wait."

"It's an idea. Have you got a small attaché case without any initials on it?"

She produced one from a pile of luggage.

"Will this do? It's very shabby."

"That's a good thing, as you'll probably say goodbye to it to-morrow. Stuff in some old magazines to give it weight. I'll take it now while it's dark"

Daphne prepared the case as he wished and handed it to him.

"Thank you for what you're doing for me," she said simply.

His inscrutable eyes stared into hers.

"Most men would be glad of the chance," he told her "You're not a fool and I don't think you're vain. All the same, you must know you're unusually lovely. Maybe once, centuries ago when I was human, your looks and sweetness would have weighed with me. They don't now. I'm as you see me, hard as steel."

"Couldn't you, for your own sake, go back to that long-ago state, Mr. Allen?" she asked almost pityingly.

"No," he rasped "And in case you think my confession means that I'm softening, watch me if you fall down on your job to-morrow through stupidity. Good night."

For a long while after the man had left her, Daphne sat thinking about him. In spirit, she shrank from the harsh gracelessness of his personality, but the woman in her was compassionate, excusing much because he had obviously suffered much. What, she could not guess, nor had she any wish to probe into his past. He had asked no unnecessary questions from her, and in turn she respected his secret and made no attempt, even in her thoughts, to unfold its dark mystery.

Of one thing she was sure; he was a man who would scorn lies as being cowardly. He could be silent concerning his history, but if he spoke, he would speak the truth. It was truth when he said he was hard as steel. Because of that, she was the more grateful that he had come to her aid. Harsh and hard he undoubtedly, was, but dependable. It was the one quality she required in man or woman at this critical time.

At ten o'clock next morning she kept her appointment. Allen was already sitting in the car. As if repenting of his softer mood of the night before, he made no response to her "Good morning."

"Glad you've had the sense to wear dark clothes," he observed after peering at her in the semi-gloom of the garage. "Tuck your yellow hair under your hat. It's too conspicuous."

Daphne obeyed with no touch of resentment, and seating herself beside him, examined the levers.

"That's right. Get the hang of the thing, and don't forget to drive on the left side of the road," he reminded her.

"I've often driven a car of this make." She turned to him. "Mr. Allen, I'm grateful for your help. In return, please count on me to do exactly as you say without question."

The man nodded.

"All right. Directly Gill makes an appearance, start your engine. I shall open the doors. Run the car out and we'll follow him."

Beside her, Allen sat with his eyes fixed on the grill through which the wide front door of the block of flats was visible.

It was not long before a well-dressed man of debonair bearing appeared in the entrance opposite, and stood looking up and down the road.

"Start her up; quiet as you can," ordered Allen, as he sprang from the car. "Wait till Gill gets into that taxi before you move out."

The maneuver was accomplished with success and the little black car trailed in the wake of Gill's cab.

"You're a good driver," Allen admitted as the girl swung deftly in and out of the traffic, keeping always at a wise distance from the taxi in front

"Ah! I know where he's making for," Allen said. "That building is New Scotland Yard. He's pretty badly scared to go there."

"If he gets detectives to follow him, I suppose it means we've failed."

"It means we'll have to park here for a bit probably. Gill dare not tell the police much. Don't worry. Drive round the block. I'll keep guard."

At the end of an hour Allen decided it was too risky to remain there any longer.

"We'll get back to the garage," he told her. "Gill has no luggage. He's bound to go to his flat."

Daphne reversed the car into the garage when they returned and Allen slid the doors across. There was no shade of impatience on his still face at the tedious delay. Silently he sat, staring through the grill at the door across the road.

It was about one o'clock when he spoke.

"Gill's come back. Give me the sandwiches and you get some food at that restaurant we went to the other day."

"Won't you go instead?" she asked. "I'm not hungry."

"Do as I say," was the man's sharp command. "If he comes out, I shall follow him. In that case, wait here until I return. I suspect he's gone in to pack up and will probably be hours. Our rat is on the run but he may wait until dark. Have a good meal. I don't know when you'll get the next one. Don't come back until half-past two. Got any money?"

"Plenty, thank you," Daphne murmured.

She was back at her post punctually.

"Any sign of a thinnish man in a fawn mackintosh?" Allen asked her.

"Yes. I walked along behind someone dressed like that a moment ago."

"Did he see you come into this garage?"

"I'm sure he didn't. He seemed to be loitering, so I purposely let him pass me before I came in here." Daphne's eyes widened in alarm. "Is he a detective?"

"Probably." Allen's tone expressed indifference. "He arrived about twenty minutes ago. I noticed him pass and repass a few times. He won't affect us and doesn't know we're in the garage. We can see out of that grill but he can't see into it. We may have a long wait. Get into the back of the car."

"I'm quite all right here," she replied.

"I daresay you are, but I'm not. If you go back I'll have more room."

XI. DAPHNE MAKES A SEARCH

Tuesday, November 20th.

THE short afternoon waned slowly to dusk. Light from a street lamp filtering through the grill showed up the silhouette of Allen's figure sitting motionless in the front seat of the car. Leaning a little on one side she could look past him and see the portico lamp at the door of the flats opposite.

"What time is it?" she asked.

"Nearly half-past six."

"Has that man in the fawn mackintosh gone?"

Allen laughed softly.

"No, he's still there. The fellow must be half frozen. He's so afraid of losing Gill that he's clinging to the area railings almost beside the front door. Can't you see him?"

Daphne shivered.

"I don't want to. It will be bad enough when he sees us. He's certain to do so if we follow Gill."

"Not if we let him get in between us and Gill," Allen told her. He twisted round and looked at the girl. "Look here, you can't afford to have cold feet. Take a good drink from this." He held a flask to her lips roughly.

"I hate spirit."

"I'm not inquiring your taste in beverages. Drink it. When you've got some brandy inside you I'll tell you my plan. You're no use in your present condition."

The raw liquor warmed the girl and made the blood tingle in her chilled body.

"I'm all right now, Mr. Allen. What are we going to do?"

"Lie down and pull the rug right over you. Stay there until I tell you to get up."

In a moment Daphne heard the garage doors slide open quietly. Allen started up the car and drove out. After turning round three or four corners he stopped the car.

"You can sit up now, Miss Ingram, if you keep well out of sight."

She peered through the windows in bewilderment. "Where are we?"

"I made a circular tour round the block. We're parked about a hundred yards behind that detective chap."

"If Gill comes this way we shall lose time in turning," she objected.

"I can't imagine that he'll want to go to Shepherd's Bush to-night! He's far more likely to go in the opposite direction and make for the West End or Victoria."

"You think he'll take a boat train across the Channel to-night?"

Something approaching a chuckle came from the man's throat.

"If Gill could have done that, he'd not have gone within miles of Scotland Yard to-day," he assured her. "His passport won't be ready until to-morrow morning. That's why I fixed to-night for our—your business."

"What luck that you found out about his passport!"

"Luck! It was confoundedly tedious work," Allen replied. "I've been following him closely for days. Once he went to the passport office and I guessed what his plan was. That night I sent him a kind of speeding-up letter in one of the envelopes that you addressed. Yesterday morning he called there again. A few hours later he went into a public call-box; there was a row of them. I slipped into the next booth and heard him positively screaming for his precious passport over the wire. 'Can't I have it before then?' he begged. They must have refused, for he said he'd call at ten o'clock on Wednesday morning."

"If we lose him now, you know where he will be to-morrow morning," commented Daphne more cheerfully.

"Yes, I know where Gill will be then," the man agreed in an odd tone. He sat up alertly and pressed the self-starter. "Meanwhile I know where he is now. There, on the steps of his house with a pile of luggage, hailing a taxi. And there is 'fawn mackintosh' getting into a cab just behind him." Again that harsh laugh came. "Gill must have seen him by the railings, and probably imagines—"

He left his sentence unfinished, and slid into gear, keeping a safe distance from the two taxis in front.

"Listen carefully," he said to the girl in brusque tones. "Gill may park his big luggage at a station cloak-room, though he probably won't if he guesses 'fawn mackintosh' is trailing him."

Daphne's brows puckered in bewilderment.

"You said Gill went to the Yard because he was frightened about something. Surely he knows this detective is there to guard him."

"By the way that chap has acted I believe he is watching unknown to Gill. He took no notice of anything or anybody else; never even glanced at this car when I drove out of the garage opposite to him. My guess is that Gill will go direct to a hotel. If he does, take your attaché case, follow on his heels, and book a single room. Get the room next to his if you can. It may have a communicating door. Use any trick you can think of to get into his room, open his cases with your bunch of keys and take what you want. I can't do any more for you."

"Suppose he remains in his room or takes the paper with him," she faltered.

The man bit his lip and thought for a minute.

"If he stays in, I must get him out somehow. To be on the safe side, directly you've booked your room, run out and let me know the number. Ask, if there's a telephone in each room. Register as Miss L. Thorpe. I'll ring you up and tell you where to meet me. Got that clear?"

"Yes, thank you," she replied in relieved accents. "You know I'm grateful. Please, isn't there anything I can do in return? Are there any papers in Gill's possession that you want?"

Allen was silent so long that she feared he was offended at her offer. His face was set in implacable lines as he stared ahead at the taxi he was following. Suddenly he pulled into the kerb near a large hotel.

"Gill has gone in and 'fawn mackintosh' is slinking after him. Shoot in quickly. I'll wait here."

Within a couple of minutes she ran out to him.

"I've got room 135, next to his. Telephone in all rooms," she explained breathlessly. "Look, they're just taking Gill's bags out of his taxi. I heard him say he doesn't wish to see his room now. He's going out. Quick, tell me if I can do anything for you?" she asked again.

The man's sombre eyes looked into hers.

"If you see any letters signed 'Maureen,' bring them," he said. Thrusting her away from the car, he drove slowly off, his eyes on Jabez Gill who was striding along the pavement.

Carrying the attaché case, Daphne re-entered the hotel and went to her room. She looked round it, calm now that the time for action had come.

Inside the wardrobe was an empty cardboard box and brown paper, discarded by a previous tenant. An idea flashed into her mind. She wrapped up the box and then slid back the bolt on her side of the communicating door. How could she get the bolt on the other side unfastened?

Presently the porter brought up Gill's luggage. Opening her door into the corridor in a few moments, she saw the chambermaid go into number 134. Daphne's heart beat fast as she prepared to carry out her plan with the empty box.

A quarter of an hour later, standing in Gill's room, she reflected that the trick had been ridiculously simple to work. By dropping her handbag she had side-tracked the maid's attention and been able to draw back the bolt on Gill's side of the communicating door. It was that doorway through which she had walked now.

Nor did her luck end there. The keys which Allen had given her unlocked Gill's two suitcases without difficulty.

In frantic haste she searched through the piles of garments. There was not a letter amongst them. She dared not waste time in re-locking the bags. At any second Gill might return.

There remained only the dressing-case as a forlorn hope. She tried a dozen keys before that lock responded to her efforts. Pyjamas, dressing-gown, collars she flung aside in despair. Nothing else!

And then her fingers touched the cold smooth surface of a large linen envelope, sealed, and evidently filled with papers of some description.

She drew it out tremblingly. Should she open it and search for what she wanted? Or dare she take the whole lot?

Swiftly she closed the case and decided to look through the papers in her temporary room while waiting for Allen to call her up.

The jarring sound of a telephone bell in the adjoining room startled her. She passed through the communicating, door and picked up the receiver.

"Any luck?" demanded Allen over the wire.

"A large sealed envelope. I can't tell—"

"Don't try to now," he snapped. "Leave your bag where it is and come to the main entrance of the Belroy Grill Room at once. You know where it is?"

"Yes, but I don't want any food."

"You're not likely to get any," he informed her. "Hurry up. Take a taxi."

Daphne left the hotel and instructed the taximan to drive quickly. He did his best, but the streets were very crowded and they were held up in several traffic blocks.

She found Allen waiting for her near the Belroy entrance.

"I thought you were never coming," he said impatiently, grasping her arm and forcing her along at a great speed. "Found your letters?"

"I opened the envelope coming along in the taxi," she explained in a depressed voice. "Nothing that I wanted was there, but—"

"Sure you didn't overlook anything in Gill's luggage?"

"I'm quite sure." She gave him the envelope. "You'd better take this. There are some letters signed 'Maureen' inside. Sort yours out and destroy the others."

The pressure of his fingers tightened on her arm and she heard him draw his breath sharply as he slipped the envelope into an inner pocket.

"Thanks," he said, briefly. "Don't lose your nerve. You may get your letters yet. Gill must have them in his pocket."

"Oh, you mean to try again to-morrow morning when he goes to the Passport Office." Her voice was shaky. "It will be very risky in daylight, won't it?"

"We're not going to attempt it in daylight," he retorted. "I intend to get them to-night—somehow."

"But you don't know where Gill is, Mr. Allen."

"What do you think I've been up to while you've been searching his room?" the man demanded.

"I thought there was no need for you to follow him when you knew he had left his luggage at the hotel."

"Stop thinking, then, and don't talk so much," he ordered roughly. "You're so wrapped up in your own troubles that you forget I too have business with Gill."

"I'm sorry. Where are we going now?"

"Back to the cinema queue where Gill is. As you were late, I had to ask a chap standing beside me to keep my place while I fetched you. He was very decent about it. He seems a good sort. We may find him useful. You see I never meant you to come here, but as those papers weren't in Gill's luggage, you have to." Allen stared at his companion. "Now do as I tell you. Be nice to this chap and wangle things so that he sits next to you. Talk in a friendly way and by some means get him to leave the cinema with you when I give you the tip. Say you feel ill or something."

"He may not go into the same price seats as ours."

"Yes, he will. I've inquired."

"Why should he leave early on my account?" she asked dubiously.

"Don't be a fool. You're a lovely girl and can work the trick if you like," Allen stated. "And you must, d'you hear? Play up to any lead I give you, mind. I'll bully you and rouse his sympathy towards you. Here's the queue. We're right behind Gill, so be on your guard."

Still grasping her arm, he led her along the row of people waiting for admission until he reached a grey-eyed man of about thirty years of age.

"Much obliged, mate," Allen said in a gruff undertone. "Here's the bit of goods that has messed up my evening. I hate girls who can't be punctual."

"It doesn't matter; you've lost nothing," the grey-eyed man answered. Moving aside, he indicated a place for Daphne next to him in the queue. "There's room for you and your friend here."

"Friend!" Allen jeered. "She's no friend of mine. I don't even know her name! Picked me up in the Park this morning, said she'd no money and tried to plant herself on me for the day. I had business to attend to and didn't want a pretty fool on my hands then. So in a soft moment I said I'd meet her for dinner and bring her here to-night. Kept me fooling round for an hour before she turned up, and now she's got the cheek to say she's had nothing since breakfast."

The grey-eyed man looked distressed. He glanced at Daphne's white face with the dark shadows under her eyes.

"It's probably true," he murmured to Allen. "She looks very tired."

"I ain't interested in sickly-looking wenches," Allen declared.

His voice was carefully modulated, Daphne noticed, so that his harsh words could be heard by no one but herself and the other man.

The latter turned to her with grave sympathy.

"I don't want to butt in," he said quietly, "but may I get you a sandwich or something?"

Daphne felt Allen nudge her elbow and interpreted it as a signal for her to act her allotted part.

"I think I shall be all right," she replied. "It's very kind of you, especially after what you've just heard about me." She forced a wan smile to her lips.

"I don't believe all I hear," he said.

"Part of it you can." She flashed a demure glance at him under her long lashes. "I've certainly had nothing to eat since a light luncheon to-day. But it was not my fault that I was late to-night."

The grey-eyed man looked from the bewitching and delicate beauty of the girl's face to the crude, unrefined features of the tall man who had spoken so roughly of her. There was no sign of poverty in the girl's clothes, if he were any judge of values. She was obviously well-bred. A beautiful girl of her type was unlikely to choose such an uncouth creature for a cavalier.

He felt strangely interested in the girl. There was a wistful expression in her eyes that drew him. Perhaps she was as lonely as he was; perhaps her unpleasant companion had some hold on her.

He took what was for him a bold step.

"Don't misunderstand me," he said under his breath. "Will you come and have some supper with me? I don't care two straws about the cinema. I was alone and at a loose end and thought it would pass an hour. My name is Michael Carlile," he added naïvely.

For a moment the girl hesitated. She was tired, hungry and dispirited. There seemed no object in going into the cinema. Allen's acting had misled her a little. She glanced up into his cold face now to know what his wishes were. His eyes were fixed on the back of the man who stood immediately in front of him It was Jabez Gill. She understood now what she had to do.

Turning to her new friend she whispered.

"The man I came with may think it strange if I leave with you now, Mr. Carlile. I'll go in with him. Please try to sit beside me. If I feel tired I'll accept your offer later."

Carlile murmured his understanding of the situation and slipped a card into her hand.

"In case we get separated inside the cinema," he said, "here's my address. If—if ever you should be in any difficulty, will you write to me? Please promise."

She tucked the card inside her bag.

"Thank you," she answered; and looked straight into his eyes. Something that she saw there made her add.: "I promise."

On her other side she felt Allen's touch on her arm.

"Excellent," he muttered. "Hide your face with your bag and look back along the queue. Is 'fawn mackintosh' there?."

"Yes," she replied. "About a dozen people are in between us."

"All right. Don't bother. We can dodge him." Allen frowned. "I wish that girl at the sweet-stall would stop staring at me. Don't let her see us talking."

"Why not?" Daphne felt a pang of fear.

"Because I mean to rob Gill of your letters, stupid," was Allen's short rejoinder. "Keep close to me and that chap beside you. Don't tell him your name or address. Come on. The queue's moving inside."

XII. IN THE CINEMA

Tuesday, November 20th.

"I'LL take your ticket," Allen muttered in Daphne's ear when they neared the box-office.

Suddenly the commissionaire put out his arm and divided the queue behind them.

Concealing her face, Daphne chanced a quick look backwards.

"'Fawn mackintosh' can't get in yet," she told Allen.

"Be quiet," he whispered. "Stick to your new pal and talk to him."

In close order Allen, Daphne and Michael Carlile walked down the carpeted gangway behind Gill.

There were four empty seats in one row. Jabez Gill went in first; then Allen, the girl and her companion.

Gill sank into his seat without a glance at his neighbours, and lighted a cigarette. On Gill's right sat Allen, hunched up so that his cap, which he kept on, and overcoat collar almost met.

Daphne tried to concentrate her attention on the film that was in progress, but the figures seemed blurred.

Once or twice Carlile spoke to her softly.

"Sure you'd rather stay awhile?" he asked, sensing that she was not following the film.

"Yes, thank you. It's warm and comfortable here." she said, inventing the only excuse she could think of.

What was going to happen, she asked herself? What could, anyhow, in a crowded cinema? Allen was still sitting in the same position and Gill was placidly smoking. Their faces were invisible but she could see the steady glow of Gill's cigarette in the darkness.

"Tell me," asked Carlile on her right, "have you any friends in London, or is that too personal a question? If so, blame it to the fact that I am anxious about you and convinced that you are worried about something."

"I've lived abroad nearly all my life and have only one friend in England," she smiled faintly. "He's the dearest person in the world but Pat isn't able to come to me just now. And, anyhow, all he could give would be sympathy."

"Does Patrick—I suppose that's his full name—know you're in difficulty?" Carlile inquired. "He's a person you can trust, I presume."

"He knows something is wrong, but has no idea what it is. I've not seen him for some time, unfortunately, but I trust him more than anyone on earth."

"That being so, why not write and explain matters to him?"

"No. He can't help me in the way I need," she replied.

Remembering Allen's instructions, she had talked to her new friend in a whisper that could disturb no one. But her mind was conscious only of Allen's still form on her left.

Some fresh people, a man, woman and child, took the recently vacated seats on Gill's left and two children pushed past Daphne to the other end of the row.

She heard the woman speak to Gill, and could detect annoyance in some reply he made. The woman was a tiresome, restless creature, and Daphne was afraid that Gill would change his seat. As the film continued the woman on Gill's left fell asleep. The row of seats behind them was nearly empty now.

Suddenly Daphne felt Allen stir and fumble in his pockets for a cigarette.

"Got a light?" she heard him ask Gill.

Gill produced a box of matches but no light was struck. Instead she heard Allen mumble something and saw him press his left hand to Gill's body.

"If you move, you're a dead man, Gill. Give me Miss Ingram's letters," he ordered.

Every nerve in Daphne's brain was strained, her senses so acute that she fancied she could detect Gill's gasp of fear.

"I give you half a minute, Gill," muttered Allen. "One sound from you and it'll be the last you ever make."

Slowly Gill drew a packet from his inner pocket and passed it to Allen. A second or two later, that seemed an eternity to the girl, she felt an envelope thrust into her hand

"Hide these and get out," Allen breathed in her ear. "Take your pal out with you, but go home alone and at once. Be sharp about it. Come past me."

Daphne cast a swift look at Carlile to see if he had observed the maneuver. He was gazing at the screen, and apparently had noticed nothing unusual.

She gave a sigh and he at once turned to her. "Like to go now?" he asked.

She nodded. Rising, she led the way past Allen and Gill.

In the gangway Michael Carlile caught her arm. "You must be starving," he said. "Come and have supper."

"I'd rather go home. I'm very tired," she pleaded.

"As you wish." He seemed disappointed. "Anyhow," he remarked as they reached the vestibule, you can't stop me from giving you some chocolates. I'll get some here and you can eat them on the way home. That will be better than nothing."

Before Daphne could prevent him he had spoken to the girl standing by the sweet-stall.

"Her goods are locked up for the night. I'll have to try the automatic machine," Carlile said, searching pockets for change. "Confound it. I've no small silver."

"It doesn't matter at all," Daphne told him. "I'll have some food when I get back. Why should you bother about me, a complete stranger?"

"Are you?" he asked, looking into her eyes. "I wonder. Anyhow, I'm determined you shall have that chocolate.

Ah, here comes your charming companion," he exclaimed; as the door from the hall opened and Allen appeared.

Carlile went across to him.

"Can you change half a crown?" he asked. Allen pushed him aside.

"No, I can't," he rasped, and hurried out of the cinema.

Carlile raised his eyebrows whimsically as he rejoined the girl.

"Your friend has engaging manners. But I forgot. He is not your friend—by his own statement, too."

Daphne was silent. She dared not mention that Allen had just risked a great deal for her sake.

Outside the cinema Carlile raised his hand to signal for a taxi.

"I'd rather go by 'bus, thank you," she said. "It's not far from that lonely monument, the Marble Arch."

"Won't you let me drive you?" Carlile begged. "At least as far as the lonely monument. I love your phrase, though, strictly speaking, I'm not sure it is a monument."

"Please forgive me. I want to be alone. I've had rather a harassing day."

"Then I'm to let you go without even knowing your name or address." He appeared so crestfallen that she smiled.

"Just like that, I'm afraid, Mr. Carlile. Think of me as the girl who spoilt your evening at the movies."

He took the hand she offered and held it closely.

"I'll think of you as a sad little pale-faced girl who had had no dinner and didn't feel confidence enough in a new friend to let him give her some."

"And I'll think of you as being very kind," she murmured, "and—a friend in whom I have more confidence than you think."

"You have my card. You've promised to let me know if I can do something for you that your pal Patrick cannot. Or is he all you want in life?"

"One can't have too many friends, Mr. Carlile. I have very few. Pat can't do all he would wish for me. Perhaps—one day—you and I may see each other again. There's my 'bus. Good-bye."

"*Au revoir*," he replied.

The cold air through the open window on the top of the 'bus stung Daphne's cheeks and cooled her aching head. Inside her bag was a precious envelope, procured by Allen's ingenuity. Antagonistic as she was to his crude ways, she was grateful to him for having lifted an immense load from her mind. Some terrible tragedy must have warped his nature and turned him into the frozen semblance of a human being that be now was. He had done her a great service. Nevertheless, with a shiver, she hoped that she would never see him again.

Getting off the 'bus, she bought a few sandwiches at a little eating-house and walked along to Barton Place. Some of the elation at the knowledge that the papers were in her possession was wearing off.

She lighted the gas-fire in her room, made herself a cup of cocoa, and tried to eat. A heavy sense of depression and loneliness was creeping over her, and almost she was afraid to stay in her room. Had it not been so late she would have rung for the maidservant on some pretext merely to have human society for a few minutes.

Over and over again she wished that she had accepted Michael Carlile's invitation to have supper with him. She was a swift judge of character and instinct told her that he was sincere. A man who could be loyal and courageous. And, by Allen's orders, she had had to refuse to give him even her name!

Why, she asked herself, was she thinking more about Carlile than she was of the envelope in her handbag? Why was she afraid to open it? Perhaps because her nerve had gone. If she found the packet did not contain the letters that she wanted, her state of despair would be worse than it was now. Later, she might have more pluck to face the situation.

Tucking her bag under her pillow, she bolted her door and went to bed. For a long while her thoughts hovered round Carlile, picturing his face, with its grey eyes and firm mouth. Not a handsome face, possibly, but one that held kindness, humour and strength. She had his visiting-card. Perhaps soon she could write him a note of thanks. With all her heart she wished that their acquaintanceship had not begun in such circumstances, when she had had to play the ugly role of vamp by Allen's wish. The success of that acting filled her with shame now.

Gradually she drifted into a light sleep, haunted by uneasy dreams.

With a violent start she awoke. There was a faint sound in her room. She felt for the switch by her bedside and, pressing it, stared round. No one was there.

Then, with fear surging in her veins, she saw the handle of her door being turned softly. The hands of her watch pointed to a quarter past two. Everyone who lived in the house must be in bed long ago.

Again the handle moved. This time it was followed by a unmistakable tapping on the panels. Pulling on her dressing-gown; she approached the door.

"Who is there?" she whispered.

"Let me in, you little fool," was the reply. Instantly she recognized Allen's voice. Of course he still had her latch-key!

"Why have you come here at this hour?" she inquired, when she had admitted him.

"Not for the sight of your face. Anybody asleep in the basement or on this floor?" he demanded.

"I was, until you woke me," she replied pointedly. "Nobody else occupies any room on this floor at the moment. I asked why you'd come."

"Get into bed," Allen ordered. "Lie facing the wall and don't move until I tell you." There was menace in his tone.

The girl slid beneath the bed covers and turned as he wished.

"Anybody on the first floor?" he asked.

"Not in the room above this. The front room is occupied, I believe. If you keep your voice down you can't be heard, if that's what you mean," she added indignantly.

"Don't talk so much," he muttered.

Lying there, silent, she heard him turn the taps on at the wash basin.

"Does the gas-fire make much noise when it's lit?" he asked after a lengthy interval.

"No, it's particularly quiet. There's very little gas, though, because I had no silver. I'm not cold."

"I don't care if you are," he retorted. A coin was pushed into the slot. He lighted the fire and the gas-ring and put a kettle on. "Got any cocoa?"

"There's a tin of it on the mantelpiece. You can have some if you like, Mr. Allen. I don't want any."

"You'll drink what I give you," he told her. "You've caused me enough trouble to make me wish I'd never met you. If you think my visit here to-night is a joy for me, you've got another guess coming. You can sit up now."

Before the gas-fire hung two wet towels, evidently freshly washed.

"You needn't have bothered to wash those. I can get clean ones to-morrow."

The man swung round.

"When will you get it into your stupid head that I've no lady manners and no use for your sex?" he demanded savagely.

In the glow of the fire his face looked white and tense.

"I'm sorry," she murmured.

"You mentioned Paris the other day," Allen remarked. "Do you live there usually?"

"Yes. I've a room similar to this. I always keep it as it's my own furniture. Why?"

"Well, you've said enough about being grateful. Let's see if you are. It's most unlikely I'll need it, but in case I'm ever in a jam, you might let me know where I can find you there."

Daphne took her handbag from under the pillow and wrote down the address.

"There you are," she said.

Allen took the slip of paper and laid her handbag on the table.

"It won't be my fault if I bother you!" he said dryly.

"You're welcome to anything I can do to repay you, Mr. Allen. By the way, where did you leave Gill?"

"In the cinema, of course. You saw me come out just after you and your fancy friend. You didn't bring him here, did you?"

"Of course not," Daphne said with spirit. "You told me not to give him my name or address."

"That ends that episode then."

"Not necessarily. He gave me his card. I can write to him if I wish. I probably shall—to apologize for my beastly behaviour, as dictated by you."

"What's his name and address?"

"His name is Carlile. I don't know where he lives. My mind was so full of other things that I forgot to look at the card he gave me."

The man nodded as if satisfied.

"Plenty of time for that to-morrow," he said. "What sort of a joint is this house? Do you have your meals here?"

"No, they only serve breakfasts. I don't have that even, as I prefer to make my own tea and toast."

"Does the maid clean your room at a fixed hour?"

Daphne was puzzled by his seemingly childish questions.

"She doesn't come until I ring for her when I'm going out," she replied.

"Huh! A nice peaceful arrangement," the man commented. "Well, lie down and turn your back again. I've got a letter to write and don't want to feel you staring at me."

For a while she heard paper rustling and the scratching of a pen. That was followed by the sound of a spoon stirring something in a cup.

"Drink this cocoa." Allen stood beside her. "It may help you to sleep. You look as if you've had none for weeks." As she looked at it uneasily, he, added, "You needn't be afraid. I didn't go to the trouble of getting your papers from Gill in order to poison you."

"I'm not afraid," she said, and drank.

He stood beside her, waiting until she had finished. "Got the letters you wanted?" he asked as he rinsed the cup.

"Yes, thank you." It would seem ungracious to admit that she had not had the courage to open the envelope yet.

"Your latch-key's on the table. Bolt the door. I'm going now and you'll never see me again if I can help it." He turned out the gas-fire. "Good night."

XIII. A TERRIBLE AWAKENING

Wednesday, November 21st.

THE room was still dark when Daphne stirred. Her head felt heavy and she could scarcely raise her eyelids. For a while she lay there, too dazed to think clearly. Then, remembering Allen's visit, she put out her hand and switched on the light. It was twenty minutes past five. She could only have slept about three hours at the most; it was useless to get up yet, though she felt terribly thirsty.

Yawning wearily, she roused herself to get a drink. On the mantelshelf beside the wash basin was a note. She read:

"You've had a harmless sleeping draught. The longer it acts, the better for you."

It took a few seconds for the meaning of the words to penetrate her consciousness. Sponging her face with cold water, she tried to reconstruct mentally what had happened. Allen had told her to bolt the door after him, and as it was still bolted, she must have done so. Of going back to bed afterwards, she had no recollection, whatever.

On the table was a latch-key. He had kept his word about that, she reflected, and could not again come and alarm her at unearthly hours. His extraordinary visit of a few hours ago seemed entirely pointless. Since his every word expressed insult, she was not under the delusion that he was concerned for her health and wished her to have a good night's rest.

Her attention was attracted by sounds of movement in the house, unusual at that early hour of the morning. The front door was opened and slammed two or three times, and footsteps went up and down the stairs. In the back yard below someone was singing.

With a puzzled feeling she put her watch to her ear. It was ticking normally and she remembered winding it last night.

Unfastening her door, she looked into the hall. The light there was burning. On her mat was a newspaper and a bottle of milk, and hung on the outside handle of her door was a card, with a message written in block letters

"Have slept badly. Do not disturb until I ring." She was looking at the date on the newspaper when the maid appeared.

"I thought you was never going to wake up, miss," she said with a broad grin. "You'll be having your breakfast at supper time if you don't make haste. I should have knocked to see if you was all right if I hadn't seen the notice you hung up."

Daphne vaguely murmured some excuse of having been awake with toothache, and closed her door.

Why on earth had Allen drugged her? She must have slept solidly for fifteen hours. Certainly she had needed rest badly, but, as he had made clear, he was not interested in her health.

Suddenly panic seized her. Her handbag was on the table. Had he tricked her and, for some unknown reason, stolen the packet of letters?

She looked inside. There was the envelope, but the seal had been broken! She pulled out the letters it contained and scanned them quickly. So far as her drugged senses could determine the incriminating missives were intact. Her troubles were at last over. What if Allen had given her a sleeping draught? What if he had treated her contemptuously? Nothing mattered now. Almost she could have knelt at his feet in this moment of intense relief.

She hummed a gay little tune while her bath was running in. It seemed ages since she had felt so happy.

Somehow the occasion called for celebration, she decided, while relaxing in the steaming water. If Michael Carlile had a telephone number on his card, she would ring him up and see what happened. Maybe he would be out. She dismissed the unpleasant possibility. This was her lucky day: he was bound to answer her call.

Running downstairs to her room, she again met the maid in the hall with the evening newspaper in her hand.

"Heard you singing in your bath, miss," the woman remarked. "Your sleep done you good. There's been a horrible murder. In a cinema, of all places. Like to see the paper a few minutes? The boss is out and won't want it yet."

Daphne took the newspaper, too absorbed in her plans to notice clearly what the maid had said. The first thing was to find Mr. Carlile's card and ring him up. It must be either in her coat pocket or her handbag.

Still humming softly, she searched. The card was in neither place. She turned the contents of her bag on to the table and went through every article carefully without success. She was certain that she had not dropped it. Indeed, now she thought intently, she remembered placing the card in her bag.

Allen must have taken it to prevent her from getting in touch with Carlile! She knew how and when he took it. "Lie down and turn your back. I've got some writing to do and don't want you staring at me," he had ordered. She had heard the rustling of paper. Why was he determined she should not meet Michael Carlile again? If only she had looked at that card last evening and noticed the address! Now she had lost touch with Carlile, possibly for ever.

Her bubble of happiness had burst. Mechanically she began to replace the contents of her handbag. In putting away the packet of letters she noticed something scrawled on the back of the envelope.

"One of these is missing. If ever you talk too much, it may come in handy.—Allen."

There was a threatening tone in that message which made her regret giving him her address in Paris. To have refused his request would have seemed churlish after all that he had done for her. To change her apartment in Paris was not so easy. Moving her furniture to fresh quarters would involve time and money, and a change of address would mean notifying the different agents who gave her musical engagements.

Perhaps, however, she reflected, she was meeting trouble half way. Allen might never go to Paris or claim her help there, and she did not think he would make use of the letter that he had taken.

Again her thoughts reverted to Michael Carlile. She recalled their conversation in the hope of obtaining a clue to his address. It might be in the telephone directory! There was one in the hall. Taking it to her room, she searched its columns. Michael Carlile's name was not there. That hope had failed.

Despondently she picked up the newspaper the maid had given her. It was a copy of the *Evening Record*. In staring headlines across the top of the front page she read:

GHASTLY CRIME IN WEST END CINEMA

The centre of the page was occupied by a photograph: the reproduction of a pen and ink sketch of a girl's head and shoulders. Underneath it was printed in large type:

DO YOU KNOW THIS GIRL?

There followed a description of the girl's height, colouring and garments. It was a description that matched perfectly with Daphne and the clothes she had worn last night! Indeed, the jaunty little hat on the girl's head in the sketch might have been copied from that which she had had on. What did it all mean? Could Jabez

Gill have observed her in the cinema—after Allen had obtained her letters—and notified the police?

Still no hint of the truth came to her. The paragraph of description below the girl's picture was set in a square bordered with black lines, and at first she did not connect it with the other news that filled most of the main page.

She turned from the sketch and sought breathlessly through the printed matter for some explanation.

Her eyes raced down the columns, picking out the salient points.

Stabbed—death instantaneous—stalls of Royal Imperial Cinema—dead man's name Jabez Gill— powerfully built man in Harris tweed coat wanted—girl accomplice—see picture.

With icy fingers she at length laid the paper down. She understood everything now. The links fitted only too well. Allen had got her papers from his victim, ordered her to leave the cinema, and then accomplished his own revenge.

Before the gas-fire steamed the two face towels which he had washed after using last night. With a shiver she flung them into a corner of the room. No wonder he had bidden her turn her back while he got rid of the evidence of his terrible crime.

One thing stood out plainly. In spite of his dreaded deed, his visit here in the night had shown a measure of protection for her. The mystery of the sleeping draught and his strange message was explained. "The longer it acts the better for you." It meant that the later she awoke the more likely was she to find full details of the story in the newspapers and be prepared accordingly.

It explained also the lines he had written on her envelope when he had abstracted the letter. "If ever you talk too much, it may come in handy."

Talk too much! She pressed cold fingers to her throbbing temples. Indeed, she was not likely to talk.

Nothing and no one should ever induce her to admit that she knew Allen. That much at least she owed him. The police could do their own work; she was not a human blood-hound. She was thankful that she did not know Allen's address or anything about him.

Suddenly consternation gripped her. If Allen was arrested, her letter would most likely be found on him. For her own sake, therefore, she must if necessary help a murderer to escape justice. The first law was that of self-preservation.

Meanwhile, Paris, which had hitherto been her refuge, might now be a source of danger, since Allen would probably seek her aid there. Even if she changed her address, he could still easily trace her, she knew.

A man who could foil Jabez Gill could soon track her down in Paris.

She read the account of the crime again, grasping the details clearly now. The main theme seemed to be a campaign against the "girl accomplice." Readers of the *Evening Record* were urged in graphic phrases to search for this girl and communicate at once with the police.

> "She may be hiding the criminal or know where he is," Daphne read. "It is the duty of every citizen to aid the cause of justice by being on the look-out for this girl. Watch for her in streets and at railway stations; or in 'buses, tubes or trains. Hotel and lodging-house keepers should scrutinize closely any of their visitors who answer to this girl's description. Shopkeepers and their assistants may help to bring her to the notice of Scotland Yard. Too many murderers have escaped justice. This time let the people of Great Britain take a hand in the matter for their own protection."

The column was headed "A Crusade against Crime."

In imagination Daphne pictured herself as a hunted animal, watched by a thousand eyes wherever she went, expecting at any moment to be pounced upon. Suppose she went to Scotland Yard now and told her astounding tale to the authorities. They would naturally demand proof. She had none. Possibly, they would reason that she must know where Allen had lived or was likely to be living at the moment. How could she explain the extraordinary dominating personality of the harsh man who had befriended her and murdered Jabez Gill?

A sense of shame came over her when she remembered that Michael Carlile had been her companion at the cinema. He, too, would read all this. How much had he seen or guessed from Allen's queer treatment of her? Would he believe that she was Allen's accomplice? And believing, would he too turn against her and go to Scotland Yard with his share of information? Fool that she had been, never for one moment to suspect that Allen had meant to commit murder.

A sharp tap on the door made her heart miss a beat. Had the police tracked her down already?

"Who is it?" she asked.

The door was opened and, the maid entered.

"It's me, miss. Have you done with the paper?" she asked. "The master'll be back presently, I expect."

Daphne pushed the journal across the table. "Yes, I've finished with it, thank you."

"Hope you haven't caught a cold after your bath, miss. Your room's chilly as a tomb. I'll turn the gas-fire on full and warm it up a bit. Does it want another bob in the meter?"

Daphne checked an hysterical laugh as she remembered who had put the last shilling in!

"It's all right for a while," she answered. The maid's words about catching a cold put an idea into her head. She dared not go outdoors, and certainly would be safer here than anywhere. To feign a cold would offer an excuse for remaining in her room. "I don't feel very well, " she added.

The maid picked up the newspaper.

"You go back to bed, miss, and I'll bring you a hot water bottle," she suggested. "The 'flu's about pretty bad, and you don't want to get it." Her eyes fell on the newspaper that she held. "Quite a pretty girl, isn't she? Poor thing, if the murderer's her husband or something, she must be having an awful time."

"Yes," Daphne agreed. She was still wearing the rubber cap she had put on for her bath. Instinct now made her pull it more closely over her forehead.

The maid glanced from the pictured face in the paper to the girl, comparing them mentally.

"I do believe you're a bit like her," she said. "Isn't that funny? Of course with your hair hid in that rubber thing you're different, but with a black beret like hers, you might be twins."

"Fair women often resemble one another." Daphne tried to speak indifferently.

The maid's remark seemed to be no more than a casual comment, nevertheless that night she cut the smart little black hat into shreds.

XIV: DEANE ON THE CARPET

Wednesday, November 218t.

THAT same evening Inspector Reynolds sat in his office with a copy of the late edition of the *Record* before him.

From time to time angry ejaculations broke from his lips as he came across some particularly lurid phrase from the red-hot pen of Bob Deane.

"Have you seen this rag, Jenkins?" he asked, as his assistant entered the office.

Jenkins nodded significantly.

"I have, sir, and I'd like to shake the breath out of that fellow. Who does he think he is? England's hope of salvation from crime?"

"Plus Dictator to the Yard," commented the Inspector with a wry smile. Lifting the telephone receiver, he called the *Evening Record* office.

"Is Mr. Deane there?" he asked. "He is. No, I don't want to speak to him on the wire. Tell him to come to Scotland Yard at once. This is Inspector Reynolds. At once, you understand."

Reynolds banged down the receiver with a sigh of satisfaction.

"I shall feel better when I've had a heart-to-heart talk with that dear little chap, Jenkins. It would be just as well if you made yourself scarce during Deane's visit. You might cramp my style."

"Quite, sir, though I shall be sorry to miss it." Jenkins pointed to an article in the newspaper, headed: 'Exclusive interview by our crime expert.' "Deane has actually tapped the Weston family. Here's the story their little girl told him."

"I saw it, my lad." The Inspector's lips narrowed. "But what annoys me most is his brutal concentration on the girl, whom he calls the murderer's accomplice."

"It puzzles me why he didn't devote his attention to the man in the Harris coat. A woman obviously hadn't the physical strength to stab Gill in that manner."

"Ever heard of playing to the gallery?" inquired the Inspector. "Deane isn't altruistically concerned with the suppression of crime. He's out to sell his paper by the million, and he knows that this girl is a more picturesque figure than the murderer. Every woman will eat this bilge and beg for more. It's melodramatic tripe of the cheapest order."

"Where on earth did he get that picture of the girl, sir? Did the sweet-stall attendant talk?"

The telephone at Reynolds' elbow buzzed. He answered the call and made a brief reply over the wire before turning to his assistant.

"You'll know in a moment, Jenkins. Miss Oliver is on her way up."

The sweet-stall girl's face wore an anxious expression as she met Reynolds. She wasted no time in preliminaries.

"Directly I saw that thing this evening," she indicated the newspaper lying on the desk, "I asked the manager to give me an hour off so I could pop along here and explain. I didn't tell that fresh guy of a reporter one word of the muck he's written," she declared hotly. "I promised you I wouldn't."

"I know," Reynolds said. "Have you any idea how he got hold of these details?"

"Yep. It's all on account of the girl's-best-friend-is-her-mother stuff," Miss Oliver said with a grin. "Mum is a sweetheart, but she can't keep her trap shut. Like a fool, I went home last night, very full of myself and your sausage and mashed, and blurted out the whole tale. Showing off, that's what I was. Mum swore she wouldn't spill the beans to a living soul. Well, this morning first you came and then this reporter bloke. I choked him off and thought he'd gone out of my young life for ever. But Mr. Clever merely waited until I'd gone out and then soft-soaped Mum. It looks as if she shot the works. Has it done much damage?"

"We can't tell yet. In any case I'm not blaming you, Miss Oliver."

"You needn't, big boy. I'm doing all that," she retorted. Her eyes rested ruefully on the picture in the *Evening Record*. "Poor kid. I'm sorry for her."

"Is this sketch more like her than the photographs I showed you?"

"In a way, because she looks scared in your album, and is bareheaded." Miss Oliver groaned. "This toddy little hat in the *Record* is exactly like hers. If I see clothes once I can describe 'em exactly. That's how Mum got hold of the doings. Pity you didn't muzzle me, mister. I'll bet that girl's having a foul time, all through me. And even though she was talking to the bloke in the Harris coat in the queue before the show, she didn't come out with him, don't forget."

"I won't forget," promised Reynolds. "I wish you could describe the man who was her escort afterwards."

"So do I," the girl confessed. "All I can say is that he was a nice ordinary type. You know, clean-shaven, cold bath every morning, likes dogs, smokes a pipe style. D'you get me?"

Reynolds nodded.

"He wasn't the fresh kind, out to pick up a pretty face, I'm sure," she went on. "He looked kind of grave and worried while he was trying to get her the chocolate, and real sorry when she said she'd rather go home alone." With her head on one side and forehead puckered, she studied Reynolds for a minute. "Gosh! I've got it. You're a bit like him. He may be a few years younger, but if you take a squint in the glass and rub that solemn look off your dial, you'll get a fair idea of him."

"I'll try to follow out your suggestion," the Inspector agreed with a broad smile. "Thank you for calling here so promptly."

"That's all right, mister. I'll buzz off now. If you see the blinking bloodhound who wrote that stuff, give him a kick in the pants for me," she urged. "So long."

Casting an amused glance at his assistant, who had thoroughly enjoyed the conversation, Reynolds walked over to a small mirror and scanned his countenance.

He saw reflected a grey-eyed, clean shaven face, a firm mouth and chin, and lips that were now crinkling with humour. Crisp thick brown hair, hair greying at the temples, and a broad forehead which a few lines showed when he frowned.

"Portrait of an ordinary-looking man," he remarked. "I'm forty-one, so we'll say the girl's companion was between thirty and thirty-five."

'You're not at all ordinary-looking, sir," opposed Jenkins stoutly. "Distinguished and—"

"That'll do, young man," his chief interrupted. "You turn my head, the next thing will be that I'll expect a 'fan mail.' And the only kind I've had were threatening letters from criminals who bear a grudge. To go back to this girl in spite of a Oliver's words, she *might* have had a hand, perhaps unconsciously, in the business of the anonymous letters Gill received."

"You said you thought a girl had addressed the envelope, sir."

"I still think so. Also I've proved that the anonymous message and the envelope were not written with same quality of ink. The latter was addressed with blue-black kind used for fountain pens; the message was written in a cheap variety of ink that soon turns to a dirty brown. If the girl only addressed the envelopes, there's a chance that she never knew what was inside them! On the other hand, considering she undoubtedly went to the cinema with the suspect, she might have known his intentions. Gill had possibly been blackmailing one or both of them."

"If only Gill had left a few papers behind!" sighed Jenkins.

"I've done my best to fill that gap by putting a paragraph in the newspapers requesting anyone who had business with Gill to communicate with the Yard. It may draw blood. To-day I've had another go at Gill's luggage and clothes. Not the vestige of a clue there, and no letters arrived at his flat." The Inspector raised his head and listened. "Hop it! Here comes the famous crime expert, I fancy."

Jenkins opened the door and muttered something under his breath as Bob Deane brushed airily past him and entered the office.

Hat well back on his head, and a grin on his impudent face, he swaggered forward and gave Reynolds a mock salute. Neither the smile nor the swagger were wholly convincing, however.

"Well, Inspector, I've done myself proud in to-night's edition, haven't I?" he demanded by way of an opening.

"You've certainly done something," was Reynolds' acid comment. "Want to run Scotland Yard, don't you?"

Deane considered the question.

"I'm too busy at present, though of course I'll continue to give you hints and help you a bit," he said in a tone of patronage. "I might run my newspaper also, if they make it worth my while."

"Or equally you might sell matches on the curb, if they feel your bright young personality is a trifle overpowering." The Inspector's eyes hardened. "Deane, you've gone too far and you know it. In your lust for sensation you've made a target of that girl. Not only that, but you've side-tracked the public's attention from the essential point—the man in the Harris tweed coat. Every reader of your scurrilous columns is busily staring at platinum blondes, and forgetting to look for the criminal."

"The girl was his accomplice," Deane submitted.

"What right have you to say that? She might be only the barest acquaintance, and perfectly innocent. I hope she sues your paper, for damages for libel. They'll enjoy paying it, I'm sure, for your sweet sake."

"If she's innocent, why hasn't she come forward to say so? Tell me the answer to that one, Mr. Reynolds," Deane demanded facetiously.

"I've no intention of telling you anything more that can be dished up and distorted into news, Deane, but I know what I should do if you were twenty years younger."

The journalist gave a shout of joy.

"Forget my years of wisdom, I implore you, and do it," he begged. "Just let me get a camera-man along first, and we'll go out into Whitehall. It would make a priceless story for the *Record*. 'Our famous crime reporter thrashed by Yard official. Motive: jealousy.' Complete with photographs. Joking aside, Inspector, I'm sorry I stole your thunder."

For the first time Reynolds' face clouded with anger.

"Thunder!" he exploded indignantly. "Do you think I'm out for cheap applause? You prate glibly of protecting the nation from crime. I'm trying to do my job and catch the criminal. You can have all the limelight you want so long as it doesn't hinder me in my task. Mind your own messy affairs and leave the police alone for the future. This is the last time I shall warn you."

"All right. What do you want me to do?" There was an artful expression in Deane's eyes.

"Drop this disgraceful attack on the girl and, if it isn't too late, follow the line the decent newspapers are taking with regard to the man we want."

"The *Evening Record* leads and not follows," Deane stated. "However, we will open out about the man in the Harris coat to-morrow." He walked towards the door.

"You heard what I said about the girl," Reynolds called after him. "Do you promise to leave her alone?"

Deane chuckled.

"Not on your sweet life," he said, and went out.

XV. MICHAEL LEARNS THE NEWS

Wednesday, November 21st.

ON the morning after the murder Michael Carlile strolled down the wide staircase of a house in Leamington Square to breakfast, humming a cheerful tune under his breath. Not for many years had he experienced this joyous feeling that something nice and unexpected might happen at any moment. A child opening its Christmas stocking was the nearest simile he could think of.

Of course the lovely blue-eyed girl with the tragic face he had met at the cinema last night was responsible for his mood. Already in his thoughts he called her his "mystery girl." Perhaps there was added attraction in the fact of her elusiveness. He knew neither her name nor address; she had refused to have supper with him and retreated into the wilderness of London. Yet, because she had his card, he did not feel that he had wholly lost her. She might write him to-day or to-morrow. The situation was full of happy possibilities.

The miracle of it was that, in an extremely prosaic world, Michael Carlile had retained most of his illusions, although life had been far from a bed of roses.

It was distinctly thorny, for instance, in this house in which he had lived for several weary years.

The house was not his, nor anything within its walls, save his tooth-brush and a few personal possessions. Sometimes, he thought cynically, that that literally was all he possessed, since his mind, soul and body had long since passed from his keeping into the tight clutches of his employer, Sir Howard Neames, and Sir Howard's daughter.

Quite a lot of Michael was claimed by Miss Neames, and it was no fault of hers that his body also—in a strictly legal way—was not included. The lady had made it abundantly clear that he might lead her to the altar whenever he wished. Michael expended considerable effort in delicately avoiding embarrassing conversations tending towards this subject.

Having suffered under Estelle Neames' domineering personality for a long time, nothing would have given Michael greater pleasure than to have told the lady firmly that the answer was in the negative.

With the dice loaded against him, that was the last thing he could do. In Miss Neames' hands rested the power for Michael to remain here in the fairly well paid role of secretary-slave to her father and herself, or go out on his ear into the street.

Michael had been there, and having no wish to go back, swallowed his pride daily as part of the routine. His own father had died, bankrupt after a Stock Exchange crash, and left Michael without a penny to start his career. For two ghastly years he did every possible kind of job in order to earn enough to eat, since his own profession was closed to him for lack of cash.

Miss Neames, during a bout of "slumming," had come across him in a Salvation Army shelter five years ago. Discovering that he had had a public school education and held a Varsity degree, she persuaded her father that he needed a secretary.

Hence Michael's induction into Leamington Square.

Hence also his indebtedness to Estelle Neames, a flamboyant brunette of some thirty-five summers.

That indebtedness had been increased within a few months of his arrival. Michael had charge of the petty cash for the household, and at times a fairly large sum was in his desk in the library.

It was no part of Miss Neames' job to check his accounts. Sir Howard, a retired and wealthy knight of the City, suffering from high blood pressure and even higher temper, was perfectly capable of managing his own affairs, and did so. Michael was responsible to him for every penny of expenditure.

But on that fateful morning nearly five years ago Estelle entered the library and, announcing that her father was indisposed, said she would check the petty cash items with Michael.

She found a discrepancy of twenty pounds. Crimson with confusion, Michael attempted and failed to account for the deficit.

"You came here less than three months ago in the garments you stood upright in, Mr. Carlile," she remarked succinctly.

"I've spent my quarter's salary that Sir Howard paid me in advance on necessary clothes," he explained, not caring to add that he had had a wild bet of a pound on a fifteen to one winner a week ago that had paid for his dinner suit.

Miss Neames raised her eyebrows.

"The salary you have received would not pay for all your purchases—if they are paid for."

"They are," Michael assured her.

"This desk is locked and you keep the key," she said. "I know your financial status—and expenditure. And my father's money is short by twenty pounds."

"I have not taken the money, Miss Neames, but if you insist, I will replace it when I get my next salary—unless Sir Howard discharges me."

"He certainly will if he finds out, and he is bound to discover it long before your salary is due."

"There seems no alternative then," Michael replied bitterly. "I can only dispose of my clothes, give you the proceeds towards the amount for which I am responsible, and return to the Salvation Army shelter in which you found me." He moved towards the library door.

There was a speculative look in Estelle Neames' eyes.

"One moment," she said. "There is perhaps an alternative. If you will write me a letter accepting the responsibility for this loss, I will advance you the money.

You can repay me later and I will undertake not to mention this matter to my father."

Michael stared at her in amazement.

"But that would be an admission of guilt. I did not take the money."

"I have only your word for it. You can act as you please, Mr. Carlile."

For hours Michael weighed up the humiliating proposition. There was no way out. Either he wrote the letter or he lost his job. The desk belonged to Sir Howard; there might be another key but he had never seen it. He could not mistrust the servants. They had been there for many years and not one of them appeared to him as likely to commit a paltry heft and lose a good situation.

He wrote and signed the letter and Miss Neames gave him the money, which he duly repaid. Then he asked her for the letter he had written.

"I think I'll keep it as a guarantee of future good behaviour," she replied with a curious laugh.

His only object in life since then had been to save sufficient money to continue with his profession—a profession which he had never mentioned to Miss Neames or her father.

It seemed as if the lady guessed his wish, if not the reason. In every way his economical intentions were thwarted. Part of his duties was to act as her escort to theatres, dances or restaurants. She never failed to allow him to pay for his share. Often, indeed, he paid for her if Sir Howard forgot to do so. These functions called for expensive suits. He was chided for meanness or a shabby appearance if he did not obey that call. Secretly he tried in vain for other posts. There were too many applicants. And, always in his heart was the knowledge that Estelle Neames did not intend him to leave; if necessary, she would use that damaging letter to prevent it.

To his dismay, her attitude changed gradually to the present one of embarrassing hints that he would be welcomed into the family. With less than a hundred pounds in the bank and little chance of adding to it, he might have drifted into matrimony. Anything was better than his ignominious position of secretary-gigolo as he styled himself.

That was up to last evening when Sir Howard and his daughter had dined with friends and Michael Carlile went to the Royal Imperial Cinema.

From the moment he met the Mystery girl, things had taken a violent turn in his life. Every man likes to be a heroic figure, and beauty in distress offers unique opportunity.

In imagination, during the small hours of the night, Michael had gone over his conversation with the unknown girl. He heard again the words of her unpleasant companion and rehearsed many scenes in which he dealt forcefully with the situation, emerging always with credit and distinction; the reward— unfortunately as yet imaginary—being the trust and friendship of the girl.

By daylight the gilt came off these romantic fancies a little, but the solid fact of his encounter with the Mystery girl remained. There also remained the buoying thought that she might write to him.

All this had taken place before he entered the breakfast-room on the morning after the murder and looked at the newspapers. Sir Howard always had a light meal in his room, and Estelle rarely appeared until Michael had nearly finished.

He had just opened the newspaper when Estelle came in with a bustling brightness.

"Good morning, Michael." She used his Christian name when they were alone, but he never called her "Estelle" although she had often urged it. "And what time did my bad little boy come back last night?"

Michael had given up resenting her coy catechism regarding his movements. This morning his mood was different. He felt cold and wary.

"I forgot to clock in," he remarked "May I cut you some ham?"

"No. I'll have an egg and you can pour out my coffee." Under the thin arch of her eyebrows she glanced up at him. "Did your best girl keep you out very late?"

Usually after a free evening Michael would amiably and truthfully deny the best girl theory. To-day a spirit of cussedness was holding him.

"Not as late as I would have liked," he retaliated. "I was in about ten o'clock. The toast is not very hot. Shall I ring for more?"

Miss Neames stared at him in surprise. This treatment was new and she didn't like it.

"Don't trouble, thanks." She sipped her coffee thoughtfully, rather at a loss through his calm acceptance of her words. She decided to express annoyance by being silent.

Apparently undisturbed, Michael turned to the morning newspaper. His expression changed suddenly as his eyes fell on a paragraph in the *Stop Press*.

> A well-dressed man of medium age was found stabbed to death in the stalls of the Royal Imperial Cinema last evening. The crime was discovered about nine-twenty while a film was in progress. The identity of the dead man was unknown up to the time of going to press. No arrest has been made but Scotland Yard is anxious to interview a tall powerfully-built man in a Harris tweed coat who left just before the murder was discovered. Also a pretty fair-haired girl who entered the cinema with him but left at nine-fifteen with another man about thirty years of age.

Michael's brain raced back over the incidents of the previous evening. Could it be a horrible coincidence? He and the Mystery girl left the cinema about that time, and the powerfully-built man in the Harris coat corresponded with her companion.

What was going to happen now? Presumably he ought to make the police acquainted with what he had heard and witnessed in the queue. To do so might incriminate the girl.

Miss Neames' irritable voice interrupted his thoughts.

"Michael, what on earth is the matter with you this morning?" she demanded. "I've asked you twice where you went last night. Of course if there is a mystery about it—"

"Mystery? Of course not," he cut in swiftly. "I spent a dull hour at a restaurant and went for a walk."

"A very long walk if it lasted for two hours," she commented. "You're a strange person this morning. Ten minutes ago you looked as if you owned the earth, and now you look as if you'd lost it."

That was exactly how he felt, Michael reflected, having no desire to let Estelle Neames dissect his secret emotions, he forced a laughing rejoinder.

"There's a dance on at the Embassy to-night," she marked as he folded the newspaper and rose. "I want you to take me, please. We ought to leave at nine o'clock."

"I've a lot of correspondence to do for Sir Howard."

"Leave my father to me. I'll deal with him. Have you ordered a new dress suit yet?"

"No, and I'm afraid I can't afford to do so, Miss Neames." Again he forced a laugh. "I really must try save for my old age, you know."

She caught his arm as he passed her chair.

"There is no need for you to save for anything, Michael," she said in a low voice. "I understand your pride—"

The entrance of the butler caused her to break off in middle of her sentence, and Michael was able to escape.

To dance at the Embassy with Estelle was unthinkable while somewhere in London a sad blue-eyed girl lay under a cloud of being associated with a murderer.

XVI. VISITORS FOR REYNOLDS

Wednesday, November 21st.

MICHAEL CARLILE was relieved that his work that day consisted chiefly of errands for Sir Howard. It enabled him to buy each edition of the evening newspapers and scan them eagerly in peace.

Gradually such details of the crime as were known were unfolded. A full description of the wanted man tallied perfectly with the individual who had insulted the girl in the cinema queue.

No, there could be no mistake. Further, both the girl and the man with whom she left the cinema were requested to communicate with Scotland Yard immediately. The girl's appearance was delineated clearly, the man of course was himself.

By chance the *Evening Record* was not among the newspapers that he had seen during the afternoon.

It was nearly six o'clock when he bought a copy of that journal and saw on the front page the picture of the girl he had met. Certainly it was not an exact resemblance, but by some trick of cunning or accident the artist had produced an effect that was a remarkable likeness.

He raged inwardly as he read Bob Deane's article. In all London probably he, Michael Carlile, was the only person who could prove that she had taken no active part in the murder. Yet, as she evidently had not come forward to say so, he might do her infinite damage if he went to the police.

Meanwhile, he pictured vividly the torture she must enduring, possibly alone. Not for a moment did he believe that she was now with the murderer.

Had she written or wired, Michael wondered? Ringing up the butler at Leamington Square he asked if any letters or telegrams had come for him during his absence, and was told that there was nothing.

Suppose she had lost his visiting card. Suppose she as too ashamed of this publicity to appeal to the man she had only met for so short a time?

That was the more likely, he decided. How, not knowing who or where she was, could he get into touch with her and assure her that he was ready to do anything he could to help her? Discretion went to the winds; gone was all fear of losing his post and facing the world on a small savings. Somewhere a frightened girl was in trouble and he meant to find her.

Then a brilliant plan evolved. He would advertise in all the newspapers. To give the address of his employer was impossible. He must use a box office number and implore her to write making a rendez-vous.

The wording of his request was not easy, since he didn't know her name and dared not use his lest police attention be attracted by it.

Suddenly he remembered that she had spoken of someone called Pat as her dearest friend, but one unable help in her difficulties. He would use her own phrase in the advertisement and trust that she would recognize it.

He took the notices to the newspaper offices himself to save any loss of time, recalling thankfully that in the cinema they had discussed daily journals, and she had named those she read.

At least, he thought, as he went back to Leamington Square, he had done all he could to assure the Mystery girl of his wish to be her friend.

Inspector Reynolds was having a busy evening at the Yard. The result of the paragraphs in the newspapers asking for information concerning Jabez Gill and the wanted man had brought an unwieldy harvest of callers to his office.

Patiently Reynolds and his assistant interviewed each one, endeavouring to find some clue. Most of the visitors were would-be detectives, full of cranky ideas for trapping the murderer. Others stated that they had known someone called Gill, who, however, bore only a faint resemblance to the victim.

One man, in evening dress, explained at great length that he had noticed a hefty individual in a Harris coat waiting outside a grill-room near the Royal Imperial Cinema about a quarter to eight the previous evening.

"That might have been the person you want, Inspector."

"It probably was," Reynolds agreed wearily. "The murdered man dined in that restaurant before he visited the cinema."

"I'm glad to have been of assistance," his visitor remarked, and made a pompous exit.

The Inspector raised his hands in a despairing gesture.

"Can nobody give me a shred of information about something that happened *after* the murder?" he demanded.

Jenkins wrinkled his brow.

"I watched Gill go into that grill-room, sir, and I'm sure I noticed a tall man in a light coat standing with his back to me near the entrance. He acted so casually that I concluded he was merely waiting for someone. There was a crowd of people about when Gill reappeared and I didn't see the man follow him. But," he paused, "I could identify him, no matter what disguise he employed."

"That's the first bit of good cheer I've had to-day," observed his chief. "Go ahead and tell me how."

"He has unusually long lobes to his ears for one thing, and he can't take a tuck in them! Also, although I never saw his face, I noticed that he had very large feet."

"Well, it's something to have that card up our sleeve," Reynolds observed. "Any more people waiting?"

"Three, sir," Jenkins replied. "An odd mixture. Lady Grace Quentin; a little Cockney chap called Taylor, whose face you'll know—we've got his streaky record; and Miss

Thelma Underwood, who looks a cross between a full-blown barmaid and a music-hall artist. The three of them arrived almost together."

"Thelma sounds as if she might be interesting. What does Lady Quentin want?"

"A good seat for the inquest, the constable thinks," Jenkins replied dryly.

"H'm. In that case we'll let her wait. Show Thelma up."

Presently Jenkins ushered in a florid over dressed woman in the mid-forties. Her absurd little hat, perched on a mass of hair that certainly never grew golden from the roots, reminded the Inspector of a pillbox on a sheaf of ripe corn.

Was she one of Jabez Gill's victims, he wondered, as he considered her carefully.

Her first words surprised him.

"When I read in the *Evening Record* that you wanted to see a blonde girl, I thought maybe it was me you were after," she stated calmly.

The Inspector veiled his astonishment.

"Were you at the Royal Imperial Cinema last night?" he asked.

"No, I was home in Archibald Road, Clapham, listening to the wireless. I am Miss Thelma Underwood and I run a board residence house."

Failing to see any link between that information and the tragedy in the cinema, Reynolds was rather at a loss how to proceed. The missing girl was young and slim, and bore no resemblance to this woman, if Miss. Oliver's statement was correct.

"What made you fancy that you were connected with this case, Miss Underwood"

"Fancy!" The woman snorted. "Reggie Vickers lodged with me and we were engaged to be married. Poor lad. He shot himself on Clapham Common." She wiped genuine tears from her blackened eyelashes. "It was because that swine Gill blackmailed him mercilessly. Reggie couldn't pay at last, and Gill threatened to expose him to his firm."

"Did you ever meet Jabez Gill?" inquired Reynolds.

"I should just about think I did. He fair hated the sight of me!" Miss Underwood said vehemently. "Reggie was in such a hole that he owned up everything. I'd often lent him money to pay Gill, I suppose. Anyhow, I went to Gill's office four or five times and told the oily scoundrel what I thought of him. I could have killed him myself if I'd had the chance. I said so to my friends at the time. That's why I thought I'd better come along here before you found out."

"Had Mr. Vickers any relatives?"

"Not a living soul."

"When you called on Gill, was anyone else ever in his flat?"

Miss Underwood nodded.

"Yes, the chap who's downstairs now. A nasty bit of work he is, too."

"That must be Taylor, sir," Jenkins interposed. "It's a queer coincidence that he and Miss Underwood should arrive here together."

"Coincidence be hanged," the woman retorted. "He's here because I fetched him an hour ago; sweating with fear he is, too. I met him in Gill's office once and he followed me back to Clapham. Wanted to borrow money. I lent him a bit because I hoped to find out something about Gill to help my poor Reggie. All I ever discovered was the little rat's address. That's where I dug him out this evening and dragged him along here."

Reynolds turned to his assistant.

"See Taylor doesn't slip off," he urged.

"You needn't bother," Miss Underwood put in. "I've already told the bobby downstairs to keep an eye on him. One of my neighbours dropped in after tea, showed me the *Record*, and asked if I'd murdered Gill as I'd threatened once. I got the windup, and went off for

Taylor. The sooner the murderer's found, the better I'll be pleased. I don't want to be suspected of it."

"Naturally. I'm obliged to you for this information, Miss Underwood."

"That's all right," the woman replied. "I'm only saving my own skin. You've got my address in case you want it for anything. Good night."

"Thelma indeed was very interesting," Reynolds remarked when Miss Underwood had gone. "Let's see what 'Slug' Taylor has to tell us "

Propelled forward by a gentle thrust from Jenkins, an undersized man presently appeared. His small black eyes, set deeply above large pallid cheeks, resembled boot buttons; a weak receding chin and a mouth that apparently had no lips, made up the unpleasant remainder, of Taylor's face.

"'Evening, sir. I hope you're well," he began smoothly. "Why that tow-'aired bit made me come 'ere to waste your time, I can't guess."

"I'll try to help, you, Slug. You worked for Jabez Gill, didn't you?"

Slug licked the corner of his mouth and did a bit of quick thinking. .

"What if I did?" he evaded. "Off and on I may have done a few jobs for him; a bit of sleuthing now and again. Watching folks ain't the exclusive patent of you gents at the Yard."

"It depends on *why* people are being watched," Reynolds informed him. "I want the names and addresses of as many of Gill's clients as you are aware of."

"I got a poor memory, sir."

"Well, you'd better stir it into action if you want to save yourself from being under suspicion in this case," advised the Inspector. "You worked for the murdered man and have a very nasty record, Slug."

Slug churned over that point in silence for a minute.

"All right, guv'ner. I'll do my best, but it won't help you much. Gill never told me anything about his business. All I knew was the names of them he told me to shadow. I'll write them down if you like."

"Take Taylor downstairs, Jenkins, and give him some writing materials. I'll see him later. Show Lady Quentin in now, if she's not got tired of waiting."

The Inspector rose when a dignified grey-haired lady was announced a few moments later. He indicated with a distant bow an easy chair that stood near his desk. Lady Quentin glanced coolly round and selected a straight-backed seat.

"You are the Inspector engaged on the cinema murder case, I presume," she observed, favouring the C.I.D. official with a penetrating glance from steely-blue eyes.

"I am, madam. Can you tell me anything about it?" Crisp formality bristled in Reynolds' tone.

"I? Nonsense. Of course not," the lady rapped back. "I've nothing to confess, if that's what you think I'm here for, and I'm not engaged in crime. Jail at my age might be rather trying."

"I was not suggesting that you had taken any active part in the crime, madam," Reynolds said. "I only wondered why—"

"If you'll stop asking questions and 'wondering,' I'll explain why I called on you," Lady Quentin reproved sharply. "I don't know the murderer, his victim, or the very pretty young woman who, according to the *Evening Record*, seems to be mixed up in the case."

Reynolds made no comment, but his face expressed boredom and his fingers tapped the desk impatiently.

There was a provoking gleam in Lady Quentin's eyes. The Inspector obviously imagined that she was a tiresome old fool who had called on some trivial, time-wasting errand. She had been kept waiting a long while downstairs and her reception here had not been of a cordial nature.

"One of my cars is black, and rather like a taxi," she remarked in a leisurely conversational manner.

"Indeed." Reynolds commented icily. "I fail to understand—"

"I'm sure you do, Inspector." Lady Quentin's voice was of honeyed sweetness now. "Having been out of town for a few days, I instructed my chauffeur to meet me yesterday. He did so—in the black car"

"In the black car," repeated Reynolds with portentous sarcasm.

"Like a taxi," supplemented Lady Quentin. "Just as I was nearing it a man jumped in."

"Thinking it was a taxi," put in Reynolds. If this interview was to resemble an absurd scene from *Alice in Wonderland*, he was determined to have his share in it.

Lady Quentin gave him a pleased smile.

"Exactly. Most amusing, wasn't it?"

"And then the man discovered it was a private car and got out?" queried the Inspector blandly.

"That's a good guess, Inspector, but the man didn't discover it. Oh dear, no. He was really rather stupid as well as rude. He gave his address to my chauffeur and in a violent manner ordered him to get a something move on. My chauffeur explained that it was a private car; the man got out, and I got in." The lady waved her hand in a comprehensive gesture.

"If the man was drunk or abusive, you should have reported him to the police yesterday. I cannot deal with cases of that description," Reynolds informed her sternly.

"Oh, really. I'm sorry if I've made a mistake. I'm not here to complain about the man, though. He was neither drunk nor abusive; merely in a hurry. I shouldn't have called on you, only," there was a malicious glint in her eyes now, "I read the newspapers this evening and had an idea that you might be interested." She rose and drew her fur coat round her. "My car met me at Waterloo Station at nine-forty last night, Inspector," she said with biting emphasis.

"Waterloo Station!" Reynolds was stung to alertness. "Did you notice the man's face or clothes, Lady Quentin?"

"His back was towards me. He was wearing a light tweed coat and cap. In appearance he corresponded with the powerfully-built man of middle age about whom you are concerned."

"And the address he gave, did you hear that?" Reynolds inquired eagerly.

"I did not. My chauffeur probably heard and might remember it." A faint smile curved Lady Quentin's lips. "Had you seen me earlier you could have asked him, Inspector. After half an hour in a rather cold room downstairs, I sent a message out to him saying I should not require him again to-night and would return by taxi."

Reynolds groaned inwardly while he made apologies that were entirely sincere.

The lady accepted them in a generous spirit and wrote down something on a slip of paper.

"That is my chauffeur's address, Inspector," she said. Her eyes twinkled as she added, "Old ladies are apt to be fractious, remember, and they are not always so foolish as you think. I overheard what the constable said, and I do not want a seat reserved for me at the inquest, thank you."

XVII. A FIND AT WATERLOO,

Wednesday, November 21st.

LEAVING Slug Taylor in Jenkins' hands, the Inspector jumped into a Yard car and drove to the address Lady Quentin had given him. The chauffeur was just going to bed when Reynolds arrived and explained his errand.

"The man told me to stop at the corner of Shalcott or Shalford something, sir. I couldn't say if it was Shalcott Road, Street or Gardens. He seemed in a desperate hurry."

"Yes, I gathered that from Lady Quentin," the Inspector observed dryly. "Did you notice anything about him?"

"I'm sorry I didn't, sir. People have often mistaken that car for a taxi, and naturally I was paying attention to her ladyship who was standing just behind the man."

"Did she have any luggage?"

"Oh yes, sir. The porter was carrying the bags, of course. He was almost by her ladyship's side."

For a moment Reynolds had a ray of hope. It was dashed when he remembered the army of porters that would have to be questioned on the off-chance of their recalling the matter.

"Could you identify that porter by any chance?" he inquired.

The chauffeur's mouth tightened.

"I could, sir, easily," he remarked feelingly. "We had a few words at the way he pitched her ladyship's dressing-case down, and I told him where he got off the organ stool. Stout ginger-headed bloke he was, with a thick moustache that looked like a couple of young carrots."

"I think I can find him after that description," Reynolds said with amusement. He obtained details from the chauffeur of the exact spot where his car had stopped outside the station, and left him.

With the help of a station official at Waterloo he was able to trace the ginger-headed porter with surprisingly little difficulty. His moustache alone would have been sufficient clue, Reynolds decided, as he saw the luxurious growth and vivid hue of the decoration on the man's upper lip.

"Ginger-head" recounted the incident of the previous night with noticeable pride.

"The bags was heavy and I gave the chauffeur an earful," he added. "And that tall chap, too, afterwards."

"What tall chap?" Reynolds demanded.

"Why, the man who got into the private car by mistake. A fair temper he was in, too. While I was putting the bags into the car he'd had a try to get into two more taxis that were already engaged. Then I stumbled over his great feet, and he went for me. If there hadn't been a crowd about I'd have had time to give him what he deserved. What d'you want him for, sir?"

"I gather that you don't read the newspapers much," Reynolds remarked.

"Racing news is all I care about," the porter confessed.

"You don't know, of course, which way the man went?"

"No, sir, not after he went to the cloak-room."

"How do you know he went there? He hadn't any luggage, surely."

"My next job was to check two bags for a party," the porter replied "I'm certain I saw the man standing near me at the counter."

There could be only one thing that the man would wish to dispose of Reynolds suspected. The tell tale overcoat! Accompanied by the station official, he went to the cloak-room.

Within a few minutes he was holding a garment made of Harris tweed in his hands.

"I must take this away for the night at least," Reynolds said.

"Shall we hold the man who owns it when he calls here?" asked the clerk.

Reynolds smiled.

"By all means. But I'm afraid he'll never claim it." He returned to the Yard bearing his queer trophy of the chase.

"There's not a chance in a thousand of any clue being found in it, Jenkins, or the man wouldn't have parked it. All the same, go through it thoroughly. What about 'Slug?'"

"He's written some kind of a list of Gill's clients. Half of the names I'm sure are spelled wrongly, and the other half he has probably invented." Jenkins sighed despondently. "I've got the slimy little beggar's address."

"Cheer up, my lad. This garment at any rate is definite proof that we're on the right track. A man doesn't leave his overcoat in a station cloak-room on a cold November night without good reason. Get the London street directory. I want you to look up Shalcott or Shalford something or other."

While Jenkins pored over the volume, the inspector examined the coat meticulously. It was obviously a ready-made garment in a large size, and bore no tag with the maker's name on it.

In a side pocket was a bottle of quinine tablets of a proprietary brand purchasable from any chemist, and a packet of cigarettes which had a curiously unpleasant odour.

The other pockets at a superficial glance were empty. Searching more carefully, Reynolds found the halves of two tickets for the Royal Imperial Cinema.

"Miss Oliver was right, Jenkins," he exclaimed. "This man evidently bought two tickets last night; one for himself and one for the fair-haired girl who went off with the other fellow. Well, it's helpful to prove even that."

"Are you sure that girl is not in our records, sir?"

Reynolds frowned perplexedly.

"Miss Oliver picked out two photographs as being rather like her. That isn't much to go upon. If I publish either of our photographs in the newspapers and it is not the girl, I'm simply causing confusion. Bob Deane has created all the stir necessary to find her. I'll concentrate on finding the owner of this coat. Judging by the evidence that he left the cinema and Waterloo Station unaccompanied, my bet is that he's playing a lone hand. Give me a large sheet of clean paper. There's some dust in these pockets."

Holding the garment carefully, he shook out the accumulation.

"That's odd," he remarked, after a moment's scrutiny. "Mixed up with fine tobacco and fluff is some gritty substance. What do you make of it?"

"It looks like sand," Jenkins replied.

"I know that. Can't you see the grains are of different shades?" Reynolds pointed out. "Now where does one find coloured sand in delicate pale shades?" He stared at the ceiling. "I've got it. There's some beach on the Isle of Wight that has sand of this description. We'll get it analysed to-morrow. What about this Shalford business?"

"There's no street or road of that name, sir." Reynolds took the directory and turned over the leaves.

"Well try what Chalcott or Chalford gives us. Ah ha! We've plenty of Chalcotts. Too many, in fact. Mercifully they're all in the same area. King's Road district." He glanced at his watch. "We can't ring people up after eleven o'clock at night asking for a man whose name we don't know. I must start on that job in the morning. Give me a duplicate list of the names 'Slug' Taylor has written down. You'd better sift through them and have another search in Jabez Gill's flat. That will keep you pretty busy to-morrow. Good night."

The Inspector locked away the overcoat and rang up the police station nearest to the King's Road area.

"I want particular watch kept for a tall, powerfully built man in the Chalcott street or road district," he said to the superintendent "No, he will not be wearing a Harris tweed overcoat."

For a moment Reynolds studied the bottle of quinine tablets and packet of queer cigarettes. He had not shown these to Jenkins and he did not intend to do so yet. Intuition was a fragile flower, and he was too sensitive to expose it to ridicule if his wild guess was wrong.

XVIII. MRS. REYNOLDS ON THE TRAIL

Wednesday, November 21st.

IT was nearly midnight when Inspector Reynolds reached his home in Highgate. Usually when he closed the gate and walked up the path to the front door he experienced the impression of a ship coming to anchor in peaceful waters.

To-night he was too tired in body and spirit to be conscious of anything save a longing to talk his problems over with his wife.

Mrs. Reynolds was the type of person with whom one could talk things over.

She was a good-looking woman in the mid-thirties, with soft brown eyes and a quiet voice. In temperament she was the perfect wife for a highly-strung conscientious Scotland Yard detective. She had quick wit and a clear brain full of what her husband called "horse sense." Above all, in his estimation, was the feeling of repose that pervaded her entire personality.

Sometimes, in restaurants, when Reynolds' ears were tortured by women's shrill conversation and strident laughter, he compared them with the low pleasant tones of his wife and felt thankful.

She heard her husband's step and opened the door before he could put his key in the lock. One glance at his weary, abstracted face told her the mood he was in. Taking his hat and coat, she hung them up and followed him into the sitting-room.

Reynolds frowned at her with mock severity. "What are you doing up at this hour, Agnes?"

"I'm making tea at the moment, dear," she replied, lifting the kettle from the hob. "You've all the signs of a man who wants to talk."

Her husband sank into an easy chair and grinned.

"Woman, with your intuition you'd have been burnt for a witch not so long ago. Phew! What a day. Have you seen the *Evening Record*?"

"I have," his wife said with compressed lips "You can save your breath. I know what you think of Bob Deane. What's your opinion of the girl he is hounding?"

"I'll be more interested to hear yours."

Mrs. Reynolds filled the cups thoughtfully.

"First, I can't believe that any girl would be a deliberate party to such a messy murder. Stabbing is a particularly nasty business from a woman's point of view. Also, and this again is in the girl's favour, would any intending murderer be such a fool as to share his secret with a woman?"

"This man showed cunning, too, in tracking his victim," put in Reynolds. "Yet, remember the girl ransacked Gill's hotel bedroom before she joined the murderer."

Mrs. Reynolds wrinkled her forehead

"Yes, that's against her, of course." She paused as an idea struck her. "Tom, suppose she was searching for something on her own account."

"I see what you mean. You think Gill might have been blackmailing her or her family. That agrees with my theory. Her acquaintance with the murderer might have been pure coincidence, or he might have fallen for a pretty face just before he killed Gill."

"What's happened to-day?"

She listened without word or movement while Reynolds told of his fruitless efforts in Gill's flat, the three interviews in his office that evening, and the recovery of the Harris tweed overcoat.

"May I see 'Slug' Taylor's list?" she asked when he had finished.

Her husband passed her a sheet of paper and she read the first two names aloud.

"Reggie Vickers and Miss Underwood."

"That's the young clerk who committed suicide and his not-so-young fiancée, Thelma," Reynolds explained. "We can cross them off at once. Vickers had no family to avenge him, and Thelma certainly had no hand in the crime. Who's next?"

"It's very illiterate spelling, Tom. Somebody called Warner or Warrener. In brackets 'Slug' has written 'divors case.'"

"I remember. We can wipe them off, too. That case was finished a year ago. Go ahead."

"Cheston and Smith, both in quod for forgery.'"

"'Slug' is right. They are. That's an old case, too. If that's all he knows, it's not going to help me."

"Here's a funny entry, Tom. 'Had to meet a girl from Paris. Missed her and got the sack from Gill.' The others seem to be mostly divorce cases. You'd better glance at them yourself. One or two sound interesting."

Reynolds studied the names which "Slug" had scrawled. "'Primrose Leveen.' Now who the dickens is she? The name sounds familiar."

His wife smiled.

"Primrose Le Vigne, my love, is a famous golden-haired revue artiste, and probably earns more in a week than you do in a year. She's supposed to be half-French. I fancy she's been touring in America for a while."

"You always manage to be a mine of information upon actresses. Where is the lady now?" Reynolds inquired.

"I think she's going to appear at the Majestic Theatre in its next show. It opens in a week or ten days."

"Primrose must be followed up," Reynolds remarked.

"Purely officially, Inspector," his wife stated firmly.

"I've always had a secret hankering for blondes," Reynolds said peevishly, rumpling his wife's brown hair. "With your jealous disposition I get no chance of indulging it." He folded "Slug" Taylor's list and put it in his pocket. "Unless Primrose can shed any light on this subject, 'Slug's' effort is a dud. Meanwhile, where on earth shall I find her?"

"You might try the stage door of the Majestic Theatre," his wife suggested practically. "She's probably in town rehearsing."

"That's a bright thought. I say, Agnes, you went to the Isle of Wight to stay with your sister last summer. What's the name of that beach there with the peculiarly coloured sand?"

"Alum Bay. Why?"

Her husband explained what he had found in the pockets of the overcoat.

"I suppose you'll have to go there, Tom, to see if you can trace this man."

Reynolds nodded.

"It's a nuisance when I've so much to do here. Another man could go, of course, but I like to see a case through if I can."

"Tom, will you trust me to go? I know your methods. Better still, I've stayed with Hettie so often that I know the district and the shopkeepers well. She'd love to have me for a day or two."

Reynolds considered the suggestion. The man might only have been there on a day trip—if at all. It would have probably been in the summer, and this was November. And it was a long chance that any information could be picked up. If there was any, he would back his wife's ingenuity against that of a good many police officials.

"All right, Mrs. Sherlock Holmes. Have it your own way. In case I've never mentioned it, you're rather a nice sort of person to have about the house. Don't forget it, will you?"

"I won't," she promised. "And see that you don't forget when you meet the glamorous Primrose! Come along. It's one o'clock and you need sleep badly."

Reynolds switched off the light and stood for a few seconds staring into the fire.

"Agnes, I've a queer feeling of anxiety for that girl Bob Deane is hunting down in his paper," he said. "The murderer will read that stuff. If, as you and I think, the girl is not in collusion with him, he'll realize that she will be a menace to him if she is found. That means he may take steps to silence her."

"He may not know where she lives."

"He may not," Reynolds agreed. "But the probabilities are that he does know. Deane has thrown a searchlight on her."

XIX. THE LONELY MONUMENT

Thursday, November 22nd.

DAPHNE INGRAM woke late the next morning. After a night that had seemed endless, she had drifted into sleep towards the early hours. Every slight sound, each creak of a board, had made her sit up in alarm, straining her ears in the darkness for a faint tap at her door.

Allen had returned her key, it was true. But had she not foolishly told him that spare keys were kept in a drawer of the hall table? He could easily have taken one when he went out. A desperate man, he would not hesitate to use her, she was certain, if she could be of any service to him.

In what corner of London was he hiding like a rat in a sewer? For all she knew, he might even live in the next street!

If she could only leave this room and go elsewhere! The *Evening Record* had made that impossible. Here, at least, in this impersonal house, she was unusually secluded. Any attempt to obtain fresh quarters would draw attention to her.

Meanwhile she could not stay in her room indefinitely, since one must eat. The landlord provided no other meals save breakfast for his clients. It was a rule from which he did not deviate or it would have meant an increase of staff. Had she been prepared for this ghastly publicity she could have laid in a store of provisions and pleaded slight illness.

Even then she might have run the risk of being turned out or having a doctor called in. Only last week a man in an upper room had been removed to a nursing home. The maid had told her it was only a mild case of influenza, but the landlord had said his house wasn't a hospital and the man must go.

No, illness wouldn't work as an excuse for remaining indoors. Nor must she change her usual routine overmuch or the maid might comment upon it to her employer.

Opening her bedroom door, she took in her bottle of milk and the two newspapers that she always read.

There was no really fresh news about Jabez Gill's murder, although public interest was being stimulated by re-hash of the known facts. They, however, had caught the *Evening Record* fever and, since nothing vital was known about the murderer, were focusing attention on the more picturesque figure of the wanted girl.

That meant danger was increasing, and soon every man, woman and child would be on the watch for her.

In spite of that, she must go out somehow. Hunger was extremely unpleasant, and for two days she had had very little opportunity to get a meal. By her own choice she had always bought her own bread and butter and made tea and toast each morning in her room. Two biscuits and a crust were all her larder contained at the moment.

The obvious thing was to disguise herself. In novels the heroine in a similar plight always had a marvellous make-up box, complete with wigs, at hand. Daphne's vanity equipment consisted of face powder, rouge and lipstick suitable for a blonde, and a brown eyebrow pencil which she rarely used. With sun-tan cream and brunette rouge she could have darkened her fair skin.

Her eyes lighted upon a tube of brown shoe polish. It was a drastic method, but hers was a desperate need. Cautiously she applied a little to her forehead and decided that it might serve until she could obtain something less primitive.

Hair was the worst problem. Even if she wore a hat with a brim, that tell-tale pale gold hue would be bound to show at the back or sides. She had no means of dyeing it, and if she did so the maid might detect some difference, although Daphne fancied that the woman had never seen her save with a hat or rubbercap on.

Suddenly a possible way out of the difficulty occurred to her. Waiting until the maid was upstairs, she looked up a hairdresser's address in the telephone directory and rang him up.

"I want to go to a fancy dress dance to-night," she said over the wire. "My costume is Spanish and I am a brunette. How should my hair be dressed?"

"With bunches of curls at the back, madam," came the reply she had hoped to draw.

"Oh dear! That's impossible," she lamented. "My hair is cut too short to make curls of it."

"We can supply a bunch of artificial ones that can be easily and safely attached if madame will make an appointment and call this afternoon."

"Madame" explained that she was engaged and could not find time to call.

"In that case," the suave voice assured her, "we will send a selection by an assistant whom madame can pay."

Daphne agreed and, promising to pay the assistant's taxi fare also if she could be sent at once, gave her address.

Her heart beat with excitement at the success of her ruse. The next thing was to dress for the part.

Hers was a poorly lighted room and the morning was rather foggy. Rubbing the brown shoe cream over her face and neck lightly, she softened the effect with face powder, wrapped her head in a towel and put on her dressing-gown.

Very soon the bell rang and the maid knocked at the door to say that a young woman wished to see her. Keeping out of sight until the maid had gone, Daphne examined the collection sent by the hairdresser, selected a large bunch of dark brown curls and paid the bill.

"May I show you how they are fixed on before I go?" the girl asked.

"I've just washed my hair," Daphne explained swiftly. "I can manage quite well, thanks."

Her spirits revived when half an hour later, she viewed the startling effect in the mirror. The blonde had turned into a gipsy brunette. Only the blue eyes remained, and here Daphne's sole asset to disguise came in useful; a pair of pale yellow tinted sun spectacles with horn rims. Behind them, she felt a little sheltered from a merciless world that was searching for her.

She chose clothes totally unlike those she had worn two days ago, and over them slipped on a thick fur travelling coat that she rarely used because of its clumsy appearance. it served now to hide the slim lines of her figure.

A smell of food from the basement soon after one o'clock signified that the mid-day meal was in progress below.

Daphne closed the front door and glanced up and down the road. Except for a few casual passers-by there seemed to be no one about.

She crossed Barton Place. At the corner, fifty yards away, appeared an apparently old man, with bent shoulders and a stoutish body, clad in a dark mackintosh that was too long for him. Head sunk into a muffler, his gaze was directed on the row of houses from which she had just come. He was coughing harshly and paid no attention as Daphne hurried by, her heart beating to suffocation.

She had noticed the man's feet and they bore a dreadful likeness to those of the murderer!

Possibly she was mistaken, she consoled herself. It might have been coincidence that a man with feet resembling Allen's should be looking at the houses in Barton Place. Surely Allen would not dare to come there lest she should warn the police.

Second thoughts were not so comforting. Allen would come to her if he needed help, secure in the knowledge that the letter he had stolen from her packet would prevent her from giving him up to justice.

She resolved to forget the matter until she had further proof.

At a small store she bought a satchel and filled it with provisions, and further along the Edgware Road made some purchases of cosmetics which would render any further use of the brown shoe cream unnecessary.

Her appearance seemed to excite no one's interest although in the store she overheard two people discussing "that yellow-haired hussy who was the murderer's accomplice."

Purchasing early editions of the evening newspapers, she ventured into a little Italian cafe and ordered luncheon. She scanned the columns that dealt with the cinema murder and then in an effort to get her mind away from it, turned to the other pages.

At the head of a Personal column was an advertisement in the nature of an appeal.

Tired by the mental strain she had been through, her brain did not at first take in the significance of the words.

Then, in a warm glow of happiness, she understood. Michael Carlile had sent her a message in the only form be could. An enigma to everyone else who would see it, to her the meaning was clear.

> *To Patrick's friend (the advertisement read) As Pat cannot help, please let me do so. Indignant at cruel attack. Shall wait daily at lonely monument at one, five and nine for half an hour. M*

The flicker of a smile hovered on her lips. So he had remembered her nickname for the Marble Arch! Little had she thought when she used it that it would serve as a bridge across the gulf that divided her from him.

She glanced at her watch. It was twenty minutes past two. Had she seen this appeal only an hour ago, she might have been with him now. This café was quite close to the Marble Arch.

A few minutes ago she had had no hope of ever seeing Michael Carlile again. And now, with less than three hours to his next appointment, she was chafing restlessly at the delay.

All thoughts of risk had flown. She would meet him at five o'clock. To talk to any friendly human being, after being bottled up with her fears in that lonely room, would be a relief worth a great deal. To talk to Michael Carlile, hear his grave low voice, look into his steadying grey eyes, would be worth a year of life.

A flash of dismay struck her. What would he think of her in this hideous guise? There was a mirror on the wall beside her. She turned and glanced at herself critically. The brown curls above her neck and ears appeared quite natural, but the shoe cream was beginning to look decidedly patchy in places. She had better go back to her room and make her face up with the proper materials she had bought or Michael might change his mind when he saw her.

The satchel of purchases was too heavy for her to carry far. Choosing a taxi as being less conspicuous than a 'bus, she ordered the man to drive to Sutherland Avenue.

Sitting well back in the vehicle during a traffic block, she saw two people turn and stare at a slim, fair-haired girl who was crossing the road. Presently more people gazed at the unconscious blonde, and one or two bolder spirits hurried up to her for a closer, study of her appearance The girl gave them an indignant glance and walked on.

Daphne shivered as her cab moved, on. That might have been her fate without the protection of the dark hair and changed complexion.

The incident waned in importance when she got out of the cab and was walking along the Avenue. A tiny bubble of joy danced in her heart. Soon she would see Michael and have the comfort of his presence. It would be easy to get in and out of her house without encountering anyone in the hall. The landlord used the area entrance and the maid was employed in the basement after two o'clock and only came upstairs, to answer the bell.

Daphne turned into Barton Place and was close to her front door when she thought of the man she had seen at the corner an hour and a half ago.

There, still, not fifty yards away, was a bent stoutish figure in a long dark overcoat. His back was turned towards her, and apparently he was watching the retreating form of a policeman.

Opening the door, she fled into her room and sank down with trembling limbs.

XX. MICHAEL FINDS DAPHNE

Thursday, November 22nd.

WHEN Michael Carlile returned to Leamington Square that day it was nearly two o'clock. He was extremely late for luncheon and Miss Neames would show her displeasure, what was worse, she would lash him with a hail of pertinent questions concerning his absence.

For the first time for years Michael didn't care what happened. He felt in a queer exalted state of tension. His advertisement had appeared in the early editions of the evening newspapers and he had kept his first tryst. The Mystery girl had not appeared, but he was not at all disheartened. His printed message to her had been too late for this morning's journals. Tomorrow it would be there, and she would see it.

On the hall table was a letter for him. He slipped it into his pocket and went into the dining-room. Sir Howard was lunching at his club; Miss Neames was alone and evidently prepared for battle.

"Sorry I'm a little late," Michael said in a casual manner, helping himself to cold beef and salad. Estelle Neames frowned. This was not the air of a penitent. Her victim was getting out of hand.

"You're very late, Mr. Carlile What detained you?"

Michael poured out a glass of water imperturbably.

"Oh, things."

"That's a bit vague," she snapped.

Michael munched placidly.

"I suppose it is," he admitted, and smiled.

"You went out on errands for my father. Did they occupy your time until now?"

"No. I had finished all Sir Howard's business by five minutes to one precisely."

"And then?" she demanded.

"And then I attended to some business of my own, Miss Neames. Every working man has his hour for his mid-day meal and half-hour for tea, you know." He glanced at the clock. "I've only seven minutes of my hour left. Lucky I've a good digestion."

Her jaws clenched tightly.

"Please don't repeat this absurd performance. I have guests for tea to-day and want you to be there."

"I have already obtained Sir Howard's permission to be absent." There was an obstinate quality in Michael's voice. "Will you excuse me if I glance at my letter while I eat?" he asked. Tearing open the envelope, which bore a French stamp and the Paris postmark, he stared at the contents with a puzzled expression. Then he re-read the document slowly.

"Michael, put away your letter and listen to me," Miss Neames' voice rang out imperiously. "You owe me a great deal. Years ago I was very magnanimous in concealing a certain deficit in your accounts from my father. I still hold an awkward letter from you that might prevent your keeping this situation or getting any other.

"In other words, Miss Neames, a delicate species of blackmail," Michael suggested.

Estelle flinched at the word and changed her haughty attitude. She continued now in the slightly whining stile of one who is hurt by ingratitude.

"Realizing your financial position, I was sorry for you and tried to make you feel that this was your home. It could be. It *can* still be your home, and you one day can be master in it, if—if you like. But if I have any repetition of today's behaviour, I shall tell my father everything. You know what the consequences will be."

The softness of her words was wiped out by the sting in the final threat. "Come to heel or get out," it said plainly.

There was a steely look in the man's grey eyes that she had never seen before.

"Marriage or dismissal?" he inquired lightly.

Estelle played a bold card.

"If you choose to pit it so crudely, yes."

He rose from the table.

"It will be awkward for both of us if I remain for the customary month," he remarked. "I'll go and pack."

"Pack! Michael, have you suddenly gone mad?" Her voice rose on a shrill note of surprise.

Michael broke into a peal of laughter.

"On the contrary, I think I've suddenly become sane after five years of lunacy! Miss Neames, had your suggestion of our marriage been made out of delicacy because I was poor and you were rich, and because you knew we loved each other, I should have felt honoured by your proposal, even if I could not accept it. But held over me as a threat, I refuse the offer indignantly."

Estelle's lips were parched. She was raging with anger which she dared not show. Every pulse in her body longed for this man and, since he had not shown the slightest attraction towards her, she had tried to get him in the only way she could.

"Supposing I say that I was unfortunate in my choice of expressing my feelings through embarrassment," she said in a low voice, "supposing I say that I care for you, love you beyond every rule of feminine reticence, Michael."

"Then I should say that I am very, very sorry, but the idea is impossible. Please let us forget the whole episode, Miss Neames. I'll leave a note for Sir Howard, resigning my position and saying that I've been called away on urgent family affairs."

"Is that true?" she asked brokenly.

"No, but it will serve." He was turning towards the door when she caught his arm.

You shan't go. I won't let you," she cried wildly. "I'll have you arrested for stealing my father's money first, and produce your letter as evidence."

He released himself from her grasp and faced her with an unforgiving expression in his face.

"Miss Neames, nearly five years ago you accused me of taking twenty pounds. The money was in five-pound Bank of England notes and I had written down the numbers. You extorted a so-called confession from me in order to keep me at my post. All those years you have held that whip over my head. To-day I can hold it over yours."

"What do you mean?" she gasped.

"Last night you asked me to change two fivers for you from the cash drawer. Your father and the butler were present. They could be witnesses if necessary. The numbers on those notes prove them to be two of stolen ones!"

"Let me explain," she began. "I had to keep you somehow, I couldn't bear—"

"It would be more dignified if you do not explain, Miss Neames."

"You can't go—you will starve, Michael. Jobs are so difficult to get. Only yesterday you said you could not afford to buy a new dress suit."

"And to-day I can," he replied cryptically. No schoolboy ever packed at the end of term with keener happiness than Michael as he thrust his garments in suitcases. That done, he had a busy hour arranging his employer's papers and writing a letter of explanation.

At twenty minutes to five a taxi containing Michael and his luggage stood in Leamington Square.

"Where to, sir?" asked the driver.

"Stop at a cloakroom where I can dump this stuff—the Marble Arch."

The short afternoon had ended in a soft dusky haze, street lamps were already alight when Daphne opened the front door at 32, Barton Place and peered up and down anxiously.

This time she was sure that no one was watching the house, for the road as far as her eyes could see was deserted.

She felt sure also of her disguise, after the care she had expended on darkening her skin.

In Sutherland Avenue she hailed a taxi and ordered the man to drive to the top of Edgware Road.

A clock boomed the hour of five as she crossed the wide street and, walking towards the entrance to the Park, stood near a pillar, scanning the passers-by.

Near the west side of the Marble Arch was the figure of a man. She could see his face clearly.

Darting between the traffic, she slipped silently behind him.

"Michael," she whispered, using his Christian name unconsciously. "Don't look at me yet or you'll get a shock."

He swung round eagerly and caught her hands.

"I've really found you at last," he said. "Let's walk in the Park for a while. Give me your name and address quickly before you spirit yourself away again."

His joyous mood infected her; almost, in those first happy moments of meeting, it seemed as though the tragedy had never happened.

"Daphne," she told him. "Daphne Ingram," and gave her address, adding: "I—I lost your visiting card."

He tucked her hand through his arm and drew her along the path away from the crowd.

"So if I had not advertised, you couldn't have found me," he said. "Well, for once I'll bless the newspapers."

"Isn't this false hair and brown stuff on my face hideous?"

"No, merely necessary. You make an adorable gypsy, but I prefer you as you were, and will be again when this disgraceful hue and cry has died down. I suppose the man was only a casual acquaintance of yours whom you had met that day for the first time. Shall we go to Scotland Yard and explain to them?"

She shrank away from him.

"I can't go to the police," she said dully.

"You mean you had met him before the day of the murder?"

"Yes. There's also another reason. Please don't be too disappointed in me."

"I'm not," Michael assured her. "Can you trust me enough to tell me all about it?"

"Not to-day," she pleaded. "I suffered a great deal before that night at the cinema. Since then I've been through such horror that I feel at breaking point. Tell me about yourself instead, please. It will take my thoughts off the ghastly affair."

They sat on a seat while he related the history of the past years from the time his father's bankruptcy had caused him to give up the profession for which he had just qualified, to to-day's final episode in Leamington Square. He dealt lightly, even humorously, with Estelle Neames' hold on him.

"What are you going to do?" Daphne asked anxiously.

"See you safely through this trouble and then take up my own job again—if I haven't forgotten all about it. It's wonderful to be free from a kind of blackmail. You've no idea how demoralizing that can be."

"Haven't I!" she exclaimed bitterly. "I've had that spectre clutching me by the throat for— No, I can't tell you to-day, Michael. Go on about yourself. What is your job?"

"I took the ordinary medical degrees, and a higher one in surgery. At the time of the crash I was going to Vienna to study surgery, which I love. There was no money. You know the rest. I never told the Neames that I was a doctor or I should have had to throw in free professional treatment!" He laughed softly. "Think of Vienna after Leamington Square!

"But you can't go to Vienna and study when you have so little money," she objected. Suddenly her face brightened. "Michael, you must let me lend you some. I have plenty for my needs and shall soon be able to earn more—when—when this trouble is over."

He kissed her hand lightly.

"You dear generous child! I shall always remember your sweet thought. I had less than a hundred, pounds in the world until I opened a letter at luncheon today."

"Did you find that a distant relative had died and left you a large fortune?" she asked.

He shook his head.

"No. After buying countless sweepstake tickets without luck, I've won a prize in the French lottery worth about six thousand pounds. It's not a huge fortune, but it means freedom from slavery, a chance to make good in Vienna, and the power to buy us an excellent dinner tonight. Come along."

XXI. AN UNCLE FROM SCOTLAND

Thursday, November 22nd.

DAPHNE'S cares slipped from her during that happy meal with Michael Carlile. The past days seemed as an ugly and unreal nightmare.

The restaurant he chose had no glaring illuminations or noisy orchestra. Each table had its softly shaded lamp and was placed far enough apart for conversation to be unheard by neighbouring clients. In the secluded corner where she and Michael were seated, Daphne felt safe.

She looked at Michael's face, that could be grave or humorous as occasion demanded, at his frank grey eyes and mouth that held strength and kindness, and felt herself fortunate in his friendship,

Knowing nothing of her save that she was acquainted with a murderer and was wanted by the police, he had promised to stand by and aid her out of her quagmire of difficulties. Even friends of longstanding might have withdrawn to high ground in such circumstances and left her to fight her way clear alone, lest they too be involved in awkward publicity.

Yet this comparative stranger, realizing the risk, even proposed to postpone his own cherished wish to go to Vienna.

In a glow of thankfulness she leaned towards him. "You're a wonderful friend, Michael," she said softly. "One day I'll try to repay you."

"Maybe one day I shall ask you to do so," he answered, looking into her misty blue eyes. "To-night you shall have an interlude of peace, but to-morrow I want you to be brave and tell me everything. Life is almost unendurable with fear destroying one's courage, Daphne. Are you afraid that some secret of yours which Gill held has, by his death, passed into the keeping of someone else?"

She nodded.

"Something like that—or worse," she murmured, and suddenly the memory of Allen flooded her brain. Allen, who was in a position to demand anything of her because of the letter he had taken. A wave of faintness overcame her and she caught her breath.

"You're ill, child," he said. "I'm going to take you home at once."

He paid the bill and, calling a taxi, helped her to get into the vehicle, noticing that her whole body was trembling.

"Please tell the man to stop at the corner of the road," she urged as he was about to give the driver her address.

Michael obeyed, but watched her with concern during the journey.

"Have some hot milk and go straight to bed, " he said in quiet firm tones when the taxi stopped. "That's a medical order, young woman; the first I've given for several years, but it's to be acted upon. Promise."

"I'll do as you say, Michael. Where are you going to stay?" she asked.

His lips twitched.

"I'd forgotten that I'm homeless! My luggage is in a cloakroom. I'll go to some hotel not too far from our lonely monument, and let you have my address tomorrow. Will you meet me at eleven o'clock?"

"At the same place as this evening?" she asked.

"Of course. It would be an insult to meet elsewhere," he declared. "After this, I shall always regard the Marble Arch as a dear personal friend."

"So shall I," she said in a low tone. "Good-bye."

"No. Good night only, Daphne. I can't lose you this time, thank goodness," he told her as they stood outside the house. "I'll wait until you've opened the door and then I shall know you're safe."

She walked up the steps, smiling a farewell at Michael, and put her key in the lock. There was a light in the front window on the ground floor. Some new guests had evidently taken the room during her absence.

The hall was empty and she walked along to her back room without meeting anyone.

She had barely removed all traces of her disguise when she heard a knock on her door.

"Who's there?" she asked, puffing on her hat again hastily.

"Only me, miss," said the maid. "I've been to your room two or three times this evening but you was out," she went on when Daphne appeared.

"I only came back ten minutes ago," Daphne told her. "Did you want anything?"

"No, miss. I thought you'd like to know that your uncle's arrived from Scotland. He was surprised that you hadn't engaged his room as he'd written asking you to."

Her uncle! Daphne had no such relative. She drew the maid into the room and clutched at the table for support.

"What time did he come?" she inquired, trying to speak naturally.

"About seven o'clock, miss. He seemed very upset that you wasn't in. Poor old gentleman, he's all wrapped up and seems to have an awful cold. The boss is out and I don't mind making some tea if you think your uncle would like it after his long journey."

"Which room have you given him?"

The maid pointed to the wall behind her.

"He's in there, next to you. I offered him the large front room on the first floor, but he said the stairs were too much for his heart. It's an easy, flight, too; the poor old thing must be pretty bad. Ain't you going in to see him, miss?"

"Not yet." Daphne's brain was whirling. What on earth was she to do now? She could not telephone to

Michael for help for she didn't know to which hotel he had gone! "You are sure he said he was my uncle?"

"Well, he asked for you by name, miss, and seemed annoyed because you weren't here. He said, 'My niece is expecting me and knew I was coming.'"

"I don't know which of my uncles has come," Daphne invented glibly. "What's he like?"

"Bent shoulders, and stoutish about the body. His face was all muffled up and he had his hat on, and he's as hoarse as a crow," the maid explained. "I noticed his feet though, and thought I'll have a tidy size pair of boots to clean to-morrow!"

"All right, thank you. I'll make him tea if he wants any," Daphne told her.

Bolting her door, she sat down and tried to think out some plan of escape. It was nearly eleven o'clock and by the time she had packed and again arranged her disguise it would be close to midnight. Where could she go at that hour without causing comment? Hotels were far too dangerous. Astute hall porters and desk clerks might detect that her hair and bronzed skin were artificial. She knew of no other rooms as safe as this.

Even if she decided to go, there were two important factors to consider. Allen would not have risked coming here unless he wanted her help. He would hear luggage being carried out and would, of course, come out and stop her. The maid, who had already remarked upon her likeness to the missing girl, would certainly have her suspicions aroused if Daphne vanished on the night that her supposed uncle had turned up! The maid would naturally tell the landlord and he in his turn, would reveal the strange incident to the police.

After that, the newspapers would request any landlord or hotel proprietor who had admitted a guest answering to her description late that night to communicate with Scotland Yard.

No, there was nothing for it but to remain here. With Michael's aid she might have managed it. Alone, she felt powerless. Oh, if she had only told him everything to-night, how much easier it would have been. His lucid brain might have foreseen this contingency, thought of some way of avoiding it.

With all her heart she longed now for the man who in this short period had come to stand for so much in her life. His quiet personality held the solid quality of a rock upon which she could rest serenely when all else was shifting sand or bog which threatened to suck her down into undreamed-of depths of blackness.

She listened for some sound from the front room. There was dead silence; not even a footstep crossed his floor. Perhaps worn-out by being hunted since the murder, he was exhausted and had gone to sleep. With luck she might be able to get out of the house early in the morning before he awoke. She could pass the hours somehow until her appointment with Michael at eleven o'clock. Then she would tell him all that had passed and leave decision in his capable hands.

At midnight she prepared to go to bed, moving stealthily across the room so that no creaking board should rouse Allen.

She started as something broke the stillness; it was the flicking of finger nails against the panels of her door. There was no doubt now. Allen had tapped in the same furtive manner on his previous visits. And with the certainty came swift courage.

Drawing back the bolt, she opened the door and confronted him boldly.

"Why are you here?" she demanded in stern accents. He thrust her aside with a rough gesture and staggering across the room, sank into a chair.

Daphne stared at him in astonishment. Could, fear and mental torture have worked such havoc? His powerful body seemed to have shrunk and his face grown haggard and pinched beneath its two days' growth of beard. There was a blue tinge to his lips and a dusky greyness on his skin. He held on to the arms of the chair for support, breathing with difficulty.

His forehead was wet, but he still remained enveloped in overcoat and muffler.

"Light the stove, fool," he gasped hoarsely.

He jerked his chair nearer the gas-fire as it glowed into warmth, and half closed his eyes.

Now that he was actually here, Daphne felt strangely calm. Terror was numbed, and she waited for the next move with a feeling that it was inescapable

"Food—have you got any?" The words came in gusts through his heavy, sobbing breath.

There was a queer sense of drama in the room.

She opened a cupboard and bringing out some of the stores bought that day, laid them before him silently. He indicated a tin of soup and one containing potted meat.

Without a word she heated the former and gave it to him. He snatched the cup from her hand and tearing off large pieces of bread, ate and drank ravenously while the cup rattled against his chattering teeth.

In a swift wave of pity such as she might have experienced for a mad dog that had been wounded; she wrapped a travelling rug round him.

A sneer distorted his livid mouth.

"Almost human, ain't you?"

She made no reply as she set the meat before him and watched him devour it.

"When did you eat last?" she asked him gently. He wiped his forehead and looked at her in a dazed fashion.

"I ate a few biscuits yesterday left over from the lunch you brought on Tuesday."

"And this is Thursday midnight."

"Nobody knows that better than I do. It seems an eternity."

"Hadn't you any money?"

He gave a harsh laugh that ended in a fit of coughing.

"Plenty. What was the good of that when I dared not go into a shop to spend it?"

"Was there no food in the house wherever you lived, or nobody who could get you any?" she pursued.

"I had a two-roomed flat near King's Road; took it furnished a couple of months ago and paid the rent in advance to Christmas. I cooked, and cleaned for myself, and fetched my own victuals—even the milk. For reasons of my own I didn't want anybody snooping round."

A shiver crept over Daphne at his phrase, "For reasons of my own."

"I understand now why you came here," she said slowly.

"That's good. You owed me a bit and I reckoned the time had come to me. Was that you who went out about half past one to-day, dolled up with false hair"

"Yes," she admitted. "I thought I saw you at the corner of Barton Place."

"How did you know? You couldn't see an inch of my face and I'd tied a blanket round my body to pad it."

"I noticed your feet. They're larger than those of most men."

There was stark frankness about their conversation, as though petty concealments faded to nothing in the light of the grim secret they shared. It was almost a relief, she reflected, to speak openly and tear aside veils of dreadful subterfuge.

"When did you know I'd killed Jabez Gill?" he asked.

"Not until I woke up late yesterday afternoon from the sleeping draught you'd given me."

He glanced at the *Evening Record* cynically. "They've got you pretty deep in the mess," he observed. "Anybody spotted you?"

She shook her head.

He leaned nearer and peered into her eyes as if he would read her thoughts.

"Tell me the truth. Have you been to the police or blabbed about what you know to anybody?"

"I've told no one." At that moment she was thankful she had not given her secret away to Michael for she felt that Allen would have detected any lie.

He gave a satisfied nod.

"I had to take a chance on your keeping quiet. I won't have to bother about that any more, though." The girl stared at him blankly.

"Why not?" For the first time since he had entered the room she experienced fear.

"Because you'll be with me," he said.

XXII. ALLEN'S STORY

Thursday, November 22nd

DAPHNE felt stunned. He meant to keep her not only as hostage but to aid him in escaping.

The futility of his plan struck her with poignant force. How could she—even if she wished—pit her brains against the skill of Scotland Yard and all its potentialities? Sooner or later the relentless net of the law would close in and trap not only Allen but her also.

Concealing a murderer from justice was a very serious offence, carrying with it penalties of a far-reaching nature.

Already she saw herself in the dock with this man; an accomplice, as the *Evening Record* had declared, who had hidden him from the police.

She clenched her teeth. At all costs she must keep calm and show no panic, or she would be doubly at his mercy. He was entirely ruthless and despised weakness. She lighted the gas ring and put the kettle on.

"I'm going to have some tea," she remarked in a controlled tone. "Do you want any?"

"Yes. It may stop my cough a bit." He watched her as she set out the cups with apparent unconcern. "You're a pretty cool one. Even murder and a situation like this don't seem to make you suffer much."

"I've suffered," she replied briefly. "It won't help to talk about it though. How did you get your cold?"

"Cold! I like that." His face distorted to a mirthless grin. "It rained the night of—two nights ago. After I left you I dared not take a 'bus. I was soaked through when I reached my flat. There was no food, liquor or milk in the place. I couldn't even get a hot bath. The gas had run out and I'd every coin but a shilling. Had to stay in bed all the next day, shivering with cold and hunger."

There was no craving for sympathy in his voice; he spoke detachedly as if he were relating a series of unpleasant events, concerning someone else.

Daphne pictured those nightmare hours he must have lived through, and again a wave of pity swept over her.

"It must have been ghastly. How did you get the newspapers?"

"I opened my door yesterday evening to see if I could pinch a bottle of milk from outside another flat. There wasn't any, but there were several newspapers chucked out by one of the tenants. how did the *Record* get hold of all that stuff describing you and giving that fake picture?" he demanded suspiciously.

"I've no idea. Probably by the same means that the other newspapers printed an exact description of you, even to your overcoat," she retorted, pouring out the tea.

"Somebody must have given us away." He frowned. "That chap who sat next to you, did you tell him my name?"

"No. Why should I?"

He seemed slightly disarmed by her reply.

"I don't know. I don't trust women an inch. Have you written to him?"

"How could I when you took his card from my bag? I told you two nights ago that I hadn't looked at it then."

"But you were interested in him enough to notice that I'd taken it!" he jeered. "Have you rung him up?"

"His name was not in the telephone book or I might have done so yesterday when I first read the newspapers and was so frightened."

"H'm. Well, you won't get his address from me. I tore his card up. He can't do much more damage anyhow."

"I don't believe he went to the police," she said warily. "He was a decent type who wouldn't have let down a girl."

"Well, if he did, he's done all the mischief he'll ever get a chance to do," Allen stated. "Those blasted detectives must have picked up a clue somewhere as to where I lived. My flat's one of a huge block in Chalcott Road. This morning there was a lot of chatter in the corridor and I heard one woman say that a detective was in the agent's office going through the list of tenants and asking for descriptions of the men who lived there. That was enough for me. I pushed some things in a bag, disguised myself as well as I could, and managed to get out without being questioned."

A thrill of horror passed through the girl. Here before her, was the desperate man for whom the entire police force were looking, and she was powerless to give the alarm. Even during the night, while he would be asleep, she doubted if she had sufficient courage to ring up Scotland Yard. How could she explain away all the damning circumstances in which she had been involved?

And, even if they were cleared up, the letter which Allen had of hers would put her in the power of the police.

"I shall lock your door outside and take the key to-night," he said, as though he had read her thoughts. "So in case you fancy handing me over to the cops, you can think again."

"I am not going to do that because you know I can't afford to for my own sake," she said clearly, using the only argument that he would understand.

"Yes, I know. I've read that letter you sent to Gill. I'm keeping it too, till I'm safely away. How did you land yourself in such a hole?

"It would take too long to explain," she answered wearily. "Were all your letters in the packet I got from Gill's bag?"

A dark flush crept over the man's face.

"They were hers—Maureen's—to him," he muttered, staring into the gas fire. "Gill and I were both crooks in Australia. Maureen's father kept a big hotel in Melbourne, and Gill and I used to meet rich mugs in the saloon bar. He worked the confidence trick on them and I supplied any rough stuff. Maureen had nothing to do with it. She was a lovely kid of eighteen; just back from school. I worshipped her." A twisted smile came to his lips. "Sort of beauty and the beast!"

"Did she love you?"

"She might have, if Gill hadn't cut in with his polished manners. Well, we worked, our tricks once too often. A wealthy bloke got nasty. Gill, to save his own skin, put the blame on me and I was arrested. Gill knew I could prove that he was in with me on the swindles, so he sent Maureen to see me in jail before the trial. I didn't know he'd sent her. I thought she came by her own wish. I was pretty soft then, especially where she was concerned. She begged me to leave his name out of it for her sake, as she loved him; said it wouldn't make my, sentence worse and she'd never forget what I'd done for her."

"But why should you let Gill get off and be free to marry the girl you wanted?" Daphne asked.

"Maureen was going to have a child," Allen replied in a dead, reminiscent tone. "I got five years. Gill married her. When my time was up I found out that her father'd gone broke. Gill had left Maureen stranded in Melbourne dying of lung trouble, while he went to London and flourished."

"Was she alive when you were released?"

"Yes. I traced her to a workhouse infirmary. She died the day after I found her. She said she'd written to Gill many times but he'd sent no money and had only replied once. She loved him even then." Allen passed his hand over his forehead.

"I think I went crazy after that," he went on. "I wrote Gill, saying she was dead. He replied saying it was a good job as he'd got his eye on a rich widow and didn't want to commit bigamy! He also said that Maureen had sent several kind little notes of gratitude for me to him as she didn't know how to send them to me in prison. Gill knew I loved her and said he'd take five hundred pounds for them!"

"You didn't send him the money?" Daphne breathed.

"No. I came to England four months ago, in July. Picked up fever on the boat and was ill for some weeks in hospital after I landed. Then I went to the seaside to convalesce. When I got fit again, I came back to London, took the flat I told you of, and tried to see Gill. He was always away or engaged or out. Once I made his charwoman let me into his office: that's how I knew his safe was foolproof. I waited for hours that day, but he never showed up. I was sick of the delay when I met you outside his door that morning."

"Then you hadn't seen him for all those years?" asked the girl.

Allen shook his head.

"No. The only time I saw Gill was when I killed him," he said simply.

XXIII. MICHAEL'S PATIENT

Thursday, November 22nd.

UNDERSTANDING of this strange being came to Daphne as she listened to Allen's graphic story.

He had made no claim on her sympathy, had not tried to depict himself in any heroic way as a wronged man carrying out justifiable vengeance.

It was an artless picture in crude colours of a primitive creature, untutored and untamed by civilization, reverting to brute force—the only force he knew—when his emotions were assaulted.

The knowledge calmed her considerably. Cunning Allen might possess, but surely her ingenuity could outwit him sufficiently for her to escape. Delilah was not a role she wished to play, but against this Samson none other seemed possible. And through her reflections ran a thread of pity such as she would have felt for some wild beast of the jungle doomed to a cage in a zoo and rebelling at its captivity.

"I'm sorry," she said at last, voicing her thoughts rather than responding to his last remark.

"That I killed him? " he sneered.

"I mean for the possible consequences, for what you have suffered and are now enduring."

Her words roused him to angry suspicion.

"Don't you worry. I'm going back to Australia where I belong. Maybe I'll have to lie low in South America for a bit first, though. Life's not particularly sweet, and I've faced death more than once, but," his fist clenched tightly, "I ain't going to the gallows for Gill, even if I have to shoot myself. Sooner than hang for him, I'd kill somebody else first."

"Don't say any more, please," she begged. "I can't bear it."

"Come all over soppy, eh!" There was a jeering note in his hoarse voice. "Well, get this straight. I don't want your pity, and your pretending to be sorry for me doesn't make me a bit less determined to have your help. Understand?"

"I understand perfectly. It's you who do not."

"If you've got any funny ideas in your head of splitting on me or running away, you can forget them. You're staying right here until we can clear off together. You can disguise yourself better than I can. I'm rough and coarse; anybody could trace me. But if I act the sick elderly uncle who leaves the talking to his lady niece, there's a chance."

"What do you want me to do?" she asked dully.

"Lie low here and pretend I'm ill until the scent grows a bit colder. Then we'll hop it to your place in Paris. If all goes well there, I'll get out of your life for ever."

"That prospect seems a long way off," she said. "Meanwhile, as it's past one o'clock in the morning, hadn't you better go to your room?"

The warmth and food had gradually eased his wheezy breathing. Even the livid colour had changed, and except for an occasional cough he seemed in normal health.

Suddenly, as he made a movement to rise, he was seized by a paroxysm of trembling that shook his huge frame. Gasping painfully, he collapsed in the chair, clutching at his collar as if for air. Veins stood out on his forehead with the strain of that dreadful choking cough.

"What can I get for you?" she asked, gazing compassionately at the man.

"You've got your chance now to beat it!" he whispered haltingly. "I didn't reckon on this 'cold,' as you called it, when I was giving you orders."

Daphne thought swiftly. Here indeed was her chance of flight. Allen was evidently helpless, at least for a while. She could hide perhaps in a railway waiting-room until

morning, when Michael would help her. But—this man
was ill and *he* had helped her.

"Have you had these attacks before?" she inquired. He
nodded.

"Asthma. Started in gaol. Had malaria years ago," he
jerked out. "Ague attacks since."

"How long do they last?"

"Few days. Started yesterday morning. No food, cold,
and wet. Must have left my drugs in flat. Ought to have
quinine for ague."

"I know. Don't talk more than necessary," she said
quietly. "I've no medicine but aspirin here. There must be
a chemist's shop open somewhere. Tell me what to get."

"No. I'll stick it. Bit of luck for you, eh! Be a sport.
Leave me with one night's freedom before you call the
police in."

"Listen to me." She looked at him steadily. "I am not
going to the police and while you're ill I shan't leave you.
Is that clear? Let me help you to bed and I'll give you my
hot water bottle."

Leaning heavily on her shoulder, he reached his room,
and fell panting on the bed. She lighted his gas fire and
brought in her rug.

"I'll manage now, thanks." A choked laugh came from
his blue lips. "Tables turned. Can you look after my grub?
Don't want maid in."

"Very well," she promised. "I'll tell her your cold is
worse and that you're staying in bed. Try to get some
sleep. In the morning I'll get any medicine you need."

"Can't, without a doctor's prescription," he replied.

She went to her room, wondering at her own decision
to stay; wondering too at the strange calm that had
replaced her former dismay. Nothing surely could be
worse than her present plight. Was she mad in pledging
her word to a murderer not to deliver him up to justice
when he had threatened to hold her as a prisoner?

Perhaps. Nevertheless, he had been of inestimable service to her, and now that he was ill and for the moment defenceless she could not betray him.

There were no additional complications when she saw the maid next morning.

"You were quite right," Daphne remarked casually. "My uncle indeed has a bad cold and I have persuaded him to stay in bed. I'll look after him. He'll be no trouble, tell your master."

"The boss needn't know, miss. He's going away for two or three days, so the poor old gentleman can take it easy."

Daphne entered Allen's room and went over to the bedside. She was shocked to see what ravages illness had made. His grating voice was now nothing but a feeble whisper and his hand shook so much that he could not hold the cup of hot milk she had brought him.

At intervals his limbs quivered violently. The blue pinched appearance of his face was more pronounced than last night, and he was far too ill to answer her questions about the purchase of necessary medicine. The aid of a doctor seemed imperative, yet she dared not call one in lest he detect who this man was.

And then in a flash she remembered Michael. He was a doctor. Would he promise to keep this man's secret if she asked him to come? Would Allen in his dazed state recognize Michael as the man she had met at the cinema? She decided to risk that if Allen would consent to see a medical man.

She bent over him and asked if he would do so.

"If I don't, the undertaker will see me," he muttered. "And if I do, I'll get my neck stretched!"

"I know a doctor whom you can trust," she told the sick man. "I will not bring him here unless he promises to ask you no questions, not even your name, beyond those concerning your health."

Allen closed his eyes wearily.

"I got to trust you," he said. "Swear you won't tell him anything about me. Say I'm a lodger sick in your house and don't want to talk of my private affairs. Swear," he insisted as she did not reply immediately.

She gave him her promise reluctantly. After all it might be the best plan. Allen was so changed that Michael, who did not know his name and had only seen him with a cap on, might not dream he was attending the murderer.

Luckily the day was exceptionally gloomy, she thought, when, after caring for the sick man's needs she hurried to keep her appointment at the Marble Arch.

A dull sense of loss pervaded her. Allen's illness and her promise to him meant that again she could not make a clean breast of her troubles to Michael Carlile. That burden must be borne alone a little longer.

Her manner was strained and nervous when she greeted him.

"Come and let's have a talk before lunch," he begged. Searching her mind for some excuse, she thought of the letter Allen had taken.

"Michael, I can't until I get a certain letter. Everything depends upon that."

"As you wish, Daphne, although I think it's a mistake. What's worrying you this morning?"

She explained that hearing from the maid that, a man was ill in the room next to hers, she had offered the invalid her help.

"He's in some kind of difficulty and won't see a doctor unless—" she repeated Allen's words.

"It's unusual in one way," Michael replied after a moment's thought, "but it really doesn't matter. A doctor's interest should be in his patient's health and not in his affairs. Do you particularly want me to call?"

"Yes. I'm sorry for him."

"All right. We'll go at once. What's wrong?" Daphne outlined the sick man's symptoms and mentioned his previous illnesses.

A little later they entered Allen's room.

"Here's the doctor," she introduced briefly, and left the two men.

In her own room she waited restlessly while Michael made his examination.

She cast a nervous glance at him when he appeared, and was relieved to see that his face wore its usual grave, kindly expression.

He sat down at the table and began to write out a prescription.

"What do you make of him?" she asked, assuming a casual tone.

"He'll be right again in a few days if he takes care," Michael replied easily, without looking up from his task. "I'll get these things made up and bring them back. He's had these attacks before and knows what to do if he has the medicine."

"Ought he to have a nurse?"

"I suggested that one should come in for an hour each night and morning but he objected, saying he hated women hanging around. I didn't press the point. He might be hard up. I suppose the maid here could give him anything he requires."

Daphne evaded a reply, relieved that the awkward situation had passed off so smoothly. Already, she observed, Michael, in his professional capacity, seemed to have a different personality. His eyes had an abstracted look and his manner was a tinge formal and aloof now that he was speaking of his patient. There was, however, neither suspicion nor curiosity visible on his face.

"I'll be along with the stuff from the chemist presently;" he told her.

She remained in her room for a couple of hours, expecting him every minute. At last, a little uneasy she went in to Allen.

He was sitting propped up in bed with two medicine bottles beside him.

"That doctor chap's a good egg," he remarked. "He asked no questions, popped back with the medicine, and washed me as good as a nurse."

"I didn't hear him come in," she said faintly.

"No. I gave him my front door key so that he could get in without ringing."

"I see. Is he coming to see you again?"

Allen nodded.

"Yes, he said he'd look in later to see I was all right for the night. I wanted to pay him but he said there was no hurry." He grinned. "Just as well he thinks I'm short of cash, or he'd have insisted on getting in a nurse, perhaps. Did he act to you this morning as if he'd recognized me as the wanted man?"

"He gave me no indication of it," Daphne assured him. "Your face looks much thinner now, and with three days' growth of beard and your voice husky, you don't resemble the strong tall man described in the newspapers. Being in bed hides your height, and you look much older without your cap. I didn't guess your hair was grey until I saw your head uncovered."

"That's true," he admitted. "Anyhow, I feel better and ain't going to worry. Busy doctors haven't time to fuss about who their patients are so long as they get their money. This chap says he's up to his eyes in work."

Busy doctors! Daphne caught at the phrase. Why had Michael pretended that he was so occupied? Was it because he wished to avoid her for some reason?

"He guessed my age as forty-eight," Allen continued.

"I let it go at that, though I'm nearly ten years younger. Prison ages a fellow: a woman, too," he added with a steely glint in his eyes. "Don't forget it. In case you try to give me away, remember two can play at that game."

"You've reminded me often enough," she answered bitterly. "I've not betrayed you yet and, as you put it, it won't pay me to do so." She bit her lip. "I've kept my share of the bargain. Will you give me back my letter?"

"And leave you free to bolt!" Alien laughed scornfully. "Not till I'm safely out of this country. Get into your room. I want to sleep."

XXIV. IN ALLEN'S FLAT

Friday, November 23rd

ON that same Friday afternoon when Allen lay ill in bed and Daphne sat unhappily in the next room, Inspector Reynolds went back to his office.

"The stars in their course seem to be fighting against me," he complained to his assistant. "Every bright little clue that I follow up peters out."

"My luck's been no better, sir," Jenkins said disconsolately. "There isn't a shred of evidence in the murdered man's flat. He either destroyed everything, or that girl who broke into his room at the hotel cleaned out his papers."

The inspector's brow clouded.

"Yesterday I noticed a small lock-up garage facing the front door of Gill's block of flats," he said. "Thinking the owner might know something of Gill's clients, I dug him out. He told me a queer story. It seems that a big strong chap booked the place last week for a month, apparently used it for a couple of nights, and hasn't been seen there since, or the car either."

Jenkins looked a little shamefaced.

"I've been on to that trail to-day, sir. The man who hired that garage corresponds with the fellow we want. On the afternoon before the murder, when I was watching outside, I'll swear that no such man went into the garage. But just before Gill appeared at half-past six, the car was driven out of it. The headlights blinded me too much to see who was at the wheel."

"Which way did it go?"

"Along the road and round a corner. Luckily I remember the number. Directly the garage proprietor described his temporary tenant I was sure he was our man."

"Where's the car now?"

"Back with its owners who lend second-hand cars. I traced it to them through its registration number. It was hired from them by a tall big chap in a Harris coat; cash and a deposit was paid in advance. The car was found empty in a side street the day after the murder, near the hotel where Gill had booked a room. The deposit has not been claimed "

"What name and address did the man give?"

"A false one."

"So that ends that!" Reynolds summed. up. "The man's taste for motoring doesn't help us a bit, though it shows us that he is not short of funds. I've been wading through houses, hotels and flats in the King's Road area, asking questions at shops in the neighbourhood, etcetera, till I'm weary of the district. Also, I've tried at the Majestic Theatre four times to see Primrose Le Vigne, the actress 'Slug' had on his list. A revue is in rehearsal but she's not put in an appearance yet and nobody knows when she will arrive. I'll ring up in a minute and see if there's any news of her. By the way, the inquest was opened yesterday on Jabez Gill. It was a very brief affair. His caretaker and landlord identified the body. Dr. Tempest stated that Gill was stabbed through the heart and death was instantaneous. The case was then adjourned."

"Is Mrs. Reynolds back from the Isle of Wight?" Jenkins inquired.

"Not yet. She went early yesterday morning. I feel lost without her," the Inspector confessed. "She wanted me to stay with you, but I preferred my own home. A nice mess I've made the kitchen in. Ever tried to fry bacon in a saucepan?" he asked with a grin.

"I've always used a frying pan for the job, sir."

Reynolds raised a finger.

"Hush! I cooked herrings in that last night and forgot 'em. They're still glued to the pan, black as a cinder. My wife will have something to say about that!" He lifted the receiver and presently was in contact with the Majestic Theatre. An inquiry as to Miss Primrose Le Vigne brought a satisfactory report. The lady had turned up.

"Good. I'll call at her hotel and see her at seven," he said over the wire. "Am I a reporter? Why on earth should I want to interview her else!" he demanded, drooping one eyelid in Jenkins' direction.

Replacing the receiver, he rummaged in a drawer for a moment and found a visiting card.

"One good turn deserves another, my boy," he chuckled to his assistant. "This is one of Bob Deane's cards, stating that he is a representative of the *Evening Record*. Miss Le Vigne will see no private callers, but is willing to receive gentlemen of the Press in her hotel suite! Ergo, I'm a reporter. If she knows I'm a detective, it may cramp her style. She's come from Paris and has had a bad crossing. Let's have another shot at Chalcott Road."

"One can't count on anything in this curious case," the Inspector commented as they drove towards. Chelsea. "In detective fiction, any one of a dozen suspects might have committed the murder. In this tragedy we've only three, people connected with it so far as I can tell: the murderer, the girl and the man with her. All three are apparently nameless and have vanished into thin air. For clues, I've an overcoat, a few grains of coloured sand, the quinine tablets—" He broke off.

Jenkins glanced at his chief reproachfully.

"I never heard of any quinine, sir."

"You weren't meant to," snapped the inspector. "It's such a frail thread of a clue that I'm afraid to mention it, but—well, never mind. You'll know if anything comes of it. We'll get out here." He knocked on the window for the taxi-driver to stop. He and Jenkins entered the building and walked upstairs.

"There are over two hundred flats here; the agent seems to be an intelligent fellow. It would have been an endless task without his assistance. He weeded out the respectable tenants and I worked on the residue. There are only two of that batch left; both are small flats, each fairly recently tenanted by one man. We'll try number 147 first," Reynolds said, pausing at a door in a long corridor.

Their summons was answered by a tall, hefty type of man with horn-rimmed spectacles, who peered at his visitors in surprise when Reynolds asked if he wished to let his flat furnished.

"Well, no, I hadn't thought of doing so," the man replied, taking his pipe from his mouth. "Still, I might consider it, as I'm arranging to go to Harrogate for a while. I haven't been in this neighbourhood long. Come inside and look round. It's in a ghastly muddle. I've been away for a few days and haven't even unpacked my bag yet."

Reynolds explained that they had another flat to see first, and after a few polite remarks, left the man.

"He hadn't the peculiar ears or big feet of the man I saw outside the grill-room, sir," Jenkins remarked, "but how did you decide so quickly?"

"Hands. They're crippled with rheumatism. He couldn't squash a fly. Let's try the other flat. Ah! here's my pal the agent," he exclaimed as an alert figure approached.

"I saw you come in, Inspector. Number 147 has just come back in a taxi with a bag," the agent said. Reynolds nodded and introduced Jenkins.

"What about number 119?" he inquired.

"He's away still, I fancy. I've been up several times to-day and can get no answer," the agent told him. "Shall we try again? I've got a pass key if it's needed. By the way, the woman who lives in 118 told me an hour ago that she had been driven crazy by the incessant coughing of her neighbour from Wednesday morning until Thursday morning. Since then she's heard nothing of him."

"H'm. That's interesting, "Reynolds replied. "Let's ring the bell."

The agent obeyed, but there was no reply.

"What name did this tenant give?" Reynolds asked.

"Allen. Rent was paid in advance to Christmas. I was on my holidays when he took the flat from the caretaker. I've seen him pass in and out many times, of course, but only spoke to him on one occasion. He was having a few hot words with another tenant who apparently had hurried past him roughly on the stairs. The tenant threatened to knock Allen down. I was about to intervene when Allen snatched the other man's thick walking-stick from him and snapped it in two like a carrot. He flung the pieces down and walked out."

An eager glint flashed in the Inspector's grey eyes. "Open the door, please," he directed the agent. Inside the tiny sitting-room, Reynolds sniffed. "D'you smell anything?" he asked.

"Not gas, I hope," said the agent, hastening to the gas meter.

"It's rather like strong eucalyptus," Jenkins suggested. "Have we found our bird at last, sir?"

"Only his nest, I'm afraid. However, cheer up. Life is brightening considerably."

The agent joined them, looking much relieved.

"There's nobody here," he told them. "No food of any description and no gas in the slot meter. There are plenty of clothes though, so perhaps Allen is coming back."

"I think not. My assistant and I will have a look round here."

"Very good, Inspector. I'll leave you. Please slam the door when you go. The latch is down."

For an hour the C.I.D. men worked patiently, examining everything minutely.

They paused at last and compared results.

"A tag on a coat showing it to have been made in Australia," said Jenkins disconsolately, "and half a steamer label, Orient line, on one suit-case; the rest appear to have been soaked off. That's all I've got. What have you found, sir?"

Reynolds raised his head with a pleased smile and again sniffed.

"One smell," he replied.

XXV. PRIMROSE

Friday, November 23rd

"MISTAIRE ROBAIRT DEANE, is it not? "asked Miss Le Vigne, in dulcet tones and an assumed French accent.

Reynolds felt an impostor as he bowed in acknowledgment.

Primrose justified her first name, he decided, after a glance at her golden locks. The scene was set in her private sitting-room at the Belroy Hotel, and had been carefully staged.

Half reclining on a couch, with the shaded lamp placed at a becoming angle, the revue actress presented an arresting colour scheme of the brighter shades.

Flowers, with visiting cards well to the fore, were banked on a table beside her. Jewels glittered on her white neck and bare arms. A tea gown of vivid brocade, edged with sables was thrown round her, and on one pretty bare ankle gleamed a chain of diamonds, above a satin slipper.

"You will forgeeve me, Mistaire Deane, if I take my rest while we talk, yes?" she murmured, as she flung aside a pile of telegrams. Favouring her caller with an enchanting smile and a coy glance from under lashes heavy with mascara, she motioned him to an armchair placed by her side.

"You weesh to interview me for your so interesting paper?" she inquired sweetly.

"I should very much like to interview you," the Inspector admitted.

The lady gave him a keen look, appraising the well-cut suit, intelligent face and crisp, cultured voice of this "reporter."

"May I pay you the leetle compliment?" she asked. "You are so deeferent, so—how shall I say"—she waved her hand as if searching for an English word that eluded her—"so 'swoyny.' You understand, yes?"

"*Si vous voulez, nous pouvons parler en francais, mademoiselle*," urged Reynolds politely, a little weary of slow action and pretence.

For a moment he saw anger in Miss Le Vigne's pale blue eyes. She was trapped and knew it. This man spoke French with a fluent, easy accent. She was not an actress, however, for nothing. Realizing how the incident could be turned into an asset, she broke into hearty laughter.

"That pose is part of my stock-in-trade, boy," she remarked. "Don't give me away, will you? That French accent's worth pounds to me in publicity, though I don't speak a dozen words of the blamed language."

Reynolds promised discretion on the delicate matter and proceeded to make tactful inquiries about her work on the stage.

"Oh, that subject's worn to rags," she exclaimed. "Everybody knows I sing songs, grave and gay, do a little dance, and several impersonations. They're my strong suit. My voice isn't marvellous and I can't afford to waste my strength on high kicks; still, I get away with it," she added frankly. "Can't you think up a new stunt for an article?"

"What about some episode in your career?" Reynolds suggested, leading the subject upon which he needed information.

Primrose poised her chin on the tips of her scarlet finger-nails and looked thoughtful.

"My railway accident, the earthquake in California, the hold-up by bandits in Italy," she enumerated. "No, they won't do. I've pulled those gags before. A Spaniard who was in love with me shot himself, but nobody would believe that, though it happens to be true!"

Reynolds was amused at the candid revelations.

"There's a good story in how my famous diamond bracelet was stolen," she went on, "only unfortunately I can't let you shoot the whole works in my own interests."

"Can't you tell me about it if I promise not to print one word more than you permit?"

Primrose weighed up his words.

"I'll risk your playing the game," she told him. "The bracelet was given to me a few years ago by a member of the Turkish Royal Family whom I met in Paris. It was worth thousands. He went clean off the deep end about me, you see. Well, I was vain as a peacock about it and always wore the thing, except in one or two of my character sketches of poorish people."

"When, of course, it would have been unsuitable,'" Reynolds commented, wondering how this recital was going to assist his investigations.

"I was much slimmer then, but not so clever at my work as I am now. In Edinburgh I met a girl very much my height, build and colouring, who did the same sort of stuff that I did, but her imitations beat mine hollow, although I was the more famous. I've a good business head, and, to put things briefly, I offered her a big salary to tour with me and teach me her work. We got on fine together. She kept dark, of course, but on several occasions, when I was tired, she'd slide on and do one or two impersonations—in costume of course—in my place. We kept it a dead secret. Not a soul detected the difference, but her work got more applause."

"Didn't your dresser know?"

"Of course, but she's been with me for ten years and wouldn't spill the beans. Well, Dodo Cray—that was the girl's name—finally said I knew all she could teach me and she'd work on her own again on the Continent. I thought she was as straight, as a die, but, would you believe it, on our last show together she pinched my bracelet!"

A speculative expression came into Reynolds' eyes. "Was that about three years ago in Birmingham, Miss Le Vigne?" he inquired quickly.

"Yes, at the Frivolity Theatre. She and I shared the same dressing-room, of course. I removed the bracelet and left it there in her charge while I did my scene on the stage. When I got back the bracelet had gone. You can bet I was first alarmed about its loss and then furious at the dirty trick she'd played on me."

"I remember the case," Reynolds replied. "Dodo Cray was arrested and sentenced to eighteen months' imprisonment. She protested her innocence although she admitted that no one had been in the room but herself. The bracelet was never found, and the prisoner, who was taken ill with influenza immediately after the trial, escaped from the prison infirmary and has not been traced since."

Primrose regarded him with admiration.

"My, you've got a good memory. That's the story, word for word. You see why I can't have it printed in full, don't you? Nobody must know that I had an understudy! I was scared it would leak out at the trial."

"Quite so." Reynolds agreed absently. His mind was racing over, the history of Dodo Cray, for she was the original of the photograph in the Rogues' Gallery which he had shown to Miss Oliver, the cinema sweet-stall assistant. She had indicated that they strongly resembled the girl who had been with the murderer on the night of the crime.

The next problem was to find out the link between Jabez Gill, this actress and Do-do Cray. "Slug" Taylor had stated that Miss Le Vigne was one of Gill's clients. He must tackle the matter with the utmost care.

"I promise you that the story, if it appears, will contain no mention of your under-study, Miss Le Vigne. By the way, it has been rumoured that Jabez Gill, who was murdered last Tuesday night, was one of your numerous admirers."

The side glance Primrose gave him this time was astute rather than coy.

"Gill was a bit soppy over me, I dare say, at one time," she admitted. "But when I could go out to supper with a duke, why should I bother with a common moneylender? I often tried to push Gill off with Dodo, but she was a funny kid; proud and distant, if you know what I mean; wouldn't have anything to do with him."

A gleam of triumph warmed Reynolds' heart. "Slug" Taylor was right. There was a link between Gill and this woman.

"Was Gill in Birmingham when you lost your bracelet?" he asked.

"When Dodo stole it, you mean," Primrose rapped back. "Yes, he was. But he wasn't near the dressing room, if that's what you're thinking. He was in the front row of the stalls and never left his place until the end of the show. I often wondered whether—" she stopped abruptly.

"Please go on," Reynolds' begged.

"I'm trusting you, mind," Primrose warned him. "I often wondered whether Gill helped Dodo to escape from the infirmary. He was at the trial with me. He was a tricky beggar and used to boast that he could do anything by bribery. If so, why did he help her? He wasn't keen on her and knew she detested him."

Reynolds knew the answer, but did not tell her. It was Gill's method of obtaining another victim for blackmail.

"Did you see much of Gill after that affair?"

"No." Miss Le Vigne's tone was emphatic. "When I was in London he used to send me messages by a miserable little rat called Taylor who worked for him, because he couldn't bribe his way through to my dressing-room or hotel suite himself. I never saw Gill after the trial or replied to his notes."

Reynolds harked back to the girl.

"Do you happen to know where Dodo lived?"

"No. I met her as Dodo Cray and that's all I ever knew. Maybe she escaped to the Continent. I've been in

America ever since, working chiefly in films. I landed at Cherbourg, spent a day in, Paris, and crossed the Channel to-day."

Reynolds pulled a copy of the *Evening Record* from his pocket.

"Then perhaps you have not seen this," he remarked, pointing to the picture of the missing girl.

Primrose stared at it and skimmed rapidly through Bob Deane's' paragraphs.

"This isn't Dodo Cray," she stated definitely. "It has many of her characteristics: fair hair, blue eyes short upper lip, but so have many blondes. Look here, Mr. Deane, Crime Expert," her eyes blazed with indignation, "if I'd known you'd done this below-the-belt-stuff, I wouldn't have opened my mouth to you. Dodo Cray was a thief, but she wouldn't have killed anybody or mixed herself up with a murderer. Don't you dare print one line about rue, or I'll swear it's a fake interview. Of all the cads I've met, you're about the worst. Get out and make it snappy."

There was a quiet smile on Reynolds' face as he walked away.

XXVI. NEWS FROM AUSTRALIA

Friday, November 23rd.

"THEN apparently it was Dodo Cray who searched Gill's luggage at the hotel," summed up Jenkins at the Yard later that evening. "If Gill helped her to escape from prison, she would certainly be in his power. I wonder what she was after."

"Papers of some kind, I suppose," replied the Inspector. "If she found them, why did she go to the cinema and join the murderer? And if he was in collusion with her, why did he trouble to kill Jabez Gill when she had the papers?"

Jenkins churned the problem over.

"I see your idea, sir. She was acting for herself, and Allen, the murderer, maybe lent a hand, but had his own grudge against Gill."

"There's no evidence that Dodo Cray and Allen were together previous to the day of the murder or since it took place. He undoubtedly lived alone in his flat."

"I saw nothing to indicate a woman's presence when I searched," Jenkins agreed. "While you were with Miss Le Vigne, I rang up Inspector Shale as you wished. He said he'd call here this evening."

"That's excellent. Any news of my wife yet? It's nearly eight o'clock."

"She hasn't rungup," Jenkins replied. "Are you going to let me in on the secret of the queer smell in Allen's flat?"

"Not yet, my lad," the Inspector said firmly. "Come in," he called out as he heard a knock on the door. His face beamed when he saw who his visitor was. "Agnes, I'm very glad to see you. Have you had a comfortable journey?"

Mrs. Reynolds smiled a greeting at Jenkins and, taking a chair, went at once to business.

"I'm all right, Tom," she said calmly. "The man you're looking for is called Allen. He stayed at a farmhouse near Alum Bay for a few weeks last August, while recovering from an illness. His landlady said he was a gloomy brute who never had a letter or a visitor while he was there, made no friends and rarely opened his lips save to snap out 'Yes' or 'No.' The only remark he ever made was, 'I've got to get back my strength as I've urgent business in London.' At times he had a bad cough and then they were nearly choked with some horrible cigarettes he smoked. And often he had attacks of shivering that shook the bed. He used to lie on that beach where the coloured sand is, in his Harris tweed overcoat all day. When he got well he went away and that's all they know of him. They don't read the newspapers much there. They're too busy."

"You've worked remarkably hard to find all that out," her husband said admiringly.

"I've not really worked at all," Mrs. Reynolds replied. "The boy from that farm delivers my sister's milk daily. There are very few houses near Alum Bay. He was almost the first person I asked. The rest was easy. I only had to call at the farm." She studied her husband's face for a moment. "Tom, you old sinner, I believe this isn't news to you. You can't deceive me."

"It corroborates what Jenkins and I discovered an hour or two ago, my dear. Confirmation is necessary and useful."

"But not vital, as it all happened before the murder," his wife retorted logically. She opened her bag and laid two snapshots on his desk. "Maybe these will cheer you up."

The Inspector pounced upon them.

"My hat, Jenkins!" he exclaimed. "They're recent photographs of Allen. Good clear prints, too. How on earth did you get these, Agnes?"

"From the farm boy. He had a new camera and experimented on Allen without his knowledge. I bought the negatives from him too."

"Rush these off and get prints sent to the newspapers at once, Jenkins," Reynolds ordered. "No Wonder Miss Oliver saw Allen's resemblance to her brother-in-law. They are distinctly alike, but Allen's face is older and harder."

"Inspector Shale to see you, sir," announced a constable at the door.

Reynolds shook hands warmly with the newcomer—a handsome man in the late forties—and introduced him to his wife.

"How are you, Shale?" he asked. "You don't look a day older than when we met ten years ago and caught that gang of forgers."

"Old enough to be pensioned off from the Australian police force, anyhow," the newcomer replied with a hearty laugh. "Still, it's good to be back in London. I'm staying with my married daughter in Kensington. What can I do for you?"

Reynolds showed him the two snapshots of Allen's head and shoulders.

"Have you ever had this man in your records?" he asked.

"Got any idea of his height or build?"

"Yes, he's the man who killed Gill in the Royal Imperial Cinema. You've read his description in the daily papers, of course."

Shale nodded.

"I've done little else!" he replied. "This looks to me like a chap called Kennedy Allen, a confidence trickster. He got five years for that and assault with violence. Another fellow was suspected of complicity but got off through Allen's confession that he had worked alone. He has huge feet, a queer gait, and very long lobes to his ears. He was ill with asthma in gaol. Let me see," Shale considered for a moment. "Allen was probably released last June or July."

"Thanks, Shale. You've cleared up that nicely. We now know our man's history. You don't know what his supposed accomplice in Australia was like in appearance?"

"A suave man-about-town type."

Reynolds produced a photograph from his drawer. "'Anything like that?" he asked.

Shale gave an exclamation.

"Why, that is the bird," he stated.   .

"That is, or was, Jabez Gill," replied Reynolds quietly. "Jenkins took a snap of him last Tuesday morning when he called at the Yard. Maybe, Shale, the kernel of the mystery lies here. Allen might have cherished a grudge against the man he shielded and come to England to revenge himself."

"It seems highly possible. If I can be of any further assistance, let me know. Good luck."

Reynolds gazed abstractedly at his desk for a while after Inspector Shale had gone.

"Planning a new course of action, Tom, now, that you know a possible motive for the murder?" inquired his wife.

"A positive crusade," Reynolds replied with a chuckle. "All based on a cough and a queer heap of bedclothes." He looked up at his assistant who had just come in. "Jenkins, did you notice Allen's bed when we searched his flat?"

"I did, sir. Every available garment, including a hearthrug, was piled on, besides the blankets and eiderdown. I couldn't understand it."

"You would if you'd been suffering from his troubles," his chief told him. "There was no sign of any medicine in the place, was there?"

"None. Only an empty cigarette packet with a peculiar smell," Jenkins answered.

"Very well. Allen was probably ill with his twin complaints, ague and asthma. They could have been alleviated with certain medicines of which he knew. The woman in the flat next to his declared that he coughed incessantly for twenty-four hours from Wednesday morning. After that, there was silence. I think he cleared out while I was actually in the building. The agent said a rumour went round that detectives were in the place. Agnes, you were a V.A.D. nurse. How long will Allen's attack last?"

An alert expression came over his wife's face.

"At least three days, Tom," she replied. "I see your idea. Somewhere Allen is still ill; possibly in London, as he wouldn't be fit to go far."

"That's it," her husband agreed. "There can't be a vast number of people needing medicines for those two ailments at the same time."

"You mean to tackle the hospitals in case Allen has gone there for relief," Jenkins guessed.

The Inspector nodded gravely.

"Also the chemists, asking for their help in tracing persons they have supplied or prescriptions they've made up. They know what complaints the formulas are used for."

"It's some task!" Jenkins responded in gloomy accents.

Mrs. Reynolds frowned at him.

"It's a good chance," she said sharply. "This isn't the moment to be depressing."

Jenkins rose to the occasion.

"I'll set the wheels in action at once, sir," he promised, and went out of the office.

Reynolds turned to his wife.

"Well, my dear, we're splashing Allen's photograph out in the newspapers to-morrow," he said, "but somehow I don't think help will come from that direction. Allen has either found a good hole to hide in or an excellent disguise."

"If your plan comes off, you will be able to dig him out," encouraged his wife.

"Providing he doesn't get well too soon!" Reynolds scribbled idly on his blotting-pad. "There's another angle I'd like to work from."

"You mean this girl, Dodo Cray?"

"No, I mean the man she was with after the cinema. If he is not implicated in any way, why hasn't he reported here? Come in," he called, hearing a knock.

A constable entered and laid a note on the desk. "The chauffeur who brought this is waiting for an answer, sir," he said.

"Tell the man to wait," Reynolds said, after he had read the brief message. "I'll be down in a few minutes and go with him."

"Any luck about, Tom?" asked his wife.

Her husband patted her shoulder and smiled.

"I'm not sure yet. But maybe that other angle I spoke of is showing signs of life. I'm going to see when I've made a telephone call." Giving the number of the *Evening Record*, he asked for Mr. Deane.

"Hello, flat-feet," a familiar voice remarked over the wire. "Does the Yard want my help again?"

"No; this time it, per myself, proposes to help you," Reynolds replied. "Ever heard of Primrose Le Vigne?"

"You bet I have," Deane sang out. "What's more, I hope to interview the little filly to-morrow."

"I've done it for you, sweetheart," Reynolds had much pleasure in informing him. "She told me some exciting incidents of an earthquake she was in, or maybe it was a den of lions."

"I'll find out about that when I call on her," Deane snapped.

"You'll get a sweet reception if you do," observed Reynolds, placing the receiver down.

XXVII. A JEALOUS WOMAN

Friday, November 23rd.

IT was half-past eight when Inspector Reynolds was shown into the drawing-room of Sir Howard Neames' house in Leamington Square.

A handsome brunette in an elaborate evening dress came forward to meet him.

"I am Miss Neames, Inspector. I gather that you are in charge of the Jabez Gill case."

Reynolds bowed formally.

"That is correct," he answered. "Your note states that you have information relating to one of the three missing people connected with it."

Miss Neames drew in a long breath. Studying her, the inspector was reminded of a swimmer about to take a deep dive. A keen observer of psychology, he knew her type well; hard and dominating, passionate in all emotions, and cruel when frustrated. Unless he was very much mistaken, this woman, under her suave social mask, was now a raging furnace of anger.

"Do you know the girl who was at the Royal Imperial Cinema last Tuesday night?" he inquired.

Miss Neames' dark eyes revealed temper immediately.

"I do not," she said with scorn. "But possibly I can tell you who her companion was when she left the cinema."

Reynolds took the chair she indicated.

"I shall be most interested to listen."

"Five years ago," she began, "I picked a young man of undoubted education out of a Salvation Army hostel and persuaded my father, Sir Howard Neames, to engage him as secretary. His name is Michael Carlile. He lived in this house as one of the family and left here suddenly during my father's absence yesterday lunch-time after a distressing scene with me. I have no idea where he is now, and no photograph of him to show you. But the description tallies pretty accurately."

"The fact that Mr. Carlile remained here so long implies that he gave satisfaction to Sir Howard," Reynolds commented dryly, noting the bitter tone the woman had employed. "I presume the scene was of a personal nature."

Miss Noames flushed.

"It was. As it had nothing to do with the case, I shall not enlarge upon it. Mr. Carlile was out alone on the night of the murder, and was in an unusually gay mood at breakfast next morning—until he read something in the newspaper that seemed to startle him. After that he changed completely. He was absent for long intervals during the day, and almost insolent when I questioned him. Usually he scarcely glanced at the evening newspapers that were delivered here. That night he had copies of all of them in his room, so the maids tell me."

"Have you an idea what he read in the morning paper to disturb him?"

"Yes. I saw his eyes fall on a paragraph. After he had gone I observed that that paragraph was the *Stop Press* announcement of the murder in the cinema."

"Of course you suspected nothing then."

"No, although Mr. Carlile's manner was odd and evasive. I asked him again later that day where he had spent the preceding evening. His reply was that he had had dinner at a restaurant, and, after a walk, had returned here about ten o'clock."

"That full explanation did not satisfy you?" Reynolds' inquiry had an acid tang in it.

"Not when one of the maids told me she had found the half of a Royal Imperial Cinema ticket in his waste paper basket."

The inspector raised his eyebrows.

"Your domestic staff seem to have remarkable qualities for espionage, Miss Neames."

"Fortunately so for you in this case, Inspector," snapped the lady. "It is also fortunate that Mr. Carlile left his old mackintosh in the hall when he packed so precipitately. To-day, inside a pocket, I discovered this." She held out a piece of paper.

Reynolds unfolded it and found a receipt from the advertisement department of a leading newspaper bearing a date two days old.

"I traced the number on that receipt to this announcement in the agony column," Miss Neames informed him.

Reynolds read it slowly, endeavouring to solve the meaning.

To Patrick's friend.
As Pat cannot help, please let me do so. Indignant at cruel attack. Shall wait at lonely monument at one, five and nine for half an hour.
M.

"If 'M' stands for the 'Michael' of this man's Christian name, it is evident that he did not know this girl's address; possibly not even her name," he commented.

"He probably does by this time if she read the advertisement and went to the 'lonely monument,' wherever that may be." Miss Neames' eyes held jealous curiosity. "Where do you think it is?"

"I have no idea," the Inspector replied shortly. "Has Mr. Carlile friends to whom he might have gone?"

Miss Neames shook her head. "He would never speak of his past life. An hour before he left the house he received a letter from Paris. That seemed to fix his determination to leave here."

"Your staff had no opportunity of discovering the contents of that communication?" Reynolds asked with mild sarcasm.

"None. The post had just been delivered as Mr. Carlile came in. One letter has arrived since he left, but as I do not know his address, it cannot be forwarded. The postmark is again Paris."

"May I see it, please?"

Miss Neames bit her lip and made no answer. Then, as Reynolds appeared blandly oblivious to her hesitation, she took the letter from a drawer and handed it to him.

"I don't think it should be opened," she observed haughtily.

Reynolds turned the envelope over and scrutinized the flap.

"There is no need, Miss Neames. Someone has already performed that operation," he replied. "As the mischief has been done, knowledge of the contents may be valuable to me. Will you kindly ring and let me ascertain which member of your staff has read it?"

The woman was caught in her own trap and realized it.

"I prefer to keep the servants out of this," she said quickly. "The—the maid who opened it told me what is inside. It is a typewritten document in French stating that Monsieur Michael Carlile will be duly informed on which day the lottery prize he has won will be distributed. This is evidently an unimportant sequel to the letter which I did not see."

Reynolds saw that she was too angry to notice the admission in her last five words.

"The document was in French!" he observed with a faint smile. "Your staff have a knowledge of languages in addition to their other abilities." He stood up. "Thank you for your information, Miss Neames. Should Mr. Carlile call, I should like to have his address. I am going to ask you a personal question, to which, of course, you need not reply unless you wish. Were you and Mr. Carlile engaged to be married?"

An expression of anguish crossed the woman's face.

"I—I always thought we should be," she murmured. "As there was a vast difference between Mr. Carlile's financial resources and my own, I had given him to understand—" she broke off.

Reynolds nodded.

"Quite," he said, comprehending the situation perfectly. "Good night, Miss Neames."

If anything, he reflected, as he left the house, his complications had merely been increased by this interview! In addition to the other extensive search, he must now rake London for a grey-eyed, clean-shaven young man of about thirty-two years of age, named Michael Carlile, who might already be in Paris!

At the corner of Leamington Square there was a taxi rank. Walking across to it, he asked the drivers if one of them had conveyed a gentleman with luggage from number eighteen two days ago

"That's Sir Howard Neames' house, sir," one of the men said. "You must mean that nice young gent who was his secretary. He's fetched cabs scores of times from this rank. We've known him for years and I was surprised when he hopped it, bags and all, last Wednesday about five o'clock. I drove him and asked if he was going on holiday. He laughed and said, 'Yes, a long one too.'" The man smiled. "He didn't go far, though,"

"Where did you take him?" Reynolds asked.

"Only to a cloakroom at Marble Arch tube, where he checked in his things," was the reply. "He had a lot of luggage—three bags, a typewriter and a set of golf clubs."

"You might drive me to that cloakroom," Reynolds replied.

Things had suddenly taken a brighter turn and his spirits were buoyant as the taxi was held up by traffic near the Marble Arch.

He watched the stream of vehicles whirling round by the Park gates. His gaze became speculative as he saw the vast columns of the Arch standing in solitary splendour. Could that be the "lonely monument" of Carlile's advertisement?

He dismissed the idea. Even if it were, it had ceased to be of importance since Carlile must have met the girl by this time and have no further need of this place for a rendezvous.

Suddenly one small point occurred to him. People often make appointments in the district where they live! Leamington Square was a full mile and a half away, but suppose the girl lived near here! She might have mentioned that to Michael on their first meeting, even if she did not give him her exact address.

"Here's the tube, sir," said the taximan, cutting in on his fare's ruminations.

At the cloakroom Reynolds explained that he was a C.I.D. official and wanted to trace certain luggage that had been left there just before five o'clock the previous Wednesday afternoon.

"Blimey! That's asking something," said the clerk. "I was on duty then. I'll do my best. I suppose you don't know the number of the ticket or how many pieces of luggage there were?"

"Three bags, a set of golf-clubs and a typewriter," replied Reynolds promptly.

"A typewriter!" exclaimed the clerk, brightening. "What was the man's name?"

"Michael Carlile."

The clerk snapped his fingers.

"I'll bet that's the same bloke," he said. "A hotel porter came here that night for a stack of luggage, and he dropped the typewriter. Knowing there might be a spot of trouble, I told the porter I'd made a note of what happened, and I saw that the initials on the handbags were M.C."

"At what time did the porter take these things away?" asked the Inspector.

"Soon after ten that night. He said that the luggage belonged to a client who had just booked a room at the hotel where he worked."

"What hotel?

"Ah, there you've got me, sir. I don't know," was the clerk's disappointing reply.

"Can you describe the porter or his clothes?"

"Dark red and gold uniform, I think. He was a biggish chap. I remember telling him he was lazy when he grumbled about the weight of the stuff. He had to make two journeys to the hotel with it."

"Excellent!" commented Reynolds. "How long was he absent before he picked up the second load? "

"Not more than ten minutes."

"I'm very grateful to you," said the Inspector, and returned to Scotland Yard.

"We've struck oil," he informed Jenkins. "If I can't track a man who is staying in a hotel within five minutes' walk of the Marble Arch, I'll change my job."

XXVIII. PAT

Friday, November 23rd.

THAT Friday afternoon and evening seemed interminable to Daphne as she waited in her room. Waited she scarcely knew why, for Michael had told Allen he would not call until late.

The calmness of despair that she had experienced last night when Allen had made his startling appearance, had changed to a sense of utter desolation at Michael's evident avoidance of her. Added to this now, an ominous tension gripped her. Into what fresh horror would Allen drag her next, she wondered dejectedly.

At intervals during the day he knocked on the wall and gave her curt orders for food or drink. His loquacious, mood of the previous night when he had been so ill was changed now to one of sullen silence. She could feel his eyes following her resentfully as she moved about his room, obeying his wishes.

Her hand shook so much when she was pouring out medicine that he snatched the bottle from her grasp roughly.

"What are you up to?" he demanded with suspicion.

"Nothing," she declared. "I'm nervous and overwrought with the strain I've been through, and there seems no end to the situation you've brought upon me by coming here."

"There'll be an end all right," he snarled, "sooner than you think and not what you're expecting."

"Is that a threat?" she asked coldly, with a flicker of courage.

"A warning maybe. You keep your mouth shut and don't try to chatter to that doctor fellow, or it'll be the

worse"—he paused and his eyes narrowed to ugly slits—
"for you both."

She fled back to her room, thankful even for that
dreary refuge so long as she could escape from Allen's
taunts. Why, oh why had she impulsively embroiled
Michael in this maze of deceit?

This morning it had seemed a providential chance; to-
night she realized bitterly how unwise she had been. An
innocent man might be placed in an invidious position
through being urged into an act of humanity by her.
Sooner or later the police would discover his share in this
matter and then the consequences might be terrible.
Even now, she felt as if their net was closing inexorably
round her in narrowing circles. Every moment of delay
would make things worse.

In her life she had known many difficulties and faced
them firmly. Cowardice should not overwhelm her now,
she determined, when the safety of this man she had
grown to care for was at stake. Despite Allen's words, she
must see Michael to-night when he called and tell him
not o come here again.

Meanwhile, the necessity of disguising herself each
time she went out and dodging into the house to her room
before the maid could see her was proving irksome and
risky.

Twice to-day she had had to go out for supplies, and
on the last occasion she had avoided the maid by barely a
second. She had scarcely removed the dark curls and
wiped the bronze cream from her face before the servant
had knocked at her door asking if she could change a ten
shilling note.

Was it her distorted imagination, she asked herself; or
did the girl glance curiously at her while waiting for the
money?

"Bad luck that your poor uncle's come all the way
from Scotland only to be shut up ill in a lodging house,
miss," the maid remarked. "Was that a doctor who came
this morning?"

"Yes," Daphne said briefly. "He'll be here again to-night though my uncle is much better."

"If he's cured the old gent's awful cough in a day, he must be real clever. I'd like to have his name, miss, in case my sciatica comes on again this winter."

"He is a very busy man and this is not his district," Daphne replied with haste. "He only came here because he is a friend of mine."

"I'm sure I don't want to know any secrets," the maid remarked in a touchy manner, and went away.

The incident added anew fear. Did the maid already suspect there was something queer about her lodgers? If so, what would she do? The *Evening Record*, far from changing its theme to-day, had redoubled its call to the public, urging them to trace the fair-haired girl without delay, and suggesting fresh places where she might be hiding from Justice.

It was after nine o'clock when the front door was opened. She hurried into the hall but Michael had gone straight to Allen's room. Pressing her ear to the door, she heard him ask the sick man how he was.

"A shade better," Allen croaked, "but it'll be days before I can get up."

"Nonsense. You'll be practically fit to-morrow." Michael's voice was brisk and emphatic. "Those attacks only last a day or two and you're a strong man."

"Who told you so?" The listening girl shivered at the tone of Allen's question.

"Nobody. I don't need to be told," came Michael's even reply. "Your muscular development is far above the average."

Allen seemed satisfied by the answer.

"Queer kind of doctor; ain't you?" he demanded. "Ask no questions and you'll be told no lies seems to be your motto."

"It's a pretty good one too, isn't it?" Michael said good-humouredly. "My job's tending bodies, not prying into personal affairs."

"Pity there ain't more of your sort about. What's your name?"

The listening girl outside the door trembled as Allen put this leading question. Now indeed the fat would be in the fire.

The sound of Michael's low amused chuckle calmed her fears.

"Let's say we're both queer," he replied lightly.

"You prefer to be—say—Mr. Smith, and I in return claim equal right to be—Dr. Jones. How's that for a fair bargain?"

"All right, by me," the invalid agreed. "What's the damage? Your bill, I mean."

"You needn't worry about that until I've got you well. In any case, I've not got expensive ideas."

"Call it a couple of quid up to now?" asked Allen.

"Call it ten shillings, if you insist on paying me."

"You'll take a pound," Allen snarled swiftly. "I don't want anybody's charity."

"As you wish." There was still no break in Michael's even tone. "That will include to-morrow's visits."

"What time will you be here?"

"Eleven o'clock will suit me best," Michael answered.

"Suit me fine, too. Don't you take any time off to amuse yourself, doctor?" To the listening girl there was guile in Allen's question.

"I get some tennis or golf occasionally."

"What about evenings?" Allen, asked craftily. "Ever go to theatres or cinemas?"

Michael parried the question, she heard, by accident or design.

"Very rarely, though I might drop in for an hour at a vaudeville show," he observed. "There's a new revue coming on at the Majestic next week. That should be good. You ought to go. Well, good-bye until to-morrow."

Daphne opened the front door noiselessly and went outside the house, reckless of being noticed, conscious only of the urgency of warning Michael.

In less than a minute he came out. Her, spirits sank as she realized that he had not troubled to go to her room first!

"Michael, I must speak to you," she said breathlessly.

His manner was entirely unruffled, but there was sternness in his grey eyes.

"Very well," he replied after a second's hesitation. "Get your hat and coat or you'll take cold. I'll wait."

"You promise not to go away?" her voice was feverish with anxiety.

"I have few qualities but I still keep my word," he retorted.

She rejoined him quickly and they walked slowly along the path in silence.

"What do you want to say? "he asked.

"You must not visit that man again." The words came in a swift rush from her lips.

"Why?

"It's—it's dangerous. For you, I mean."

"You've thought of that a bit late, haven't you?" he inquired almost indifferently.

"I've thought of little else all through this dreadful day," she murmured with a catch in her voice. "Oh, Michael, you don't know how you've hurt me. After your wonderful kindness I'd grown to depend on you so much. You're right to blame me and decide to have nothing more to do with me. You needn't. I quite understand. Only— you mustn't go to that house again."

He caught her arm, and still holding it, swung her round facing him under the light of a lamp.

Tears brimmed over from her troubled blue eyes and dripped down her cheeks. He mopped them with his handkerchief.

"Stop crying,'" he ordered.

"That's better," he went on as she gave a wintry smile. "Now listen to me, young woman. You and I seem to be at cross purposes. When I decide to see no more of you, I hope I'll have the frankness to say so and state the reason."

Daphne choked back a sob.

"But you've been to the house twice to-day without making any attempt to see me, so you must be blaming me."

He shook her arm gently.

"I'm blaming you because you didn't give me credit for a particle of intelligence, and refused to trust me. Do you take me for an utter fool?" he demanded.

'Her eyes widened in alarm.

"You mean you knew the—the sick man was Allen?" she asked incredulously.

"I knew he was the man who was at the cinema the moment I saw him, of course. I didn't know his surname until now. It's put me in the dickens of a hole professionally. You ought to have told me before I visited him."

"He wouldn't let me; he made me swear not to say who he was."

"If he has such a ghastly hold on you, he can't be much of a friend for you to guard so preciously."

"A friend!" she exclaimed. "He's my worst enemy. I'm terrified of him, but I must do as he orders."

"Because he's committed murder for your sake?" demanded Michael bluntly. "You're more fickle than he is, apparently. Once he was your dearest friend; now he's your worst enemy. Poor, beloved Pat!"

She drew away from him in amazement.

"Pat! What on earth are you talking about?"

"Please don't put on that surprised pose," his voice had hardened again. "The moment I saw Allen this morning I knew who he was, and the meaning of the tragic farce you and he performed for my benefit in the cinema queue was clear. You were the decoy duck; I was to be your alibi. A pretty low trick."

"It certainly would be if it were true. You are insinuating that I was in Allen's confidence and knew he was going to kill Jabez Gill."

Michael Carlile shrugged his shoulders.

"What else am I to think? No wonder you couldn't give me your confidence this morning!" he observed cynically.

"I said I couldn't until I had a certain letter."

His expression was sceptical. "When do you expect it to arrive?"

"It is already there. In Allen's possession, " she said in desperation. "If he is arrested before he gives it to me, I too shall be arrested—possibly as an accomplice to this horrible crime, and certainly as an escaped prisoner, convicted of theft and due to serve a sentence of eighteen months. Now, are you satisfied, Mr. Carlile, or would you like to torture me a little more?"

Michael was dumbfounded.

"There's a police station close by. You'd better go there and do your good deed for the day," she added wildly.

A smile flickered on his grave face and his grey eyes twinkled as he tucked her arm through his and led her firmly round the corner of Barton Place.

"Bless the dear child," he said calmly. "How well she knows me. It's a cold night; we might drive there and save time." Stopping beside a small closed car, he opened the door. "In you go," he ordered.

She looked from him to the car, bewildered.

"Whose is it?"

"Mine; or rather she will be when I've drawn my prize money in a fortnight. I borrowed her to-day from an old friend who's buying a new 'bus. Thought a car might be handy if we—you and I—wanted to get off in a hurry. When I discovered the identity of that sick man this morning I was anxious about you—although I'm still annoyed about something. Hop in, young 'un. You're going to do a whole lot of explaining before I let you loose again."

Sitting by Michael's side in the car, she told him the story that Primrose Le Vigne had told Reynolds concerning the missing bracelet; of her meeting with Allen outside Gill's flat and their subsequent adventures.

"Dodo Cray is only my stage name," she explained. "When I was arrested I never told anyone my real name. My passport was made out as Daphne Ingram, so it was easy to get to Paris. I work there in cabarets."

"Jabez Gill planned your escape from the prison infirmary, of course?"

"Yes. Later he traced me to my address in Paris and blackmailed me. That's how I came to write letters to him. For a while I paid his demands. Then when they increased, I risked coming to London twice in the hope that I might strike some final bargain with him. The first time was six months ago. He was away and I had to go back alone to fulfil some engagements. The second time was three weeks ago, when all this tragedy happened." She twisted round and looked into his eyes. "Michael, it's a horrible story. Remember, I was alone in that dressing-room when the bracelet vanished. Aren't you ashamed to be with me, a convicted thief?" she asked after she had given him full details concerning the affair.

"Don't be absurd," he replied. "I'll admit, though, that I'm puzzled. and maybe a bit annoyed about a phrase you used a moment ago. You said that you had to go back alone to Paris six months ago. Who had been with you previously?"

Under her long lashes she peeped at him with mischief.

"Why, Pat, of course. You remember I told you he was my dearest friend," she replied. "We have not been parted for years. We came to England last May together; I wouldn't trust him with anybody else. If I could have cleared up this affair I should have remained here. As it was, Pat stayed in England and I had to go back alone."

"I'm sure you must miss him very much," Michael said savagely.

"It's been terrible for us to be apart. I'm longing to see him again."

Michael glared at her.

"And this precious friend, who deserted you when you needed him so badly, is to be welcomed back with open arms, I suppose," he pursued.

She nodded demurely.

"Of course. I adore him." Her, face clouded to seriousness. "It hurts me so much to know he could be with me now only I dare not fetch him."

"Fetch him!" Michael exploded wrathfully. "Can't the lazy pampered blighter come to you, or is he an imbecile?"

"He's neither." She broke into soft ripples of laughter. "Pat is my dog; an Airedale. The poor darling's been in quarantine since May. He's due for release to-day. Are you still annoyed?"

"So much so that I'm going to punish you," Michael said softly and kissed her. For one long moment he held her in his arms, then he drew away and stared ahead, absorbed in thought.

"Was Pat with you when you were helping Miss Le Vigne, Daphne?"

"Yes. He slept in my room all night, travelled with me and waited in my dressing-room always."

"What happened to him when you were arrested?"

"He stayed with the dear soul who was my dresser at the theatre. She was very kind to me during the week before the bracelet was stolen. Afterwards, all through the trial, she was the only one who believed I was innocent. She and her husband helped me after my escape. She is married to the stage doorkeeper of that theatre in Birmingham where it all happened."

"What is her name?"

"Mulligan. She and her husband are both Irish and the kindest people I've ever met. But, Michael, they can't help me. She was out on an errand for Miss Le Vigne when the bracelet vanished."

"I see." Michael changed, the subject brusquely. "Like motoring?"

"I love it. Why?"

"Never mind. Give me the receipt for your dog," he said in brisk tones. "It will be safer in my care. Allen may get at it."

She took it from her handbag and passed it to him. "Do you mean you'll fetch Pat for me to-morrow?" she questioned.

"Maybe, if it's safe to do so. Now, listen to me carefully." He gave her a few swift instructions. "Got that all clear?"

"Yes. I'll do exactly as you say."

"You'd better, angel. It will train you for being an obedient little wife," he told her. "Run along to bed now."

XXIX. A BUNDLE OF MISCHIEF

Friday, November 23rd.

MICHAEL CARLILE drove slowly along Sutherland Avenue after he had said good-bye to Daphne. He was in an uneasy frame of mind. The memory that the girl he cared for was in the next room to a murderer made him shiver.

Yet where could he take her, without causing comment, at this hour of the night? Her altered appearance might not be sufficient disguise. In hotels, with public, attention centred on the missing girl, she might be recognized. And, until the bracelet business was cleared up, she was safe neither from Allen nor the police. That Daphne was innocent of the charge of theft he was convinced, but belief and proof were very far apart.

He had a curious longing for companionship at the moment, although time pressed if he meant to fulfil the task he had set himself. Should he waste half an hour in a yarn with his friend Langley, or, should he go back to his hotel, pack a, bag and push on with his job?

Pulling up the car at a telephone box, he solemnly tossed a coin. Heads, Langley; tails, the hotel.

"Heads" turned up twice. Fate having decided as he wished, Michael entered the box and rang up his friend's number. In case he were out if would save time.

"Hello, 'Lanky.' Can I blow round for five minutes or are you busy? he asked over the wire.

"Thank Heaven you've rung me up! I'm not busy and particularly want to see you at once," came Langley's swift reply. "Listen to me, Michael; something has broken loose. Come straight here, and don't call at your hotel or anywhere else en route."

"Right you are," Michael promised, and drove in haste to his friend's bachelor flat.

Langley was a black and white artist who did clever cartoons for a leading London daily and earned good money. He and Michael had graduated at the sane college. Later their ways had divided by their differing professions, but the old friendship was well founded. In Michael's bad financial patch after his father's bankruptcy; he had avoided Langley through pride. Afterwards, a semi-prisoner as secretary in the Noames ménage, he went round whenever he was free for an hour or so.

The two men greeted each other now with that cheery abuse peculiar to Britishers when they are really friendly. A fashion that foreigners never cease to marvel at.

"Smashed up my old 'bus yet?" demanded Langley with a grin as he opened the door.

"I'll manage it in time. Got your new car?"

"Took delivery to-day. When she's run in she'll be a snorter" Langley poured out a drink. "Say when."

"Don't drown it. I need bottled courage to-night," Michael said feelingly as he sank into a chair and put his feet on the table.

"Hi! keep your shoes off my famous work," Langley ordered, removing a drawing-board tenderly. He raised his glass towards his friend. "Here's mud in your eye, old son."

"I'm stuck in the mud all right. What are prisons like to live in?"

"Up to now I've escaped personal experience. Are you thinking of trying 'em?"

"I may be forced to!" Michael replied with a whimsical smile. "I wasn't thinking primarily of my own fate," he went on seriously. "Gaol must be horrible for a well-bred girl—if—if she doesn't deserve it."

Langley regarded him over the rim of his glass.

"British juries are pretty sane. Don't get any fancy ideas into your head," he warned. "The chances of a convicted person being innocent are very remote."

"I know all that. Nevertheless circumstantial evidence can play queer tricks." There was an obstinate line to Michael's jaw. "Anyhow, I'm going to have a try at being smarter than police and jury combined."

"Like to take me along to play Dr. Watson, Sherlock?"

"Better than anything in the world, Lanky. Do you mean it?"

"I do. When do we start? Now?"

"To-morrow morning. Birmingham. Does that put you off?"

"Not a bit. There's a pub there dear to my heart, where I've shifted many a luscious quart." Langley's eyes became reminiscent. "Why can't we start to-night?" he demanded plaintively.

"Because I've got to make a journey in another direction."

Langley stretched his long legs and kicked a log on to the fire.

"Sounds mysterious and enticing. Going to invite your little boy friend or are you fixed up?"

"It's a dull job and I was going alone. I'll be darned glad of your company, but you'll miss your beauty sleep."

Langley pursed his cadaverous face to an affected simper.

"Since I've used my new chin strap and skin food I can take almost any risk," he stated. "Here, young fellow-me-lad, why does Scotland Yard want a heart to heart talk with you?" he asked in casual tones.

Michael sat upright and whistled.

"It's the first I've heard of it. Where did you get hold of that tale?" He reached for an evening newspaper.

"You won't find it in there—yet," Langley told him. "I was in the Press Club an hour ago and a noisy young oaf from the *Evening Record*, one Bob Deane, blew in very full of himself as usual. He informed all present that

Scotland Yard had sent a message to the papers requesting a Mr. Michael Carlile to come forward at once in connection with the cinema murder case. Deane added that he meant to sit on Inspector Reynolds' head until he learnt who Carlile was and why he was wanted."

"Did you mention to Deane or anybody that you knew me?" Michael asked anxiously.

"Did I!" Langley exclaimed with wrath, flinging a cushion at his friend. "Of course not. Me, I was asleep!"

"Thanks, Lanky. I ought to have known you better. So that's what has broken loose!" Michael looked grave. "I'd like to know how."

"Your late employer's daughter, I fancy, was responsible. It appears that Deane has annoyed this Inspector by his disgusting and unprofessional stunt in featuring the girl in the case. Said Inspector closed down on Deane sharply. Diplomatic relations and dainty snippets of news being cut off, Mr. Clever Deane has been sleuthing Inspector Reynolds in order to get a few crumbs to make into a smelly pie for his paper. Incidentally Deane boasted that he'd trailed Reynolds to Sir Howard Neames' house at eight-thirty pip-emma this evening, and fished out—from the chauffeur probably—that Miss Neames had sent her car to the Yard for the Inspector in charge of the Jabez Gill murder case. That's all I know," Langley ended. "But it occurred to me that meanwhile the Yard might make a few inquiries at hotels in case you didn't hop along to see them."

"I'm jolly grateful to you," Michael replied. "Look here, I'd better get out. I didn't commit the murder, but I'm involved up to the hilt. You can't afford to be mixed up in a spot of bother with the police."

"Oh, can't I?" snorted Langley. "You try to keep me out of any fun, and I'll put you across my knee as I did twenty years ago, you great boob. Heaven only knows why I trouble about a fool like you, but we've all got our weak points. Besides, I rather fancy myself rescuing a fair damsel in distress."

"I'm doing that particular bit of rescuing, if you don't mind," Michael replied firmly.

Langley made a grimace.

"Go ahead, Sir Galahad. I won't cramp your style," he promised. "But, as a penalty, you can buy my liquid nourishment from now on, or I'll refuse to act as best man. And, believe me, I can sink beer in grand style. Let's get on the road, whichever way it is."

"Dover; to fetch a dog from quarantine," replied Michael succinctly, pulling on his overcoat. "The pubs will be closed. You'll have to carry any rations you want."

"Quarantine places also will be closed," his friend reminded. "What d'you propose to do about that?"

"Bang on the door, or alternatively sit in the car until morning," retorted Michael. "Anyhow, I'm going to Dover now, either alone or in company. Your old 'bus is outside."

It was a cold November night, with occasional gusts of rain beating against the windscreen, yet both men were singularly happy and unconscious of the weather as the car sped towards the coast.

In curt sentences Michael made his friend acquainted with the situation in which he was entangled, knowing that Langley would not violate his confidence.

"You see, I'm in the dickens of a mess. I'm virtually concealing a criminal because I can't and won't let Daphne suffer."

"If the balloon goes up, you can plead the delicate point that a doctor does not betray his patient," Langley suggested.

Michael groaned.

"That doesn't hold good in murder cases, I'm sure. Also, after the murder, when he was not my patient, I didn't go to the police with my information for Daphne's sake."

"According to the newspapers, that girl at the cinema sweet stall gave them an excellent description of Allen," Langley urged logically. "Anyhow, you're working on the right lines now, old lad, so don't worry. If, by a miracle, you can clear that girl's name, she will be automatically free from Allen's clutches and you can open up to the police. How do you propose to set to work in Birmingham?"

"Go to the theatre first and find Mrs. Mulligan who was Daphne's dresser, unless you have any brighter ideas."

"Your plan's all right, but it doesn't go far enough." Langley pulled at his pipe for a moment. "What time do you want to start to-morrow?"

"After I've seen Allen. I'll call for you at a quarter to twelve."

"Make it noon at my garage," Langley said. "I don't promise, but I might be able to help you. My brother who died last year was an actor, as you know, and through him I met lots of folks in his profession. I'll nose round to-morrow morning. Hello, there are the lights of Dover. Let's drink its health." He produced a bottle of beer from the back of the car. Have some?"

"Not now. One of us had better appear sober, or we won't get delivery of the dog."

"We must, and to-night if possible, late as it is." Langley's voice was urgent. "If we wait until the morning papers come out, it might be difficult. Primrose Le Vigne might have mentioned 'Dodo Cray's' real name to the Inspector, or Bob Deane might have dug it up."

Michael shook his head.

"The dog is registered to 'Daphne Ingram,' and she is positive that Primrose never knew or heard that name."

"I don't want to add to your troubles, but if Daphne had this dog always with her, the fair Primrose must have seen it and heard its name. Ergo: if she spoke of an Airedale called Pat to the Inspector, the fat indeed will be in the fire. We don't know what is going into print to-morrow, so we'll play for safety. Somebody will have to sign for the dog, and if Michael Carlile does so, half England and all the police force will know to-morrow. You stay in the car and I'll collect the animal."

Without difficulty they found the veterinary establishment. It was well past midnight but 'lights were visible in two or three windows.

"This is where you fade out of the picture," Langley informed his friend. "I'll pick you up at the end of the road later."

Michael walked ahead as directed.. The waiting interval seemed interminable. He could see the lights of the car from where he stood, fretting impatiently and imagining every possible kind of trouble.

At last he heard voices and a dog's excited bark. Then the door of the car was banged and the lights drew nearer. Langley thrust his head out of the window, and a dog's soft muzzle appeared hanging over his shoulder.

"All aboard," he sang out cheerily. "You might take charge of the menagerie. He's knocked off my hat and is now nibbling gently at my right ear. Pat, stop washing my face and save your spit for the other bloke." He chuckled as Michael climbed in beside him and the dog leaped on to his knees with whimpering cries of joy. "No wonder your Daphne missed her Pat. He's a corker and worth the trouble he's given me."

Michael fondled the soft warm head that nestled confidingly against his shoulder, its body sprawling awkwardly in his arms.

"Pat caused me quite a bit of trouble too," he commented, "but not in the same way. Did you have to answer any difficult questions to get him?"

"No. I stalled 'em by telling a few dozen lies first; positive whackers," Langley informed him. "Luckily for our purpose, a valuable dog is very ill so they're up late looking after it. You've got a handful of canine mischief there, boy. One of the kennel men gave me Pat's character. 'Not a spark of vice in him, sir; very sweet-natured and obedient, but full of tricks. He's a devil for chewing and hiding things.' When do you hand him over to his owner?"

"To-morrow morning," replied Michael contentedly. "Daphne's coming with us. I arranged it all with her this evening. While I'm with Allen she's going to walk out and get into the car."

"And afterwards?" questioned his friend. "When we get back from Birmingham, I mean, where is she going then?"

"That is on the knees of the gods," was Michael's answer.

Langley turned the car adroitly.

"Bunkum. It's up to us, of course," he said. "I'm going back to town now, and you're going to spend the rest of the night at my place. Your hotel might be risky. Who knows what line the newspapers will take about you to-morrow?"

XXX, PRIMROSE SPILLS THE BEANS

Saturday, November 24th.

INSPECTOR REYNOLDS and his assistant had more trouble than they anticipated in finding Michael Carlile's hotel. It was after eleven o'clock on Saturday morning when Reynolds struck the trail.

"Did you fetch some luggage from the Marble Arch cloakroom for a gentleman called Carlile on Thursday night?" asked the detective of a hotel porter dressed in red and gold livery.

"I did, sir. He's staying here," was the reply.

"I should like to speak to him, please."

"I've not seen Mr. Carlile go out this morning, sir. I'll send a page to find him."

Evidently the man had not seen the paragraph in the morning papers concerning Carlile, or had not connected it with his client.

After his long quest, it all seemed too easy, Reynolds thought, as he followed the porter into the lounge hall and sat down. Michael Carlile might easily be any one of the thirty odd men who were scattered about reading or writing letters. He scanned the visitors with interest, listening to the page boy's treble voice shrilling out, "Mr. Carlile, please."

Not one of the guests responded to the call, and the boy returned to the porter after a search of the other reception rooms.

"Run up and see if he's in his bedroom," ordered the porter.

"You're sure he has not left the hotel?" asked Reynolds with a touch of anxiety. "Ask if his luggage is still in his room."

In a few minutes the boy came back.

"The gentleman is not in his room," he reported. "He's not had breakfast and his bed's not been slept in. But all his luggage is there, the chambermaid says; even his razor and brushes."

The hall porter was not disturbed by the news.

"Perhaps Mr. Carlile stayed the night with a friend unexpectedly. He'll probably be in soon. Would you like to leave a message for him, sir?"

"No, thanks. I'll call again later," Reynolds told him, considerably worried by the result of his visit. What had happened to Carlile? Could he suddenly have feared that the police net was closing round him, and fled? Or had some ill befallen him?

Leaving Jenkins to watch over that end of the situation, he proceeded to the Majestic Theatre and asked for Miss Le Vigne at the stage door.

"She's probably at her hotel, sir," the man replied. "Dress rehearsal is at two o'clock this afternoon. Miss Le Vigne won't be here until then."

Michael Carlile's friend, Langley, renewed an old acquaintance that morning when he called on Primrose Le Vigne at her hotel.

There was nothing sychophantic in his greeting of this spoilt darling of the footlights.

"Halo, trooper; how's time serving you?" he demanded. He tilted her chin up impudently and studied her face with a critical air. "H'm, a bit fat around the gills! Your eyes are as alluring as usual, but you've overmuch paint on."

She kissed his cheek lightly and laughed.

"Your manners are even worse than they were, my dear, but I'm glad to see you all the same. It's years since I saw you last. You're famous now, and making pots of money, I suppose." She raised her heavily mascara'd lashes and flashed the appealing glance that was her specialty at him. "Going to do a caricature of me?" she inquired with an eye to business.

Langley patted her hand in an abstracted manner.

"Too easy," he told her with a grin. "Did you ever find that diamond bracelet? Your arm looks quite bare without it."

"No, it was never discovered. That girl must have smuggled it out of the dressing-room with the aid of an accomplice. Like to give me one to replace it?"

"The urge isn't noticeable at the moment," Langley coolly replied. "I say, Primrose, did that girl really steal it, d'you think?"

"It couldn't have walked out alone, could it?" She frowned suddenly. "Look here, what's the game? That rat Deane from the *Record* asked me no end of questions about her last evening. I sent him packing, the nasty skunk. Even though she escaped gaol, Dodo got punished enough without his rotten attack on her. Deane wasn't bad looking; never should have thought a chap who could write that muck could have had such a distinguished appearance. He was extremely well-tailored, too."

Langley was surprised. Nobody could apply the word "distinguished" to Deane's cheeky countenance, with its retroussé nose and sharp black eyes. As for clothes, Deane was notoriously and invariably badly dressed.

"Sure it was Deane?" he questioned. "What was he like?"

"That was the name on the card he sent in," Primrose stated. "He's about five feet ten or eleven, has fine grey eyes, good features, hair slightly grey at the temples. Kind of stern, serious type. I'd told him all about Dodo, unfortunately, before he showed me the stuff he'd written. He simply lapped it up too."

"I see." Langley chatted idly for a few moments and then took his leave. He was distinctly perturbed by the thought of the mysterious visitor to Primrose, who most certainly was not Bob Deane.

The problem was unexpectedly solved. Immediately outside Primrose's door he saw a page boy, and a man who tallied perfectly with the presumed Deane.

Langley glanced at him in passing, and strode down the corridor. Directly the newcomer had gone into the sitting-room, Langley tiptoed back, and listening for a minute or two, heard one all-important statement from Primrose.

There was no time to lose. The Yard was definitely on the track of "'Dodo Cray." Soon they would unearth the link that connected her with Daphne Ingram.

It was nearly noon when the Inspector reached the Belroy Hotel and was taken to Miss Le Vigne's suite. The page paused outside her door.

"Agent's there now, sir," he told Reynolds. "Shall I knock or will you wait until—Oh, it's all right. He's just leaving."

A tall, thin man, upon whose lean face a sardonic smile still lingered, came out of Primrose Le Vigne's sitting-room and, with a keen glance to Reynolds, hastened along the corridor.

"I'll announce myself," Reynolds said, dismissing the boy.

He disliked the unpleasant task that was before him, but it had to be performed. With a sharp preliminary knock, he opened the door and went in.

Primrose was standing by the fire, looking distinctly less attractive in daylight. Her face darkened as she recognised her visitor.

"Well, of all the nerve!" she exclaimed. "How dare you march in here after I told you to get out and stay out? I've a good mind to ring up your editor and tell him what kind of a reptile his precious Mr. Deane is."

Reynolds suddenly saw a way to palliate the lady.

"My name is not Deane, although I know the young man. I deeply regret that it was necessary for me to use his card yesterday. Will you accept my sincere apologies? You were quite right to resent what Deane has published in his paper, Miss Le Vigne."

"That's a handsome apology, anyway." Primrose appeared to be considerably mollified. "Who are you?"

Reynolds gave her his card with a smile.

"It really is my name this time," he observed.

The lady's finely plucked eyebrows shot up to a startled angle as she looked at it.

"Inspector Reynolds of New Scotland Yard, eh!" she read aloud. "So that's why you wanted all that dope about Dodo Cray!"

"Yes. You might have been alarmed had you known I was a C.I.D official,'.' Reynolds explained. He handed her a small object resembling a coin.

"Have you ever seen this before?"

Primrose turned the article over.

"I don't think so. What is it?"

Reynolds did not tell her it was the token which "Dodo Cray" had given to the chambermaid in mistake for a shilling at Jabez Gill's hotel the previous Tuesday.

"I have reason to believe that it belonged to Miss Dodo Cray," he said.

"Then you know more about her things than I do. She never wore jewellery; either on the stage or off, to my knowledge, and she certainly wouldn't wear a brass disc!"

"Did you share the same rooms during the time she toured with you?"

Primrose shot him a curious glance.

"No; she liked a quiet life, and I'm all for a bit of fun in a jolly hotel. Besides, I couldn't stand that great dog of hers with his dirty paws all over my dresses. She lived for that animal; couldn't bear it to be out of her sight."

"What breed was it?" There was an eager light in the Inspector's grey eyes.

"Ah, there you've got me. A big black and brown thing. A Peke's my fancy, if people must have a dog."

"Do you remember what Miss Cray called it?"

"Don't I!" Miss Le Vigne laughed. "It was chiefly 'Angel,' or 'My lovely,' with odd 'darlings' thrown in.

Sheer waste of affection, I call it. If it had a real name, I've forgotten it."

"Miss Cray never gave you any hint either before or after the theft of the bracelet as to where she intended to go when she left you?" he asked.

"No, but I gave her a darned good hint to keep out of the British Isles and America as our work on the stage was so much alike. I know she'd taught me her tricks, but I'd paid her two hundred pounds for it and all expenses."

"But she had to earn her living, hadn't she?" inquired Reynolds, with a sudden sympathy for Dodo Cray.

"She had all the Continent to work in," Primrose retorted. "She was educated abroad and spoke French, German and Italian fluently."

The Inspector left the hotel in a puzzled mood. Some chord of memory had been vibrated by Miss Le Vigne's last words. Slowly he worked his mind backwards over the witnesses he had interviewed during the last few days. At Slug Taylor's name he paused mentally. On the list that Slug had written was a queer entry. "Had to meet a girl from Paris; missed her, and got the sack from Gill."

At that time the words had seemed to be pointless. Reynolds wondered now if they fitted in with this case. Was Dodo Cray the girl whom Slug had been sent to meet? If so, and she had brought her dog with her, a whole slice of the mystery was automatically cleared up. The animal would be in quarantine at one of the ports. The girl might visit the dog which she obviously loved so much. In that case her address would be known there.

The next thing was to see Slug and find out the date and railway station when and where the girl arrived.

XXXI. SLUG TAYLOR'S DISCOVERY

Saturday, November 24th.

SOON after eight o'clock that morning, Daphne heard three thumps on the wall, it was Allen's signal that he was awake. She thrust the note she had written into an envelope and hid it with her handbag and attaché case under the divan.

Allen was sitting up in bed when she went in. His glance travelled from her dressing gown to her eyes that seemed to sparkle with happiness.

"Thought you always got up early," he grumbled, studying her curiously.

"I'm a bit late this morning. I was just going to have my bath but if you'd like some tea, I'll make it first." Her voice had a nervous breathlessness.

"I can wait," he replied. "There's no hurry. Give me the papers."

She brought them in, drew the curtains back and poured out his medicine while he scanned the news quickly. Almost immediately his eyes noted the paragraph asking Michael Carlile to communicate with the police.

Closing the journal, Allen watched Daphne's brisk movements speculatively.

"Been up long?" he asked.

"No. I—I only woke when you knocked. I'll have my bath now and then bring your breakfast. Are you better?" she asked, carefully avoiding a direct look at him lest he should see the joy that was almost suffocating her. Only a few hours and she would be with Michael, racing along the roads in clean fresh air away from this man who had caused such havoc in her life. She intended to keep her promise to Allen not to desert him while he was ill;

indeed, unless a miracle happened in Birmingham, she must return here to-morrow because of the letter that he held.

It was the terribly damaging communication, written to Gill from Paris soon after she had escaped. In it she had thanked him for his help, enclosed some money and promised to send him more towards his expense in arranging her escape. The money, of course, Gill had taken. The letter remained for the police to read what had occurred, and link Daphne Ingram with the prisoner, Dodo Cray.

"I'm still far from being fit," Allen answered. "When the doctor comes at eleven o'clock he'll say whether I can get up. If so, I'll clear out on Monday and you shall have your letter." He cut short her expressions of gratitude. "All right. No need for thanks. You've been a good sport."

She gathered up her towels and sponge bag and went upstairs to the bathroom.

Listening intently, Allen waited until he heard the water running in before he pulled on his overcoat and slipped cautiously into her room. The gas fire was alight and on the table lay writing materials and her pen.

His lips tightened grimly. Just awake, was she? Lucky he'd noticed ink on her fingers as well as a radiant look in her face. What was she up to, he wondered? Searching round, he found the case and her handbag. Beneath the bag was an envelope. It was not addressed, and tearing it open, he read the contents.

> *Please believe that I am not going to break my word. I have to go away unexpectedly for a short while but I promise to return. Don't worry; it is on business that has nothing to do with your affairs. D.*

A cruel smile crossed the man's face. This message was meant for him to receive later. The girl intended to push off on the sly, did she? Well, she had another guess coming.

Pulling a blank sheet of paper from the writing-pad, he folded it into one of the envelopes on the table and, sealing the flap, placed it on the case under the bed. The note she had written he took with him to his own room.

He was in bed, apparently still occupied with the newspaper, when she brought in his tray.

"Look here, kid," he said. "I've been doing a bit of thinking. I've been pretty tough on you, but I had to try you out and see if you were playing fair."

"I understand," Daphne said gently. Allen's white fate with its thick growth of grey stubble gave him the semblance of a very sick man. She did not realize the immense strength of his physique that was only lightly touched by his sudden illness. "Have you thought out some plan?"

He nodded.

"A good one, if you'll help me to get away. I know a lonely spot in the country where I can go on Monday and lie low, but I'll need grub. A whole lot. Could you slip out now and get the stuff? Better bring it back in a taxi with you as it's Saturday, I may get off early on Monday, morning before the shops are open." He paused a minute. "If you'll do this, I'll give you your letter when you bring back the things. Here's the list. I wrote it out while you were in your bath."

"Thank you. You don't know how much it will mean to me," she said eagerly. "Of course I'll help you. I'll go at once. There's a big store in the Edgware Road. That will be the safest place to go."

He pulled out a thick roll of pound notes and gave her a handful.

"Here's the money. No need to stint things. I've got plenty. How long will you be gone?"

"Let me see." She looked at the lengthy list thoughtfully. "It's nearly nine o'clock. I can be back by half past ten easily."

"Don't be later," he said with a laugh. "I want to get that stuff hidden away here. The doctor will come at eleven."

Her heart sang with joy as she put on her make-up and hurried from the house. If all went well, in little more than two hours she would have her incriminating letter and be with Michael. And, if Allen had these stores, perhaps he could get away alone on Monday, and claim no further assistance from her. She was too numbed by the recent days and nights of terror to have a clear perspective of her actions now in aiding a criminal to escape.

The moment she left the house, Allen dressed himself, and packed his bag. Clad in cap, muffler and overcoat, he rang for the maid.

Giving her a large tip, he asked if she would pack his niece's luggage at once.

"Miss Ingram has gone out to do some errands," he explained. "I'm taking her back to Scotland with me as London suits neither of us. I'll pay both bills."

Having arranged that matter, Allen occupied himself with a classified telephone directory. Presently he made a call, speaking in discreet tones so that no one should overhear.

At ten o'clock a large black car appeared, of the old-fashioned roomy variety. The man who drove it went into Allen's room, and after a short conversation and the receipt of a fair sum of money, he walked away, leaving the car in front of the door.

At the back of the car was a receptacle for luggage into which Allen placed Daphne's bags. His own he put inside on the seat. From time to time he consulted his watch and glanced anxiously up and down the road. It was already half past ten and the girl had not returned with her purchases. If she didn't come soon and the doctor was a little early, all would be lost.

He was relieved to see that Barton Place was empty save for one unkempt individual; a man with a flabby white face, who was lounging idly at the corner, reading a crumpled newspaper.

Allen's nerves were on edge when at last a taxi arrived and Daphne got out.

She looked bewildered to see Allen on the pavement, and was beginning to ask a question about the car. "Hush," he checked her. "I'll explain later. I want to clear off before the doctor comes. Get the stuff you've bought transferred from the taxi to the back of this car. When everything is ready, drive me as far as the Marble Arch and I'll give you your letter. You'll be back in plenty of time to catch the doctor and explain that I'm called away."

Leaving her to carry out his orders, he went into the house and called the maid who was watching from the front window.

"Can you make us some sandwiches?" he asked, producing half a crown. "It will save us time on our long journey North."

"I'll run down and get them ready at once," the maid agreed. "You won't let the young lady go before I've wished her good-bye, will you?"

"She shall come in and fetch the sandwiches," Allen promised. "Oh, by the way, give the doctor this note if he calls this morning." He added in a confidential tone, "I'm afraid he's been trying to flirt with my niece, and as he's a married man, I'm annoyed about it. So if he asks any question about her, you'll know how to manage. She's been very upset about it, and that's why I'm taking her home with me. It might be wise to lock both our bedroom doors and not mention that we've gone away."

"I'll lock them at once, sir," the maid promised. "It's a shame that nasty-minded doctor should lead a sweet young lady on. He'll get what for if he starts asking me any questions," she assured him fervently, and went downstairs to the basement to cut sandwiches which Allen had no intention of eating.

Things had gone with remarkable smoothness so far, Allen thought, as he closed the front door. The maid was out of sight, Daphne evidently suspected nothing, the taxi had disappeared, and the boxes of provisions were stowed away in the car.

He walked down the steps to the pavement. And then he saw the pasty-faced man, who had been lounging at the corner, on the offside of the car, in the act of shutting the back door.

Allen scowled at him

"What do you want?" he demanded roughly. Daphne came forward.

"The taxi driver refused to lift the heavy cases, so this man offered his help," she explained.

"All right," Allen said, giving the man a shilling.

"S'pose you can't give me a job, sir?" whined the man, staring at Allen with bright beady eyes.

"No, I can't," he said shortly. "Jump in and take the wheel," he added to the girl in a low tone. "This fellow may be a nuisance and I want to be off."

Daphne got into the front seat, with Allen by her sides and started the engine.

The car was on the move when the pasty-faced man sprang on to the running board and thrust his head in at the window nearest Daphne.

"Fancy I've seen you before, miss," he said with an ugly leer, and caught hold of the wheel. "Sent to meet you, I was, when you come from Paris a while ago."

Chill fear gripped the girl's heart.

"You've made a mistake," she said coldly. "Get off the car or you'll fall."

The man tried to wrench the wheel towards the pavement.

"Oh no, I haven't," he persisted. "I told my boss a lie and said I'd missed you. He sacked me for being careless." Again the leering smile twisted his pallid face. "But I didn't miss you. Followed you here, and thought I'd get something from you for keeping quiet."

"Push on and he'll fall off," urged Allen.

"No," breathed the girl in an agonised whisper. "I must find out what he means. Give him some money, please."

The car was moving round the corner now at a fair pace, but still the man hung on firmly.

"The Yard flatties tried to get me to talk, but poor old Slug didn't tell 'em where you lived," the whining voice continued.

Allen leaned forward and held out a two shilling piece.

"Take this and go," he ordered. "If you're out of work, I'm sorry for you. You've never seen this young lady before and you know it. If you try any dirty blackmail tricks on her, it'll be the worse for you."

The man transferred his attention to Allen.

"Will it?" he demanded. "Call a cop and see. She's called Ingram and ought to be doin' time in jail. My employer was Jabez Gill who got murdered last Toosday night. Two bob!" he jeered. "Gimme ten quid or I'll call a copper. Stop the car—"

Slug's threat was unfinished. With one terrific blow under the jaw from Allen, he fell backwards and rolled in the gutter.

"Drive like blazes," barked Allen, "Keep in these side streets until we get to Hammersmith. I've looked up the route on a map."

The girl slowed up near the kerb.

"No," she said firmly. "I'm going back. I've got to leave a message."

"For Dr. Michael Carlile?" Allen's tone was menacing. "Thought you and him had tricked me, didn't you? Well, he'll get a message when he calls: the one you wrote for me!" He pressed something hard against her side. "Feel that? It's a revolver, loaded and likely to go off at any minute. One squeal from you and you'll be nobody's trouble any more. Get into top gear and make her shift."

XXXII, THE THEATRE DRESSING-ROOM

Saturday, November 24th.

SLUG TAYLOR for a few seconds lay dazed where he had fallen. Then he sat up, touched his jaw tenderly and felt extremely sorry for himself.

Three shillings, all told, plus a blow that might have felled an ox, was a poor recompense for his earnest efforts. He had demanded ten pounds without much hope, but had counted on getting at least a fiver. It might have paid him just as well, he reflected sadly, if he had "come clean" when that Yard flattie had made him write out a list of Jabez Gill's clients.

There might be money in the business yet if he acted carefully, but at the moment his head ached too much for the perfect clarity of thought that the occasion demanded. His tongue moistened his dry lips What he really needed was a long drink.

He wiped the mud off his face and garments and strolled to and fro aimlessly. There wasn't much point in going back to the house in Barton Place since the girl was not there, but for want of a better idea he turned in that direction.

His mind dwelt with some bitterness upon the recent episode, which had been ended so abruptly by the elderly man in the car. Who was the man, Slug wondered? He was all muffled up except for his eyes, and looked quite sixty, but the blow that he had planted on Slug's chin had tremendous power behind it. The question had no answer so far as Slug could find.

He didn't recognize the girl at first when he had offered to lift the cases into the car, although her blue eyes and neat figure resembled the girl he had tracked from Victoria Station to this address. But while he was arranging the boxes on the seat, her hat had been knocked crooked, and in straightening it she had smeared her glove across one cheek.

And then Slug knew who she was: he had caught a gleam of golden hair beneath the brown curls, and the cheek where her glove had touched it was dead white. What on earth was in those three cases? Heavy as lead they were.

Suddenly he stopped and pulled the morning newspaper from his pocket. Searching the columns he found the paragraph that gave a description of the presumed murderer and the missing fair-haired girl who had been with him at the cinema. The paper had the name of the man now: "known as Allen," it said. The girl was called Dodo Cray, and she had escaped nearly three years ago from prison in Birmingham.

Slug felt a shock go through him. "Dodo Cray" must be the girl Ingram; she, too, had escaped from gaol—Gill had told him so. Dodo Cray had been at the cinema with the murderer. She might have been with him since; comrades in crime. Slug decided he was clever to have thought all that out.

The truth flashed upon him. If Miss Ingram was Dodo Cray, the man who had driven off with her was probably the murderer! They had slipped through his fingers and apparently there was nothing to be done about it. The departure of the girl had set a period to his hopes of blackmail in her direction.

With finances in their present precarious condition, Slug was not at all troubled by any moral scruples about informing the police in the interests of justice. His sole anxiety pivoted round one problem: was there any money in it for him?

Having lived for many years on what is commonly called his "wits," and the stingy supply granted him by Nature being always less than the demand, Slug admitted to himself now that he was stumped.

His mournful eyes, turning to the house from which his last hope had just vanished, noticed a car stop a little distance away. From it emerged a man who walked briskly along until he reached number 32. Inserting a key in the lock, the newcomer was just going to open the front door when Slug darted up to him

"Shall I mind your car, sir?" he asked, assuming an eager whine.

The man, who was Michael Carlile, was on the point of giving a negative answer when something about the forlorn figure in the mud stained suit made him change his mind. The poor chap looked as if he were down and out.

"Very well. I shan't be more than a quarter of an hour. I'm expecting a young lady," he told Slug "It's quite all right for her to get into the car and wait for me."

Slug touched his tattered cap and felt things had taken a slight turn for the better.

"I'll look after the lady, sir," he promised.

He watched Michael go into the house, and then took a peep into the interior of the car. Sometimes a tin of cigarettes was lying around handy.

Slug spied some on the front seat. While extracting a few, he noticed a slip of paper fastened to the dashboard. A billey-doo for the lady, Slug thought with a smirk, and bent forward to read the brief message.

Pat is well, sends his love, and hopes to see you at noon to-day.

The words conveyed no meaning to Slug, but such as they were he remembered them.

Casting a glance backwards he saw the front door of Number 32 open and the owner of the car appeared on the steps with a letter in his hand. Behind him stood the maid, and her irate voice reached Slug's ears clearly.

"Her door's locked and you ain't going in," she shouted belligerently. "It's no business of yours where she is. You won't give me your name or address, so I ain't telling you anything. Fishy! That's what I call it, you coming here, asking me a pack of questions."

She slammed the door, indicating that the conversation, so far as she was concerned, was ended.

Michael thrust the letter into his pocket and strode back to the car, where Slug stood in an attitude of devoted attention.

"The lady's not come, guv'ner," he observed unnecessarily.

"So I see." Michael's tone was abrupt and Slug saw that his former gaiety had changed to depression.

"Going to wait for her, sir?"

"No." Michael dropped a coin into Slug's extended palm abstractedly, and switched on the engine.

"Like to leave a message with me for the lady, sir? I ain't got no work, worse luck, and I'd be thankful to earn the price of a bed." Slug's voice rose to a final wail. "I've just had a nasty fall and feel as weak as a perishing rat."

Michael's keen grey eyes ran over the man swiftly. Less drink and more soap would cure the trouble probably, he diagnosed

"Bad luck," he remarked evenly. "Where did you get that crack on the jaw?"   .

Slug weighed up the delicate points of truth or invention and decided on a mixture. He put one foot on the running-board and settled down to tell a picturesque story in which he had been a gallant defender.

To his intense surprise, his victim took the bait and seemed interested.

"Which house did you say this lady and the man came from? " he asked.

Slug did a little rapid thinking. If this fish was biting so easily on a semi-fairy, tale, there was no need to give the truth away. That might be worth something if the girl Ingram came back, or the police offered a reward.

"Number twenty eight, sir," he invented "As I was saying, I was faint with lifting those heavy cases into the car, and then when the gent bullied the girl, I ups and defends her, and he hit me a punch that laid me. out. He drove off in a large car and left me."

"Yes, I don't doubt that," Michael interrupted with a faint smile, and put his car into motion.

Another bright star of hope was fading on Slug's horizon. Too late he realized that he had rather overdone his romantic story. He made a last desperate effort.

"About the lady you was expecting, sir," he tried on another tack. "I heard that servant shouting at you and thought perhaps she wouldn't deliver a message honest as I would."

A hard look came to Michael's face suddenly as he remembered the paragraph in the morning papers concerning himself. This loafer was becoming importunate with his fantastic lies and sly offers. What was he up to prowling round watching Barton Place? Had he been spying on Daphne or Allen?

"The lady knows where to find me, thanks," he said curtly.

Michael drove away in a bewildered frame of mind. Daphne's note urged him not to worry, but why had she gone off in this mysterious fashion?

Langley was waiting in the garage. One glance at his friend's face told him that something was wrong; also the car contained no lady passenger. He listened closely while Michael hurriedly told him what the maid at number thirty-two Barton Place had said.

"Here's the note Daphne left for me," Michael added.

Langley read it.

> *Please believe that I am not going to break my word. I have to go away unexpectedly for a short while but I promise to return. Don't worry: it is on*

business that has nothing to do with your affairs.
D.

"Odd wording, isn't it?" he commented.

"What do you advise me to do?" Michael asked. "I feel like going to Scotland Yard and telling them everything."

"That would have been the wisest course in the first instance," Langley replied. "As you've left it so late, we'd better carry on with the programme and shoot for Birmingham. We may do no good, but should we have a streak of luck, Daphne will be cleared." His eyes narrowed thoughtfully. "You didn't stay long enough at Barton Place for anyone to spot you?"

Michael shook his head.

"I only saw the maid as I opened the front door, with Allen's key. She gave me Daphne's note together with a hefty slice of her tongue. I read the message and came away. Oh, I forgot. There was a weed of a chap who minded my car and told me a preposterous yarn about a man and a girl driving off in a car after a quarrel."

"Indeed; where did they go?" Langley carefully veiled his interest.

"I don't know. They came from another house, he said, and anyhow he probably made the story up."

"H'm. He minded your car, did he! Well, if it's all the same to you, my lad, we'll park it here in the garage and do our trip in my new 'bus. I'm taking no chances. He might have been a Yard man and have made a note of the car number."

"As you like," Michael agreed indifferently. "Where's the dog?"

"He's already in the car, chewing up anything he particularly fancies. Come on and I'll lock up the garage. Lucky it's my own."

"You're as fussy as an old hen," Michael told him. "Who on earth can connect me with your car?"

"I've no time to think, but—I'm locking the garage and we're using the Chrysler. By the way," he said. when they, were moving, "did Daphne take any luggage with her?"

"How can I tell? Both rooms were locked, the maid refused to open them and demanded my name and address," Michael said desperately. "I had to beat it, of course."

"Then so far as you know Allen might have been inside his room."

"He probably was. I'm sure, however, that Daphne was out. I spoke loud enough for her to hear my voice, and the maid was shouting."

"We might ring 'em up later," Langley remarked in a casual manner. "Got the telephone number?"

"Yes, it's Maida Vale 4X04. Daphne told me yesterday."

Langley drove on for a while. Outside a tobacconist's shop in the suburbs he pulled up.

"Want some cigarettes," he said. "Shan't be a minute."

He returned presently with a set look in his eyes and, flinging his purchases into the back of the car, plunged into a cheery conversation about the dog.

"Sounds as if he's rabbit hunting by the noise," he laughed. "Better stop him before he digs through the floor boards."

Michael twisted round.

"He's terribly busy burying something under the carpet," he said, bending down and producing an article, indented with teeth marks. "I'm afraid he's had rather a good time with this."

Langley regarded it ruefully.

"My favourite pipe! I say, Pat must have brought that along with him. I left it on the coffee table where my papers are. You might tell Mrs. Carlile-to-be that her animal has very taking ways."

A sad little whine came from the back of the car as Pat was deprived of his new treasure and felt he couldn't suffer the bereavement. The whine rose to a melancholy howl, then, as he caught sight of his toy, he rose on his hind legs and licked Langley's neck frantically.

"Here you are," said the owner of the pipe, thrusting it into the dog's eager mouth. "You may as well finish your work and polish it off."

"Got any plans?" Michael asked when they were entering the busy streets of Birmingham some hours later.

"Only one, but it's a good 'un. I browsed round this morning after leaving the fair Primrose, and managed to see the man who's leased this theatre. He knew my brother. There's no show on until to-night and I've got written permission to have the run of the place up to seven o'clock. First we'll find the stage doorkeeper and his wife."

"You're a good egg, Langley"

"Keep your compliments until I've earned them. Let's try the theatre first You've more native charm than I have, so you talk and I'll butt in when required."

A burly Irishman in shirt sleeves was cleaning out his office inside the stage door.

"Is your name Mulligan?" Michael asked.

"It is, sir. And what can I be doing for you?" came in a rich brogue.

"A whale of a lot, possibly," Michael told him with a smile. "You and your wife were very kind to Miss Dodo Cray."

"Ah, the poor little lady. How is—" Mulligan broke off and frowned. "Is it the police ye are?"

"We certainly are not," Michael stated. "I am Miss Cray's fiancé. My friend and I want to see if we can get at the truth of that mysterious bracelet case."

"Then ye're welcome to all the help me and my wife can be giving you, sir, but it's a divl of a task you'll have, though I'll swear on the Saints, that she never stole it. What would Miss Cray be wantin' with a diamond bracelet fit for royalty? A swate girl she was, with simple tastes. Never a bit of jewellery did she wear, and no drinkin' and late parties for her. All she cared was to go for walks with that handsome great dog of hers when she was free. My wife's up in one of the dressing-rooms doing a bit of mending, if you'd like to be seeing her, sir."

Langley stepped into the conversation. "We should," he said, handing Mulligan a letter. "Read that first and then you'll understand what we want you to do."

The man read the communication authorising him to help Mr. Langley in any way that he was requested, particularly in arranging a certain dressing-room exactly as it had been when occupied by Miss Primrose Le Vigne.

"I'll put a man on to my job and help you meself," Mulligan promised. "Will you follow me, please?"

"Come and see a pal of yours who is outside in my car," Langley remarked. "He may like to go upstairs too."

A little mystified, Mulligan went and saw Pat's head thrust out of the open window. After a preliminary sniff the dog yelped with joy at meeting his old friend.

Mulligan took the soft warm muzzle and shook it lovingly.

"Ye old rascal, I'll bet you remember me," he said with twinkling eyes. "And would you mind telling me what you did with my best 'baccy pouch, for never have I clapped eyes on it since you went."

"He probably chewed it up," Michael suggested.

"Or buried it?" Langley put in questioningly.

"More likely that, sir. We found things we'd lost hidden all over the house after he'd gone."

"Bring Pat in," Langley told his friend. "Bring that pipe too," he added quickly.

While Mulligan arranged the now empty dressing-room with his wife's assistance, Langley strolled round examining everything.

"You understand," he said, "I want it exactly as it was on the night of the theft. Was this window open or shut?"

"It was shut and fastened when Miss Le Vigne came back from the stage. She hated a breath of air," Mrs. Mulligan replied.

Langley opened it; he and the dog looked out together. There was a low wall a few feet beneath, and then a yard with a padlocked door, of which one panel was broken.

"Who owns the yard?" he asked.

"It's been locked up for years, empty. A brewer once had it, I believe, and stored his goods in the cellar below. It's nothing but a home for rats now."

"Miss Dodo Cray was staying with you that week, wasn't she?" Langley pursued.

"Yes, sir. She had a bedroom and sitting room."

"Was Pat here with her, on the night the bracelet was stolen?"

Mulligan shook his head.

"No, sir. We'd thought of that. Pat had been here with her, each evening up to then, but the day before he'd torn one of Miss Le Vigne's dresses and she wouldn't let Miss Cray bring him again. He was left home in the sitting-room alone. And he was still there when we got back that night."

"How far away do you live?"

"About four minutes' walk, sir. The dressing-room's ready."

Langley nodded.

"I see." He laid his pipe on the table. "Is this where the bracelet was left?"

Mulligan moved the pipe a little.

"Like that. Miss Le Vigne was on the stage for twenty minutes, and Miss Cray was in here alone reading. She admitted in court that nobody entered the room until Miss Le Vigne came back."

"All right, thanks," Langley replied. He sat down in the chair which Daphne had used. "Will you all go out and shut the door, please? Take the dog round to the outside of that yard door, Mulligan, let him loose and watch what happens. I'm going to try an experiment and you might pray hard."

Mulligan called the dog who was standing with his eyes fixed on the beloved pipe which rested temptingly on the corner of the table.

"Come on, you villain," exhorted Mulligan, and dragged the reluctant animal out by his collar.

"Wait outside the yard door and when I wave my handkerchief at this window, whistle for the dog," Langley ordered his friend.

"But Pat will be with us!" reminded Michael. Langley's face puckered comically.

"Never mind. Just humour me and do as I ask, old son."

XXXIII, THE MISSING BRACELET

Saturday, November 24th

LANGLEY waited in the dressing-room for a few minutes to allow the others time to get round to the yard door. Then he gave the low clear whistle that Pat already knew and obeyed.

Through the open window, he could hear the dog give an excited bark. There was a scuffling sound and a few seconds later the animal bounded through the window at Langley's feet.

Beyond a perfunctory lick, Pat's behaviour showed that his mind was on quite another subject. Langley watched him trot around the room and pause at the corner of the table. Presently the dog rose gently on his hind legs and pawed the pipe near enough for him to grasp it in his mouth.

Directly Langley saw that the pipe had gone, he signalled with his handkerchief, and heard Michael reply with a whistle.

Pat cocked his head on one side, ears pricked alertly at the sound. As if uncertain what to do, he glanced at his temporary master, and meeting with no objection, leapt back through the window.

Leaning out, Langley watched the lithe animal jump down from the wall to the yard. Then there was a longish interval when the dog was out of sight. At last he appeared again—still in the yard—forced his way through the broken door and rejoined the waiting men.

Langley beckoned to them to come back to the dressing-room.

Michael grinned ruefully as he entered.

"As an exhibition of Pat's powers of jumping, it was perfect," lie observed, "but we've not gained much else, have we?" He scanned the table. "Hello, where's your pipe?"

Langley glanced significantly at the dog's empty mouth.

"Exactly," he retorted. "Where is my pipe? Pat came in and fetched it. It was in his mouth when he leapt through the window and it was gone when he scrambled through the yard door, wasn't it?"

"I'll swear the varmint hadn't got it then," Mulligan put in. "Are ye thinking it's a cat burglar he is and fetched the bracelet and gave it to a thief outside?"

Langley shook his head.

"No. Pat doesn't like parting with his treasures easily and would have made a row about it. His motto is: what I have, I hide." He turned to his friend. "I watched him last night after you went to bed, Michael. He took away various articles from a table and hid them carefully. That put an idea into my head which, we've now tested."

"Could the dog have got out of your house and found his way here that night?" Michael asked the Irishman.

"Certainly he could, sir. The kitchen window was always left open for him to get into the garden, and he knew his way here and back alone as well as I do." Mulligan rubbed his head. "I'll bet that four-footed bunch of trouble missed Miss Cray that night and came along to see her. He'd jumped in and out of that window two or three times during the week, and as the stage door was shut on the Saturday night, he must have remembered he could get in by the yard. He might have taken the bracelet without her knowing it."

"Can we get down there?" Michael asked eagerly.

"By this window is best, sir," Mulligan, told him. "The padlock's rusted and we mightn't get the door open for ages. I'll fetch a short ladder."

"And a torch and stout bar if you have one," added Langley.

They waited in tense silence while the man obtained the necessary things. It was an easy descent but already the daylight was fading rapidly.

The yard contained nothing but half a dozen, rotting barrels, and a few mouldy boards half covering a flight of steps, dank and moss grown, leading to the cellar. Langley caught the dog's collar.

"Good lad. Find it," he urged.

Frantic with excitement, the dog led the way down to the cellar past rows of mildewed kegs to a corner. There he squatted down and wriggled partly under a large cask.

"Bring the light," Michael said, crawling after the animal. He pushed the dog aside and flashed the torch into the narrow crevice. "I can see your pipe, Langley," he exclaimed.

Mulligan pulled up his shirt sleeve.

"Let me have a go at it, sir," he said. Stretching his arms underneath the cask, he gave a startled exclamation. "That four-footed divil must have had a positive nest here, sir. Will you be taking these?" He withdrew his hand two or three times and dropped several small articles into the hat Michael held out. "That's the lot, I think."

By the aid of the flashlight the three men bent over Pat's hoard, turning the earth-stained things over impatiently. Langley's pipe, packets of cigarettes, several odd gloves, vanity cases, a necktie, sundry bones, a shoe, and a bracelet from which gleamed dazzling rays.

"There it is, sir," Mulligan exclaimed with glee, wiping away some of the mould that covered it. "No you don't, you son of wickedness," he added, snatching it from the dog's eager mouth. "You've brought grief enough on your poor mistress and she loved you and all."

"That's the end of your troubles, my son," Langley said quietly to his friend. "We'll get Mulligan to sign a letter saying how and when we found this."

"I know exactly when it happened," said Michael. "All along Daphne declared, that nobody else could have entered the dressing-room. She did, however, stand at the door for a few moments and send the call boy for some cigarettes. During that brief interval she closed the door but stood quite close to it in the corridor. That was when Pat must have entered by the window. Not finding her there, he jumped out again, taking the bracelet with him. Well, what is our next move to be?"

"We'll beat it for London and Scotland Yard as fast as we can pelt."

Mulligan's signature was appended to the brief statement that Langley drew up, and the two men set out on the return journey.

"You're sure it's wise to go to the Yard before we've seen Daphne?" Michael asked. "She might be back in Barton Place by now."

His friend's expression was serious.

"Get a grip on yourself, old lad. I'm afraid you're going to have a nasty jolt. On the way to Birmingham I rang up the maid at Daphne's address. She didn't want to talk at first, but after I'd given myself a fictitious title and a pompous tone of voice, she toned down. I found out that Daphne and her presumed uncle went off in a private car at a quarter to eleven this morning; bound for his home in Scotland, Allen told the maid. He had hired the car, while Daphne was out shopping—all their luggage went with them."

Michael drew in his breath sharply.

"Why didn't you tell me at once, so that we could warn the police or something? "

"And have the girl arrested on a double charge of being an escaped prisoner and a murderer's accomplice!" Langley shook his head. "No, we had to snatch this chance to clear Daphne first, and we've done it. Now you see why I'm going to the Yard at once."

"Then there was a streak of truth in what that dirty little blighter who minded my car told me this morning," commented Michael.

"I feared so when you told me. That's why I rang up the maid and got confirmation."

"He might know where they're gone," Michael said with a groan. "I'd give a lot to see him again."

The "dirty little blighter" had done a considerable spot of thinking that morning after Michael had driven away.

"There goes the second busted flush," he soliloquised bitterly as he watched the retreating car.

Slug Taylor's brain was well-stocked with cunning, but it was rather overlaid by a stupor caused by an intensive course of alcohol. He was rarely drunk, but just as rarely was he sober. A perpetually fuddled state required grave, mental effort to produce a worthwhile idea, he discovered now.

He was about to give up the struggle when he recalled the maid's angry words to his departed client. Slug scratched round in his mind and then decided to take a chance after he had had a little sorely-needed nourishment at a near-by pub.

Half an hour later he returned boldly and rang the bell at Number 32, Barton Place.

"Scuse me, miss," he said to the maid who opened the door. "I s'pose you can't tell me where that young gent lives—him as you had a few words, with a while ago?"

"No, I can't," she replied with a snort. "He's a doctor; and that's all I know except I'm told he's a married man and tried to get fresh with a nice young girl. He got more than he reckoned on with me."

Slug's boot-button eyes tried to express admiration.

"I'll bet he did. The stingy beggar made me chuck up a good job to mind his car here. Said he was expecting a lady! She never turned up, and all he give me was, a lot of 'lip."

The maid nodded understandingly.

"He's been after Miss Ingram, and wouldn't he just like to know where she's gone!"

"Off with another bloke, an old man," laughed Slug, hoping to draw her out. "I saw 'em go."

"That's her queer old uncle. He's been ill here for a couple of days. He's taking her home to Scotland. A bit batty, but he's rolling with money." The maid assumed an air of importance. "Miss Ingram must be in with the swells 'cause a few minutes ago a Lord Claridge or Claritch rang up and wanted her to dine with him. He seemed most disappointed when I said she'd gone, bag and baggage, and I didn't know her address."

Slug memorised these details and stowed them away for a future occasion when they might be profitable.

After a few more trifling questions he left the maid and ambled away, disconsolately. Here he was, bursting with valuable information, and unable to think of anyone who would buy it.

A casual chat over a purchase of cigarettes sent his spirits up to undreamed-of heights. The conversation had turned to the topic so dear to Slug's heart—murder and the trapping of criminals.

"A pity there ain't a reward," Slug muttered gloomily. "Now I know where to lay me hands on two desperate murderers this very minute. Did it all with me own brains, too, when the Yard flatties failed. But as they're too jealous to pay me to talk, I ain't going to tell 'em a thing."

The tobacconist winked at another customer and leaned across to Slug.

"Why, haven't you heard? There's a new law just been passed," he exclaimed earnestly. "One hundred pounds' reward cash down and no personal questions asked if anybody catches a murderer."

"Go on!" Slug was deeply impressed. "What d'you advise me to do?"

"Take a taxi to Scotland Yard at once," counselled the tobacconist. "You'll be a rich man before the pubs shut tonight. Some folks have all the luck."

Slug missed the roar of laughter that followed his exit. Solemnly he counted his cash assets. Cabs cost real money, but with a hundred pounds in the offing, what did it matter?

With a lordly air he hailed a taxi.

"Drive to Scotland Yard and be smart about it," he ordered.

The taxi man looked Slug up and down.

"Sure you've got the price, mate?" he demanded with a grin.

Slug produced a few coins as being the quickest way to settle the question, and entered the vehicle.

A short while later he was shown into Inspector Reynolds' office and felt that indeed the die was cast. Worse still, there was a cold look in Reynolds' grey eyes before which the preface concerning the reward that Slug had intended to make died a premature death.

The Inspector plunged him straight into the theme of his story. Moreover, that gentleman seemed to have an unerring instinct if Slug deviated from the truth, and deftly pulled him back.

"Now, then," Reynolds said briskly when Slug's breath had given out, "the facts you've told me are these: the murdered man, Jabez Gill, employed you to meet a client coming from Paris called Daphne Ingram, and find out where she was going to stay. You tracked Miss Ingram to Barton Place but, hoping to touch her for a little personal blackmail, you told Gill that you had missed her. In consequence, he sacked you. Is that right?"

Stated in those bald words, it sounded very unpleasant, but Slug, with a wriggle, had to admit that it was substantially correct.

"Quite so. Next, Miss Thelma Underwood of Clapham, fiancée of the cashier called Vickers who shot himself because Gill was persecuting him, dragged you to the Yard in case she was suspected in any way. At my request, you wrote out a list of Gill's clients, carefully omitting the item of the greatest importance which was Miss Daphne Ingram's address and her link with Gill."

"I wrote down Miss Le Vigne's name," Slug protested in injured tones. "I read in the papers that you'd had an interview with her."

"Miss Le Vigne had nothing to do with the crime and was not being blackmailed by Gill," Reynolds replied. "Then we come to this morning and your intention to see Miss Ingram as funds were running low. You recognized her, disguised with brown hair and darkened complexion, going off in a large private car loaded with luggage and three heavy wooden cases. Her companion was an apparently elderly man, tall and heavily built. You annoyed Miss Ingram by threatening her and he knocked you off the car." Reynolds waited questioningly.

"That's right, guv'ner. He fair knocked my block off!" Slug confessed, mopping his forehead.

"Shortly afterwards," Reynolds continued, "a gentleman arrived and, parking his car a little distance from the house, told you he was expecting a lady. He entered Number 32 and a few minutes later you heard heated words between him and the maid. He came out and drove away. After a while you called at the house and learned that Miss Ingram had driven off with her supposed uncle, who was rich, to Scotland; that the second man was a doctor who was anxious to see her, and that a Lord Claritch had rung up after she had gone."

"Quite true, guv'ner," Slug agreed. This seemed the moment to cash in on his reward. Casting a wary eye at the Inspector's inscrutable face, he sucked in his breath and launched out boldly. "Putting two and two together and finding it very suspicious, I hopped in a taxi and come here to tell you all I'd found out."

"Why?" inquired Reynolds blandly.

Slug appeared entirely nonplussed by the crude question.

"In the interests of justice, sir," he. faltered, "and of course, being very hard up, there's the reward for catching murderers. The new law, a hundred quid down."

"Indeed!" Reynolds observed. "It's the first I've heard of it. The murderer is not yet caught, in any case. He might have been, had your interest in justice outweighed your love of blackmail. There is a law, however, Slug, which you seem to have forgotten. A person can be arrested for concealing important evidence relating to a crime. Did you notice the number of the big car in which Miss Ingram and the man drove away in?"

"No, sir." Slug's tone was depressed. "But I wrote down them that was on the doctor's car." he said, putting a dirty scrap of paper on the desk.

Reynolds glanced at it and nodded towards the door.

"You may go."

XXXIV, THE NET DRAWN TIGHTER

Saturday, November 24th

INSPECTOR REYNOLDS and Jenkins reached the Yard almost together at seven o'clock that evening.

In view of Slug's information, the two C.I.D. men had made exhaustive inquiries.

"Well, how did you get on?" Reynolds asked.

"I've found the garage from which Allen hired the big car this morning, sir. He ordered it by telephone, paid the man who brought it a deposit and a fortnight's hire in advance, and gave a false name and address."

"He's pulled that trick off twice," commented the Inspector. "Anything else?"

"The registration numbers which Slug Taylor noticed belong to a car, owned by a Mr. Anthony Langley."

"I suppose that must be the well-known cartoonist. Are he and Carlile friends?"

Jenkins shrugged his shoulders.

"I can't say, sir, but the car is now locked inside Mr. Langley's private garage, which is large enough to hold two cars, I see. I climbed up and looked through the garage window. Mr. Langley's flat is also locked up and nobody knows where he is. The caretaker says that Mr. Langley went out this morning with another gentleman and an Airedale dog which has never been seen there before."

"That was Michael Carlile with him, definitely," Reynolds replied. "I've rung up several quarantine places. At one of them I discovered that an Airedale belonging to a Miss Daphne Ingram was fetched away very late last night by a tall thin gentleman who signed his name as Langley. That the lot?"

"I've got a bit of news about the queer weapon used by the murderer," Jenkins told him. "Allen got it from one of the dining stewards on board his boat which has just come back from another trip since then. It was a very long carving steel. This steward admits grinding it to the shape of a stiletto at Allen's request and selling it to him for a pound. Alien told him he meant to use it for killing cattle on his ranch after he had put a strong spring lever handle on to it. He actually demonstrated to the steward how it could be driven through an animal's skull without raising his arm for the blow."

"All I want is the man who used the weapon," Reynolds said anxiously. "We're nearly up to date with past history. I've raked up everyone I could get hold of this afternoon who was on the liner with Allen. I'm expecting one of the deck-stewards to come here at any minute. He was out when I called at his home to-day."

"As you ordered, I've sent round messages for the police to keep a sharp look out on all roads for the car Allen was in," Jenkins said.

"That's right. Only Allen won't be driving it now, I fancy! He's had nearly eight hours' start. By this time he'll have abandoned it, or hidden it somewhere. He knows it can easily be traced and stopped." Reynolds drummed his fingers on the desk impatiently. "Why doesn't that fellow Carlile report here? I can't make him out. I don't believe he had anything to do with the murder. The meeting at the cinema must have been accidental. Come in," he called as he heard a knock on the door.

"Man to see you by the name of Emmetts, a ship's steward, sir."

"Bring him up at once," ordered Reynolds. His eyes lost their troubled expression at this fresh chance of discovering a useful clue.

"Sorry I was out when you called, sir," said the newcomer, who bore an air of the sea in his fresh complexion and clear eyes.

The Inspector was pleased to hear that the man remembered Allen perfectly.

"Second-class passenger he was, sir, and I never want another like him," the steward stated. "Surly wasn't the word. While sitting at table, they said, he bolted his food and never spoke to a living soul, except another deck-steward and one dining-room steward from whom he bought a carving steel."

"We've already had a chat with the latter," Reynolds explained. "Did Allen ever talk to you?"

"Just a snarl about his chair occasionally; not a word else," the man replied. "But he had long, queer talks with my mate, Bowden, the other deck-steward. Bowden was a mysterious bloke, too; never had anything to do with any of us nor spoke of himself in any way."

"So he and Allen chummed up during the voyage," commented the Inspector. "What do you mean by 'queer' talks"

"Well, sir, you'd see the two of 'em huddled together, talking quiet and serious, away from everybody. If anyone came near, they'd stop talking or part company. I went for Bowden one day for neglecting his job and wasting his time with Allen, and he replied, 'Don't be a spoil-sport. I've got a chance to let a lonely little shack I own and never get the time to live in. Allen's going to give me fifty quid for the use of it while I'm away on voyages.'"

"Thanks, Emmetts. I shall be glad to have Bowden's address."

The man grinned.

"Sorry, sir; I don't know it. Bowden was taken sick in Melbourne and died in hospital there the day before we left for home this trip. Nobody knew as much as I did about him, which is all I've told you."

The Inspector made a hopeless gesture towards Jenkins.

"Try to think of any casual reference Bowden may have made concerning this 'shack' of his," he pursued. "Take your time."

Emmetts thought for a few moments.

"Once—after Bowden talked to me of hoping to let his place—I heard him say something to Allen about the marshes being bleak and deserted and the sea mist bad at times."

"H'm. That sounds like the Kentish coast." Emmetts' face brightened.

"It must be, sir. Allen asked if there were any houses near. Bowden laughed and said 'No,' but there were often aeroplanes overhead, the lights of France were visible from the side windows, and a round stone tower stood between his house and the sea. Is that going to be any guide to you?"

"A whole jugful," Reynolds assured him. "Any more bits you can rake up?"

"That's all I overheard, sir, except that I know Bowden had a nice packet of money soon after that, so evidently the deal came off."

"Bowden never discussed this house of his with you?"

"No, sir, except the time I went for him. Once, months before that, he spoke of the chimneys, but that's no use to you."

"Never mind. Let's hear it," Reynolds urged

"We were talking about smoky chimneys. He said he had a funny old barn of a place and had had to have a chimney made taller and a lobster cowl put on and still the blamed thing smoked."

The Inspector wrote down the details that Emmetts had given and dismissed the man. For a while he sat silent, turning over and rejecting various ideas.

Then he lifted the receiver and, calling a number, glanced whimsically at his assistant.

"Like to have a night flight over the marshes? he asked, while waiting for his call to be answered.

Jenkins shuddered, remembering previous experiences that had treated him worse than a bad Channel crossing.

"I'd hate it, sir, but if you're going, I'm coming, too," he replied heroically.

"Stout lad!" his chief retorted. "Ah, is that Croydon?" he inquired as a voice came over the wire. Receiving an affirmative, he stated his requirements and after a short conversation, replaced the instrument with a look of disappointment.

"Visibility very bad; low-lying fog hides the ground," he remarked. "No joy ride for you to-night."

Jenkins' expression registered thankfulness. He suggested going by car that evening.

"I'll think about it," Reynolds promised."Meanwhile—"

His sentence was interrupted by the hasty entry of a constable, who was obviously struggling to repress his excitement. In an undertone he breathed a few words to the Inspector.

The effect was magical.

"Yes, bring them here at once," Reynolds ordered.

He could scarcely restrain his impatience during the short delay before the constable reappeared with two visitors.

"Mr. Langley and Dr. Michael Carlile," he announced in portentous tones.

The Inspector spared only a glance for the very tall man whose lean cadaverous face was known to him in the pictorial Press as Anthony Langley, the cartoonist.

Then, with an inward sigh of relief, he scanned Langley's companions, whom the cinema sweet-stall girl had said was not unlike himself.

Reynolds now noted the resemblance and the difference. He himself was a shade taller than Carlile and several years older, but they both had the same grey eyes and contour of countenance. Only, whereas Reynolds' face was outwardly calm and his eyes steady, Michael Carlile was obviously showing signs of intense nervous strain and he looked haggard with anxiety.

"Please sit down," Reynolds invited them genially. "I need not say how glad I am to see you, Dr. Carlile, and your friend also. Mr. Langley's work has given me many a pleasant chuckle."

The Inspector's easy, manner had the desired result on Michael, whose taut expression relaxed as he received this unexpected greeting.

"That's a very gracious reception, Inspector," he said. "After the abominable way I've acted, I deserve instant arrest."

Reynolds grinned.

"Well, tell me what you've both been up to," he suggested. "I'll decide on the penalty afterwards." Bit by bit the two men revealed the story of the past few days, from the time of the murder to this afternoon's discovery of the bracelet in Birmingham.

"Directly we had cleared Miss Daphne Ingram's name," Langley remarked, "we raced back here to you. You can appreciate Dr. Carlile's anxiety for her. If he had come here before, she might have been arrested on the previous charge against her."

Reynolds' eye twinkled.

"I think Dr. Carlile's interest in Miss Ingram is not entirely impersonal," he observed dryly, "in which case much can be forgiven. Even detectives are human, though few people credit us with anything but eagle eyes and a pair of handcuffs. Miss Ingrain, of course, will, after a few formalities, be free from the charge of theft. By the way, you made a slight detour before calling on me tonight, did you not?"

Yes," Michael confessed. "I persuaded my friend to call at Barton Place in the faint hope that Miss Ingram had telephoned. It was a useless errand. She had not done so, and the maid said that the rooms were already let."

"I 'took' them this afternoon!" Reynolds said with a smile. "It was the only way to get a quiet search for a chance clue left behind by Allen. A detective is in one of the rooms now. He has found nothing, unfortunately, but he advised me by telephone half an hour ago that Lord Claritch had called to see Miss Ingram!"

"My elevation to the peerage was sudden and purely temporary," Langley gravely assured him.

"As will be my tenancy of the rooms in Barton Place," supplemented the Inspector. "What is it?" he asked as a constable appeared at the door.

"The dog in this gentleman's car is howling her heart out, sir," the man replied. "I might be able to quiet her if I knew her name."

"The animal is called Pat," Langley explained, "but I understand he is usually addressed as 'my lovely.' You might try that, officer, if all else fails."

"I think we'll have Pat up here," the Inspector observed. "I'd like to see the rascal, and I'm particularly fond of Airedales."

In a few moments the burly constable returned, towed by a magnificent specimen of that breed, full of boundless energy. Leaping towards his temporary masters, Pat alternately licked and nibbled their hands gently as a reminder that he had been shamefully neglected.

The bribe of a lump of sugar tempted him to Reynolds, who fondled him in an understanding way.

"Much must be forgiven you because you're an engaging scoundrel," the Inspector told Pat solemnly as fifty pounds of dog jumped on to his knees and settled down calmly. "Now, Dr. Carlile, I'll tell you how far I've got in this case."

Michael and his friend listened in awed surprise as the Inspector unfolded the difficult means by which he had acquired his knowledge of the details of the crime.

"Indeed, you've made remarkable progress over thorny paths," Langley commented. "You've practically caught up with facts."

"Not quite," Reynolds replied. "There remains the little formality of arresting the criminal. Still, by the aid of the steward's useful information, and now that Dr.

Michael Carlile has materialized, I'm feeling distinctly more hopeful."

Michael moved restlessly.

"Can't we motor down at once and rescue Miss Ingram from that scoundrel's clutches?" he asked. "I'm terribly worried."

The Inspector caught Langley's eye with a significant glance.

"I understand perfectly, Dr. Carlile," he said, and then, choosing his words carefully in order not to alarm Michael, added "Miss Ingram, I feel sure, will be safe while Allen sees no signs of police activity. We must proceed cautiously. Allen is a desperate man, you see."

Michael buried his face in his hands.

"What a hopeless position!" he said. "Here am I powerless to help her, while she is at the mercy of that brute."

"Things are not quite so bad as that," came the Inspector's calming words. "I've discovered that those cases contained provisions, so Allen obviously intends to make a stay. Haste, at the moment, would be most unwise. Whereas the longer the lull, the more Allen will imagine he has eluded us, and therefore perhaps slacken his guard on Miss Ingram. Judging by what you have told me, she is not lacking in courage."

"If only we could get a message to her saying that we are close at hand trying to rescue her!" Michael exclaimed.

"That she will have quicker than you imagine," Reynolds observed. A twinkle gleamed in his grey eyes. "I promise you that a few minutes after we locate the house she shall know you are near."

Carlile looked at him wonderingly.

"I accept your word, Inspector, but it beats me how you're going to manage it."

"The lady understands French, I believe, Dr. Carlile?"

"As well as she does English, but how is that going to help?"

"I think I'll keep that little secret," Reynolds told him with a smile. "Consider it as your punishment for not coming to me sooner. I suggest—" he spoke a few words in an undertone to Langley.

"Right," the latter agreed. "We'll be there. Come on, Michael. You're going to bed early for once in your life. We've a big day's work ahead of us. Good night, Inspector."

Reynolds nodded to the two men as they moved towards the door.

"Oh, Mr. Langley," he called out. "Bring the dog tomorrow."

XXXV, THE HOUSE ON THE MARSHES

Saturday, November 24th.

TWICE in traffic blocks that Saturday morning Daphne had tried to make signals of distress to pedestrians, in spite of Allen's revolver which was pressed against her side.

Once they were out in the comparative desolation of the big arterial road leading to the coast, he ordered her to pull up.

"Get into the back of the car," he snarled.

Watching until no other vehicle was about, he gagged and bound her tightly, forcing her to lie in a cramped heap on the floor boards. Then flinging a rug over the girl, he climbed into the front seat and drove on.

Half suffocated, Daphne struggled vainly to free herself from the cord that bit into her wrists and ankles, and seemed to jar and tighten with every jolt of the car. Exhausted, at last she gave up the effort, and lying still, tried to concentrate upon the direction in which they were going.

To make sure of that, too, was impossible. The choking gag that Allen had forced into her mouth made breathing very difficult.

Suddenly the thought of Michael came to her in a comforting flash. She was not fighting this battle alone now. He would use all his ingenuity to trace her as he had done in his advertisement about the "lonely monument." A man who could think of that could devise other things. Something of his steadying influence came to the distracted girl now as she lay trussed and helpless under the rug.

At all costs she must show no fear and conserve her strength for future emergencies. She would keep the "even keel" that Michael had said was such a help in facing trouble Relaxing every muscle that her bonds permitted, she lay still.

They seemed to have been travelling for hours when she felt a terrific jolting as though they were moving across a ploughed field. The car stopped after a while and in the distance she heard the faint wash of sea on shingle.

For a second she wondered if Allen was going to drown her as he picked her up, rug and all, carrying her as easily as if she were a baby. She counted thirty-two stairs that he mounted. Then he lowered her on to a bed.

With clumsy but not rough movements, he pulled off the rug and removed the gag and cords. He stood looking down at her, apparently expecting frightened tears or indignant rage.

Showing no sign of the pain she was experiencing in her aching limbs, Daphne yawned and gave a bored smile.

"Does your hospitality run to a drink of water and a cigarette?" she inquired, making no attempt to move.

Evidently nonplussed by her cool attitude, he stared perplexedly.

"All right I'll fetch some," he said sullenly. "Don't dare to get up."

"I've no intention of doing so," she remarked, and closed her eyes.

Presently he placed water, cigarettes and matches on a chair beside her.

"Stay there while I get the stuff in and run the car out of sight," he ordered.

She lighted a cigarette as if she had not heard his words.

Allen locked her door on the outside and clattered down the stairs. His indifference to the noise he was making assured her that there could be no neighbours within earshot.

Directly she judged that he was on the ground floor, she dragged herself to the window.

The sight was not cheering. Her attic, she realized, must be at the top of an old, tall house, for it was a great height from the barren ground beneath. No other houses were visible, except a round stone tower that stood out against the background of a grey wintry sea beating on a deserted stretch of beach. A whirling flock of seagulls were the only signs of life in her radius.

The bedroom was barely furnished. There was nothing except a couple of thin blankets that she could knot together for a rope, which would not have been long enough for the big drop.

Oh, for a few of the ingenious tricks she had read of in sensational novels, the girl thought, as she surveyed the dismal prospect.

She had no idea where she was. Somewhere on the coast of England was a trifle vague. Allen had provisions sufficient for a lengthy siege.

From the ground floor came muffled sounds of hammering that continued for over an hour.

The short winter afternoon was fading. rapidly now, and although it was only half-past four, the room was already dusk.

Going to the window once more, she saw far across the sombre sea two beams of light. They must be from the lighthouses of Northern France, and this house therefore must be somewhere on the lonely waste of Kentish marshes opposite. The knowledge was of no particular value, but at least she knew in what corner of England she was imprisoned; also that dense fog was creeping up.

Allen's feet sounded on the stairs, and, unlocking the door, he entered, bearing a candle. Pulling the thick curtain across the window, he set the light on the table.

"You can come down now," he told her awkwardly.

"Why?" Her tone was disinterested.

"You've got to eat, haven't you? I can't afford to have a sick female on my hands." He sneered. "Your doctor pal ain't nice and handy this time. Thought you was going to do a nice little bunk and leave me in the lurch, didn't you?"

Daphne raised her eyebrows.

"We all make mistakes. I was merely going to try to clear my name of a false charge, and I should have kept my word and returned. You probably read my note."

Allen nodded.

"Yes, and I wasn't taking any chances. You know too much. Here we are, and here we stay until we can safely cross to France. Once we're in Paris, you can go your way and I'll go mine."

"And what happens if you're discovered first?" she asked mildly.

"I told you I wasn't going to hang for Jabez Gill. If the police come here I'll shoot you first because of the tricks you played on me, and then shoot myself."

The girl rose from the mattress on which she had been lying.

"In that event," she observed, "I seem to gain more by helping you to remain hidden until it is safe to move. Can lights from any of these windows be seen?"

A twisted smile came to Allen's face.

"There isn't a house or road in sight. I've nailed the shutters over all the windows except this one, and blocked up the backdoor. The only exit will be by the front door, and I'm putting my mattress right across it inside, in case you fancy doing any running away while I'm asleep."

"You're wonderfully thorough in your methods," Daphne drawled. "Nothing seems to have been forgotten, so we may as well have some food."

He led the way down two steep flights of rickety stairs into a large kitchen.

"You can unpack that stuff," he said, pointing to the cases of provisions.

"Very well. Take my luggage upstairs meanwhile," Daphne replied. Seeing him hesitate, she added scornfully, "Lock the front door and take the key if you're afraid I shall try to bolt!"

"I can't make you out," the man remarked. "Most girls would be scared to death in your place."

She stooped over the boxes and began to take out the food.

"Really! Well, don't flatter yourself that I'm afraid of a man who is cowardly enough to hide behind my skirts to protect himself. Would you rather have tinned tongue or salmon?"

Allen lifted her bags quickly.

"I don't care," he mumbled, and went upstairs.

The moment he had gone Daphne quietly opened the various doors which led from the kitchen. There was a wash-house, coal shed, and larder. The small window of each was securely blocked up except that of the larder, which had a narrow aperture far too small for a human being to squeeze through. This opening was covered with rusty perforated zinc, some of which bad been broken.

As a means of escape it was hopeless, yet Daphne regarded it with interest. With a strong tug she tore the rusty zinc still more.

The girl prepared their meal and ate heartily. Allen seemed to have less appetite, and eyed her in uneasy silence, responding to her casual conversation with curt monosyllables.

Overhead at intervals came the droning whine, and throb of aeroplanes.

"There must be an aerodrome near," she remarked. "I suppose these 'planes are crossing from Holland to Harwich."

A pleased glint came to the man's eyes. So she thought they were on the East Coast! That was all to the good.

"That's it," he agreed. "You can see the North Sea from these windows."

Daphne helped herself to tinned peaches and smiled inwardly.

"Very bracing and healthy, but a trifle cold. Are we going to freeze or dare you risk lighting a fire?"

"I'll think about that to-morrow. There's plenty of oil and a couple of oil stoves. You can have one in your bedroom to-night. I'll fill it and take it up."

While he was carrying the lamp upstairs, Daphne rolled up some old newspapers and thrust them under her coat. Exactly what purpose they would serve, she didn't yet know, but perhaps she could light them as signals if Allen had not nailed up her window.

And then she heard again the sound of hammering and knew that that plan had failed.

"How do I get any air?" she demanded when she went up to her room and looked at the closed shutters.

"It's a cold, foggy night. You can leave your door open if you like," he retorted.

Sitting on the mattress after Allen had gone, Daphne lighted a cigarette and reviewed her position. For some queer reason she was entirely unafraid. Even in this desolate place Michael seemed very near her in spirit, urging her to be calm and wait patiently until he came.

Yet how could he find her? She glanced round the bare attic with the plaster walls stained with damp patches. There was no skylight, and as Allen had locked her in she could not investigate further on this floor. The nails he had driven in to the shutters were far too firmly fixed for her to take them out, even if she had had the necessary tools.

There was a tiny fireplace with broken bars to the grate. She pushed back the damper and a cloud of dust fell down. No soot was visible so probably the grate had never been used. Maybe there was not even a chimney.

By straining her head into the small space, she could look up a narrow flue, and felt cold air beat on her face. Up there was the sky and freedom!

With a sigh she rolled herself in her coat and went to sleep.

XXXVI, AT BAY

Sunday, November 25th.

SHE was roused by the strange sound of a man's voice. Thinking it was Allen, she lighted the candle and looking at her watch, saw that it was barely, six o'clock.

The voice came nearer. It seemed to be just over the roof of her attic now. She could hear words booming out above the drone of a 'plane.

Her heart beat wildly as she distinguished two words. "Lonely Monument." "Lonely Monument." "Lonely Monument," reiterated in her ears.

In an instant she understood. Michael, by some miracle, had found her and was in an aeroplane sending her this signal. In France she had often heard things being advertised by this means. A portable wireless set with an amplifier attached to a microphone on one side and a loud speaker on the other was used for the purpose.

The voice was dying away now, and her spirits sank as she feared Michael had given up his quest. No, the 'plane was returning, and the voice came even clearer now: Michael's voice.

"Lonely Monument. Lonely Monument," he cried. "*Tout va bien. Nous sommes ici. Ou etes-vous?*"

Over and over again the 'plane circled, with Michael's voice repeating the same phrases, assuring her that they were there and asking where she was.

How could she signal to him? To attempt to do so from the larder window downstairs would be madness. Allen must be awake and would surely shoot her if she attempted to send a message.

Suddenly her eyes fell upon the oil stove. Snatching up the newspapers, she swamped them with oil and, reckless of what happened, thrust them alight up the chimney as she heard the 'plane coming back.

There was a fierce roar, and crackling. For a moment she was nearly choked by a cloud of oily smoke. But she continued desperately to keep her flaming signal alight by pushing up fresh supplies of blazing paper.

And then, when her strength was giving out through the suffocating fumes, she heard the words of her message from the skies change.

"We understand," Michael's voice came again, still speaking French. "The roof is on fire. Get out of the house. We are landing."

Outside her bedroom door came the roar of Allen's voice, furious with anger.

"The place is choked with smoke. What on earth have you done?"

She laid the lamp on its side quickly.

"I tipped the lamp over. Some papers caught fire and I had to push them up the chimney," she explained.

He unlocked the door and came into the room which was thick with smoke.

"What's that fellow in the aeroplane yelling?" he demanded suspiciously.

"How do I know? I was locked in here." She bit her lip. "I smell wood burning."

"You've probably set the place on fire," he retorted, peering at the roof through a skylight on the landing. "Yes, you have! We must put it out."

Grasping her arm, he forced her to a step ladder.

"If there's any danger you're going to share it," he snarled. "Up you go! Now stay there while I fetch a bucket of water."

Out on the roof, she stood swaying and half-dazed on a small platform close to the edge. Not far off in the faint dawn she could see an aeroplane swooping towards the ground.

In a few moments Allen was beside her. He hurled water on the flames, which came from the woodwork of the gabled roof.

The 'plane had landed by now and men were rushing towards the house. One of them, Daphne could see, was Michael.

Flinging aside the bucket, Allen drew his revolver, and pulled the girl nearer the edge of the roof.

"Tell them to go away or I'll shoot you," Allen ordered gruffly as the sound of crashing blows against woodwork down below became audible and flames rose higher against the grey sullen sky.

In desperation, she obeyed.

"All right. We'll go," was Michael's surprising answer. "But," he added immediately in French, "call your dog."

The girl gave a long low whistle.

"Stop that!" snapped Allen, peering down at the ground far below. "This is the end for both of us if they don't go."

Once more the girl whistled, expecting every second to be shot.

Suddenly, as Allen raised his revolver, a form scrambled through the skylight. It was her dog.

Swinging the gun round, the man pulled the trigger but missed the animal. With a bark of fury, Pat leaped at Allen's throat. He struggled to fight it off, but the weapon fell from his hand.

Daphne snatched at it, and as two men came through the skylight, she called the dog off.

Allen looked from the gun in the girl's hand to Pat standing defensively beside her. Twisting round quickly, he saw the men advancing towards him across the roof.

"The game's up, Allen," Inspector Reynolds said.

Allen faced him with bloodshot eyes.

"Yes, it's up. But I'm not going to swing for Jabez Gill," he declared, and dived head first off the roof.

THE END

Other Resurrected Press Books in *The Chief Inspector Pointer Mystery* Series

Death of John Tait
Murder at the Nook
Mystery at the Rectory
Scarecrow
The Case of the Two Pearl Necklaces
The Charteris Mystery
The Eames-Erskine Case
The Footsteps that Stopped
The Clifford Affair
The Cluny Problem
The Craig Poisoning Mystery
The Net Around Joan Ingilby
The Tall House Mystery
The Wedding-Chest Mystery
The Westwood Mystery
Tragedy at Beechcroft

MYSTERIES BY ANNE AUSTIN

Murder at Bridge

When an afternoon bridge party attended by some of Hamilton's leading citizens ends with the hostess being murdered in her boudoir, Special Investigator Dundee of the District Attorney's office is called in. But one of the attendees is guilty? There are plenty of suspects: the victim's former lover, her current suitor, the retired judge who is being blackmailed, the victim's maid who had been horribly disfigured accidentally by the murdered woman, or any of the women who's husbands had flirted with the victim. Or was she murdered by an outsider whose motive had nothing to do with the town of Hamilton. Find the answer in... **Murder at Bridge**

One Drop of Blood

When Dr. Koenig, head of Mayfield Sanitarium is murdered, the District Attorney's Special Investigator, "Bonnie" Dundee must go undercover to find the killer. Were any of the inmates of the asylum insane enough to have committed the crime? Or, was it one of the staff, motivated by jealousy? And what was is the secret in the murdered man's past. Find the answer in... **One Drop of Blood**

AVAILABLE FROM RESURRECTED PRESS!

THE EDWARDIAN DETECTIVES
LITERARY SLEUTHS OF THE EDWARDIAN ERA

The exploits of the great Victorian Detectives, Poe's C. Auguste Dupin, Gaboriau's Lecoq, and most famously, Arthur Conan Doyle's Sherlock Holmes, are well known. But what of those fictional detectives that came after, those of the Edwardian Age? The period between the death of Queen Victoria and the First World War had been called the Golden Age of the detective short story, but how familiar is the modern reader with the sleuths of this era? And such an extraordinary group they were, including in their numbers an unassuming English priest, a blind man, a master of disguises, a lecturer in medical jurisprudence, a noble woman working for Scotland Yard, and a savant so brilliant he was known as "The Thinking Machine."

To introduce readers to these detectives, Resurrected Press has assembled a collection of stories featuring these and other remarkable sleuths in The Edwardian Detectives.

- The Case of Laker, Absconded by Arthur Morrison
- The Fenchurch Street Mystery by Baroness Orczy
- The Crime of the French Café by Nick Carter
- The Man with Nailed Shoes by R Austin Freeman
- The Blue Cross by G. K. Chesterton
- The Case of the Pocket Diary Found in the Snow by Augusta Groner
- The Ninescore Mystery by Baroness Orczy
- The Riddle of the Ninth Finger by Thomas W. Hanshew
- The Knight's Cross Signal Problem by Ernest Bramah

- The Problem of Cell 13 by Jacques Futrelle
- The Conundrum of the Golf Links by Percy James Brebner
- The Silkworms of Florence by Clifford Ashdown
- The Gateway of the Monster by William Hope Hodgson
- The Affair at the Semiramis Hotel by A. E. W. Mason
- The Affair of the Avalanche Bicycle & Tyre Co., LTD by Arthur Morrison

RESURRECTED PRESS CLASSIC MYSTERY CATALOGUE

Journeys into Mystery
Travel and Mystery in a More Elegant Time

The Edwardian Detectives
Literary Sleuths of the Edwardian Era

Gems of Mystery
Lost Jewels from a More Elegant Age

E. C. Bentley
Trent's Last Case: The Woman in Black

Ernest Bramah
Max Carrados Resurrected:
The Detective Stories of Max Carrados

Agatha Christie
The Secret Adversary
The Mysterious Affair at Styles

Octavus Roy Cohen
Midnight

Freeman Wills Croft
The Ponson Case
The Pit Prop Syndicate

J. S. Fletcher
The Herapath Property
The Rayner-Slade Amalgamation
The Chestermarke Instinct
The Paradise Mystery
Dead Men's Money

The Middle of Things
Ravensdene Court
Scarhaven Keep
The Orange-Yellow Diamond
The Middle Temple Murder
The Tallyrand Maxim
The Borough Treasurer
In the Mayor's Parlour
The Saftey Pin

R. Austin Freeman
The Mystery of 31 New Inn from the Dr. Thorndyke
Series
John Thorndyke's Cases from the Dr. Thorndyke
Series
The Red Thumb Mark from The Dr. Thorndyke Series
The Eye of Osiris from The Dr. Thorndyke Series
A Silent Witness from the Dr. John Thorndyke Series
The Cat's Eye from the Dr. John Thorndyke Series
Helen Vardon's Confession: A Dr. John Thorndyke
Story
As a Thief in the Night: A Dr. John Thorndyke Story
Mr. Pottermack's Oversight: A Dr. John Thorndyke
Story
Dr. Thorndyke Intervenes: A Dr. John Thorndyke
Story
The Singing Bone: The Adventures of Dr. Thorndyke
The Stoneware Monkey: A Dr. John Thorndyke Story
The Great Portrait Mystery, and Other Stories: A
Collection of Dr. John Thorndyke and Other Stories
The Penrose Mystery: A Dr. John Thorndyke Story
The Uttermost Farthing: A Savant's Vendetta

Arthur Griffiths
The Passenger From Calais
The Rome Express

Fergus Hume
The Mystery of a Hansom Cab
The Green Mummy
The Silent House
The Secret Passage

Edgar Jepson
The Loudwater Mystery

A. E. W. Mason
At the Villa Rose

A. A. Milne
The Red House Mystery
Baroness Emma Orczy
The Old Man in the Corner

Edgar Allan Poe
The Detective Stories of Edgar Allan Poe

Arthur J. Rees
The Hampstead Mystery
The Shrieking Pit
The Hand In The Dark
The Moon Rock
The Mystery of the Downs

Mary Roberts Rinehart
Sight Unseen and The Confession

Dorothy L. Sayers
Whose Body?

Sir William Magnay
The Hunt Ball Mystery

Mabel and Paul Thorne
The Sheridan Road Mystery

Louis Tracy
The Strange Case of Mortimer Fenley
The Albert Gate Mystery
The Bartlett Mystery
The Postmaster's Daughter
The House of Peril
The Sandling Case: What Would You Have Done?
Charles Edmonds Walk
The Paternoster Ruby

John R. Watson
The Mystery of the Downs
The Hampstead Mystery

Edgar Wallace
The Daffodil Mystery
The Crimson Circle

Carolyn Wells
Vicky Van
The Man Who Fell Through the Earth
In the Onyx Lobby
Raspberry Jam
The Clue
The Room with the Tassels
The Vanishing of Betty Varian
The Mystery Girl
The White Alley
The Curved Blades
Anybody but Anne
The Bride of a Moment
Faulkner's Folly
The Diamond Pin
The Gold Bag
The Mystery of the Sycamore
The Come Back

Raoul Whitfield
Death in a Bowl

And much more!
Visit ResurrectedPress.com
for our complete catalogue

About Resurrected Press

A division of Intrepid Ink, LLC, Resurrected Press is dedicated to bringing high quality, vintage books back into publication. See our entire catalogue and find out more at www.ResurrectedPress.com.

About Intrepid Ink, LLC

Intrepid Ink, LLC provides full publishing services to authors of fiction and non-fiction books, eBooks and websites. From editing to formatting, from publishing to marketing, Intrepid Ink gets your creative works into the hands of the people who want to read them. Find out more at www.IntrepidInk.com.